The Meaning of Home to Jess Trujillo

♥ *A mother's loving arms*

♥ *A house filled with the scents and sounds of childhood*

♥ *A place where the sins of the past are forgiven and any future is possible*

♥ *Anywhere that Caitlin is*

ΛΛΛΛΛΛΛΛΛΛΛΛΛΛ

❧FAMILY❧

~ FAMILY ~

Marilyn PAPPANO

The Lights of Home

Make me a Match

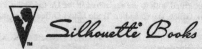

Silhouette Books

TM

Published by Silhouette Books

America's Publisher of Contemporary Romance

SILHOUETTE BOOKS
300 East 42nd St.,
New York, N. Y. 10017

ISBN 0-373-82165-4

THE LIGHTS OF HOME

Dear Reader,

Family and home. Those are two of the most important things in my life. As I followed my husband from state to state in his navy career, I always kept that connection to my family back in Oklahoma, in the place that always has been and always will be home. When we got the opportunity to return there, we did, this time to stay.

Jess Trujillo left his home and family, but he was never able to leave behind the longing—the connection. Now it's drawing him back to the New Mexico town where he was born, where he learned about life, love and heartbreak.

Caitlin Pierce never had the courage to leave her home or her family. After foolishly allowing her father to force her to choose between him and Jess, she's given up her dreams of love, marriage and a family of her own, for the only man she's ever loved is Jess and the only children she's ever wanted are his. If she can't have him, she'll settle for no one.

But just as family drove them apart, now it's bringing them back together, and along with the lessons life has already taught Jess, he's about to learn another one: forgiveness.

I hope you enjoy the journey.

Marilyn Pappano

Please address questions and book requests to:
Silhouette Reader Service
U.S.: 3010 Walden Ave., P.O. Box 1325, Buffalo, NY 14269
Canadian: P.O. Box 609, Fort Erie, Ont. L2A 5X3

Chapter 1

It was the end of another long day in the hot Louisiana sun, and Jess Trujillo was tired and craving a shower, dinner and his bed, in that order. On the way to his truck he stopped to get a Coke from the machine outside the ramshackle building that served as Southern Oil's field office. The can was cold, and condensation quickly formed on its sides. It felt good when he held it to his forehead, temporarily lowering his skin temperature a few degrees.

His co-workers walked past him in small groups, laughing, making plans for the evening. None of them invited Jess to join them. Most of them didn't even seem to notice him. He told himself it was all right; he didn't mind. Sure, he was lonely sometimes, but those men couldn't relieve the ache inside him. Only two people could make him forget his loneliness, and they were two states and hundreds of miles away. They weren't a part of his life anymore.

He smiled slowly. It was a rare and not entirely pleasant smile, heavy with bitterness. Caitlin and Lupe weren't part of his life because he had no life—simply an existence. Their lives had gone on, and his had ended. It had been his choice, his doing. He had no right to be bitter about it, but he was.

He had reached his truck when the foreman stepped out of the office and called his name. In his hand were several pieces of paper. Jess recognized the top one. Several members of the crew had received them lately, and he had figured it was only a matter of days until he got his. He was being laid off.

The oil price slump had turned the Louisiana economy upside down. Oil companies were going under with frightening regularity, and those that managed to survive did so by cutting expenses to the bone.

Jess didn't mind. Better that he get laid off than someone with a wife and kids to support. He had no one depending on him, no one counting on him for food and a home. He was responsible only for himself.

The foreman handed Jess his final paycheck. "Sorry, Trujillo," was all he said on that matter; then he held out an envelope. "This letter came for you. It was sent on from the last place you worked."

Jess folded the check and stuck it in his back pocket, then accepted the long white envelope. Letters for him were rare, since he moved often and sometimes didn't have an address for weeks at a time.

He stared at the return address. There was no name above it, but he knew the street number. Caitlin's. Why would she write to him after eight years? After what he had done? After what *she* had done?

The foreman noticed how pale Jess suddenly seemed, even though his bronzed skin was as dark as ever. "Are you okay?" he asked sympathetically.

Still staring at the letter, Jess didn't respond. Then he saw the envelope move and realized that his hands were shaking. He spun quickly and got into his truck, tossing the letter to the far side of the seat. It teetered on the edge before sliding slowly toward the floorboard. He leaned over and scooped it up before it landed. He laid it on the seat next to him, one corner under his thigh, and started the truck's engine.

His room at the local boardinghouse was small and dreary. Its single window was open wide, admitting insects through the holes torn in the screen, and a small fan turned back and forth, circulating hot, humid air. The mirror over the sink was mottled and cracked, and the linoleum that covered both the counters and the floor was worn and faded. Handmade curtains, old and too short, covered the doorless cabinets. There was a wooden table with uneven legs but no chairs, a sofa with rips that showed the stuffing, and a single bed several inches too short for Jess's long frame.

It was a shabby and depressing place, but Jess didn't mind. He lived there alone, and he had no friends or lovers to impress with his home.

No lovers. He'd bet that Caitlin had lovers. A woman as passionate as she was would never choose celibacy, as Jess had done for so long. After trying unsuccessfully to find a woman who could make him forget Caitlin, he'd decided it was easier to forget the desire. It was never very strong with anyone else, anyway, not like it had been with her.

He lay in the narrow bed, his thick black hair wet from the tepid shower he'd taken in the communal bathroom down the hall. It left a damp spot on the flat pillow he had folded in half to prop up his head.

Across the room was the envelope, leaning against a can of shaving cream on the table. If he squinted, he could make out the neat strokes that formed his name.

Why had she written? He rarely allowed himself to think of her anymore, except in his dreams, where he had no control. Only occasionally—like today, when he had admitted to himself that he was lonely—did Caitlin Pierce gain access to his conscious thoughts. Now he couldn't shut her out. He had to read her letter.

He rose from the bed, still naked from the shower. Droplets of water clung to his chest and arms, and he reached for a towel to dry them at the same time his other hand picked up the letter.

The bedsprings squeaked as he lay down again. The fan continued its monotonous back-and-forth hum, and a mosquito buzzed near his ear. But Jess heard none of those noises. He was staring once again at the letter, half-afraid to open it.

He wished she had put her name over the return address. Was she married? Did she have a last name he would recognize, possibly that of one of their friends? Or had she, like him, chosen to remain single? Alone.

The single sheet of paper inside the envelope offered no information about its writer. It was plain white typing paper, bearing lines of hot-pink ink that crossed the paper at an angle, dipping lower on the right side. Jess didn't need to see the signature to know that it was Caitlin's. Odd that he recognized her handwriting after so many years.

It was dated a month earlier, and it contained four lines, counting his name at the top and hers at the bottom.

Jess,
Your mother is very sick. Please come home as soon as you can. She needs you.

Caitlin

Jess dropped the letter and stood up. It was 1,170 miles from New Orleans to Isabel, the small New Mexico town that had once been his home. He knew the distance to Isabel from every place he'd ever been, inside the United States and out. It would take him at least twenty-three hours to get there, since his old truck refused to go faster than fifty miles an hour. If he left as soon as he was packed, he would be home Thursday.

He pulled a battered suitcase from the closet and began throwing his belongings into it. There wasn't much: some worn clothing, a couple of books, shaving gear—and a box. He tossed everything in haphazardly, except the wooden box. He laid it against the back of the case and arranged the clothes around it, to cushion it. That box was his only valued possession. Inside it were a few photographs, and some cards and letters bearing perfectly detailed miniature paintings in the margins. As hard as he'd tried to convince himself that he no longer cared for Caitlin, he hadn't been able to destroy those papers. Or the ring. It was in the box, too, inside a small green velvet case. He hadn't been able to get rid of it, either. Together, they were all he had left of their long-ago love.

Would he come today?

The question was routine, automatically popping into Caitlin's mind first thing every morning. It had been over a month since she'd written to him, and there had been no response. She was disappointed. She realized that Jess had built another life for himself, one that didn't include her, but surely he wouldn't forsake Lupe. Surely he would at least call to see if his mother was all right.

She hadn't told the older woman about her letter. She had been afraid that it might not reach him, or that he might choose to ignore it, and Lupe was in no condition to bear such a disappointment. So Caitlin kept quiet, and prayed every morning that Jess would come. She went to bed every night with her prayers unanswered.

She shut off the alarm before it rang and got out of the bed. Her long hair fell over her bare arms, tickling her soft skin. Impatiently, she brushed it away and walked across the cool tiled floor to the bathroom.

Caitlin was an early riser, a habit she had learned as a teenager—from Jess. It wasn't yet 6:30, but she didn't consider returning to bed. She wouldn't be able to sleep, and she didn't want to think, so she busied herself with her morning ritual.

After catching her hair in a large clasp, she pushed it over her shoulder and bent over the sink to wash her face. Her skin was smooth and tanned, her eyes brown, her long hair dark brown. Most people found her coloring pleasing, and sometimes surprising—especially if they knew her blond-haired, blue-eyed father. That was because Grant Pierce wasn't her real father. Her natural father was Indian, a man her mother had met years ago in one of the nearby Pueblo villages.

She knew nothing of her natural father, except that her mother had loved him deeply. He had died only weeks before Caitlin was born; a few weeks after her birth, her mother had also died. Her death had been officially considered an accident, but there had been rumors—tales that Lupe, her mother's best friend, had believed—that Claire had lost interest in living when her lover died. Why else would a woman still weak from a difficult birth wander off into the desert on an unusually hot summer day?

So Caitlin had been raised by her mother's husband, and she had grown up believing that Grant was her father. Until that night eight years ago.

Resolutely, she put all thought of that night out of her mind. Her face washed, her teeth brushed, she divided her hair into three sections and began braiding it—one plait on the left, one on the right, one in the center. When that was completed, she gathered the three braids together at her nape and fastened them with a bright-yellow rubber band.

She removed her knee-length nightgown and hung it on a hook behind the door. As she walked naked to the bureau in her bedroom, she glanced out the sliding door. Out there was the desert, her home. Beyond the mesas to the north and east was the city of Albuquerque, some fifty miles distant. To the north and west were the Laguna and Acoma Indian reservations. Her father had lived on one of those reservations. Caitlin herself had never lived anywhere besides the desert, here in the small town her great-great-grandfather had settled, and now she had no desire to. As long as she was home, her world was all right. Not perfect, not always happy, but all right.

She got undergarments from the top drawer, a lemon-yellow sweater-knit tank top from the second and a pair of tailored white shorts from the third. She pulled on the clothes and got a pair of brown huaraches, sandals woven from narrow strips of leather, and a bright-yellow belt from her closet.

A glance in the mirror confirmed that she looked passable. She wasn't a vain woman, so she didn't touch the tray of makeup on the bathroom counter. She knew it made her look better, but who was there to notice? Only Lupe, and she insisted that Caitlin looked wonderful no matter what.

Her world was small, consisting of Lupe, her father and a few friends she saw occasionally. When she gave it any thought, she decided she was happy enough with it. Lupe and Grant filled her emotional needs, and her art filled her creative needs.

Other than Grant, there were no men in her life. She had learned her lesson with Jess. It had taken years to get over him—years before she was able to face another day without him. She wouldn't give another man the power to hurt her the way he had. She wouldn't give another man her love.

Early as it was, Lupe was already in the kitchen and two places had been set at the breakfast table. Caitlin picked up the orange juice at her place and sipped it as she crossed the kitchen. "Good morning, Lupe," she greeted, hugging the woman.

Lupe Trujillo was in her early fifties, but she looked fifteen years older. Her soft brown face was lined; her eyes were weary. She had lost weight since the onset of her illness, and although she was still plump, she looked shrunken, as though she didn't fit her skin.

She'd had a bad night, Caitlin noted, and her heart contracted. If God had to give this awful disease to someone, why couldn't He give it to anyone besides Lupe? The kindly woman was like a mother to Caitlin—the only person who loved her unconditionally. Grant's love was largely dependent on how good a daughter she was. Jess's love had easily disappeared when put to the test that night eight years ago. Only Lupe looked at her faults and loved her anyway. She didn't deserve this illness, and seeing her looking so frail and weak made Caitlin sad and bitterly angry. God had no right!

She was instantly ashamed of such thoughts. If Lupe heard her voice such an opinion, she would chide her with her gentle brown eyes and remind her to have faith, to trust and believe. Lupe was a devout Catholic, and her faith had been a great comfort to her in dealing with her illness. Caitlin guessed she simply didn't have enough faith herself to attract God's attention, or He would answer her prayers and bring Jess back before it was too late.

Lupe raised her cheek for Caitlin's kiss, then smiled. "You brighten my day," she said, a hint of an accent in her soft words.

"Sit down, Lupe," Caitlin said. "I'll finish breakfast."

Usually the woman protested, but this morning she handed over the long cooking fork and shuffled slowly to the table. A bank of wide windows and French doors made up the outer wall of the kitchen, offering the same marvelous view as Caitlin's bedroom: the wild, rough desert landscape. It was to that view that Lupe turned.

"Do you suppose he's all right?"

Caitlin lifted the last slice of bacon from the skillet and set it to drain on a paper towel. Lupe rarely spoke Jess's name, as though she feared it might offend Caitlin. It made Caitlin feel guilty. He was Lupe's son, and Lupe loved him. But only once in the last few years had she posed the question that was always with her to Caitlin. "Have you ever regretted it—not going with Jess?" she had asked. And Caitlin had, after much thought, given a negative answer. Sometimes she was lonely for what they could have had, the love, the happiness, the children—especially the children. But if she'd gone with Jess that night, she never would have forgiven him for causing her to lose her father. She had some regrets—she still resented both Jess and Grant for forcing her decision—but she thought she had made the best choice possible under the circumstances.

She drained the bacon fat from the skillet, poured in the eggs Lupe had prepared and began stirring. "I'm sure he's fine, Lupe." It was her standard answer. Jess could take care of himself.

Green and red peppers and green onions added color to the mass of scrambled eggs. Spooned onto plates with slices of crisp bacon and wedges of tomato, they made a meal that was appealing to the eyes as well as the mouth.

"I'm sorry," Lupe said as Caitlin carried the plates over. "I know it must displease you to have to listen to me talk about him, but—" She fingered the silver cross around her neck and whispered, "Dear Lord, I miss him."

Caitlin bent to hug her. "It doesn't bother me, Lupe."

"Really?"

That was also a routine exchange. Lupe loved Jess dearly, and she needed to talk about him, to keep his memory alive, but she feared the constant reminders might irritate or anger or possibly even hurt Caitlin.

"Really, Lupe, I don't mind."

"He didn't mean to hurt you, Caitlin."

The denial was both true and false. His words that night, spoken in a burst of anger and resentment, had been directed at Grant. It was Grant he'd wanted to punish, not Caitlin, but he'd known she would be hurt, and he had done it anyway. He had made accusations and demands, knowing he was hurting her, and he had destroyed their love.

As she ate her breakfast, Caitlin wondered why Lupe's thoughts centered on Jess that morning. Because she'd had a restless night? Did nights without sleep make her more aware of her illness, of the short time she had left? Did she fear, as Caitlin did, that she would die without seeing Jess again?

Caitlin closed her eyes briefly, and her lips moved in a silent, familiar prayer: Dear God, please let him come today.

Soon after breakfast, Lupe left for the small shop where she worked. Caitlin offered, as usual, to drive her, and Lupe, also as usual, refused. Driving represented a small measure of independence to her, and it gave her a few minutes alone to think, she said, so she stubbornly refused to give it up as long as the doctors said it was safe. Since the shop was only a few blocks away, down the steep hill in Isabel's tiny business district, Caitlin usually gave in to her on the matter.

What did Lupe think about? Caitlin speculated as she did the few dishes they had dirtied. She was sure Jess was at the top of the list. She knew that Lupe blamed Grant for driving her only child away, but she'd never placed any of that blame on Caitlin. Still, there were times when Caitlin couldn't help feeling guilty. Did Lupe think about dying? At twenty-nine, the thought of death frightened Caitlin, but Lupe, knowing that each day could be her last, seemed serene and accepting. "My only sorrow," she had told Caitlin once, "is that things never worked out between you and Jess. I wish you two could be happy." It was typical of her—no complaints about her own unhappy love, or about the disease that was slowly eating away at her, but concern instead for Caitlin and Jess.

Caitlin sighed. Thinking about death was depressing. Thinking about Lupe's death was guaranteed to have her in tears in no time. She had to put it out of her mind for now.

It was Caitlin's habit to clean house thoroughly every morning, though with Grant out of the country on business, it never really got messy. By the time the last tile floor had been swept, the heavy wooden furniture dusted and the final load of laundry put into the dryer, the sun was shining brightly in a cloudless sky, and she was anxious to get outside. She rarely went to her studio, a renovated detached garage at the edge of the backyard, before eleven, so that left her almost two hours to laze in the sun on the deck out back. She fixed a glass of iced tea, got the novel she had started the night before, picked up her tape player and went outside to relax

Jess rubbed his eyes to ease their weariness. He'd left Tucumcari early that morning, and now he was almost in Albuquerque. From there it was about fifty miles to Isabel. He was almost home. He savored the sound of that. Almost home. He'd stayed away so long, but now he was back.

The interstate cut through the Sandía and Manzanos Mountains and dropped into the city of Albuquerque, situated in the Río Grande Valley. The city had grown a great deal in the eight years he'd been gone, and it seemed to take forever to get through it. Once he reached the west side of the river, it wasn't far to Isabel. He would be home within an hour.

Home with his mother. For two days he had worried about her, but now the excitement of seeing her again was taking over. He knew she would be pleased to see him—she was the most giving, most loving person he knew. No matter how badly he'd hurt and disappointed her, she would welcome him.

Unlike Caitlin.

The corners of his mouth tightened and turned down. Not yet. He wouldn't think about Caitlin yet.

He had gotten this close before. One December three years ago, he had been moving from a California farm town to a Texas oil field, and he had passed through on the interstate. The desire to see his mother had been so great that he'd almost forgotten about Caitlin. Almost.

Jess rubbed at his temples, gave up, and let Caitlin take over his mind. Would he see her? Had she and his mother remained close? She had written the letter, which indicated that they were still friends. Jess hoped it was just a casual friendship. He didn't want her to be an important part of his mother's life.

He didn't want to see her. The hurting had stopped a long time ago, but it had left its mark on him, and seeing Caitlin would only reopen old wounds. She meant nothing to him but bad memories and renewed pain.

What he had done that night eight years ago had been rotten and unkind and foolish, but he had acted in anger, provoked by Grant Pierce. Grant had mocked and taunted him until he couldn't stand it anymore. What *she* had done that night had shown a complete lack of trust and faith and loyalty to the man she'd claimed to love. If she had loved him, she would have stood by him; she would have gone with him. But she hadn't loved him—at least, not enough. In the end, Grant had won, because without Caitlin's help, Jess couldn't fight her father's hatred anymore. And she had refused to help. Peace with her father had meant more to her than marriage to Jess. That was something he wouldn't forgive.

His dark eyes grew bleak with remembrance. He'd been a fool eight years ago, and he had suffered for it long enough. He had given up his mother—the only family he had—and his home. But today that was coming to an end.

He exited the freeway onto a narrow paved road that looked as if it led nowhere. After going fourteen miles south and one mile west, he remembered, he would crest a hill, and the town would be there below him.

The sign on the edge of town was rusted and filled with holes; someone, probably after a little too much to drink, had used it for target practice. Welcome to Isabel, N.M., it greeted. Founded 1868. Population 6,231.

Isabel was the perfect place for a man like Grant Pierce, Jess thought bitterly as he drove along the main street. It was small, not too prosperous, not too advanced. The people were still impressed by the fact that he was the great-grandson of Amos Pierce and his wife, Isabel, for whom the town was named. Even if he'd done nothing worthwhile in his life, his name alone would have assured him of the respect and admiration of the townspeople, something that Grant needed to feed his incredible ego.

Jess turned onto the street that led to his house. Little had changed. For the first time since he'd left, he realized just how much he missed his home. Just seeing the town filled part of the emptiness inside him.

When he pulled into the driveway of the house where he'd grown up, the sense of homecoming was wiped out by shock. In the center of the lot, where their modest two-bedroom frame house had stood, was an old, cracked concrete slab—the foundation of their home. Nothing else was left, not even debris from the house that had stood there for years.

Thought and feeling slowly returned, drawing Jess from the truck. The formerly neat yard was overgrown, littered with beer cans and broken bottles. The place looked lonely and desolate, and for an instant Jess felt the same way. What had happened to their house? What had destroyed it so completely? Why hadn't Caitlin told him in her letter? And, more importantly, where was his mother?

He walked around the lot, looking for answers, for clues, and finding none. With a sigh that was almost despair, he returned to his truck and reluctantly started the engine.

He was angry when he left for Caitlin's house. She should have told him in her letter. It wasn't right, letting him find out like this. Would it have been too much to ask that she write one or two more lines explaining that his house was gone and where his mother was living?

He made the turns that would take him to the Pierce house on the edge of town. A few minutes later he parked in the driveway next to a late-model Jeep. For a moment he simply sat there and looked. In the middle of an already yellowing lawn was a cactus garden, its round borders defined by rust-colored stones. The desert plants looked appropriate against the pale-buff house.

Jess got out of the truck and faced the house, his hands on his slim hips. It was a traditional adobe, but instead of the flat pueblo roof that was so common in New Mexico, the roof showed the California Mission influence in its sloping lines and red tiles. The walls were thick, but not the usual two feet or more. The windows were shuttered, the wood painted dark brown. The double doors located in the center of the house were also dark brown, solid wood and intricately carved with the sunbursts that were popular in Mexico.

Jess headed toward the front door, but the sound of music coming from the backyard stopped him. He went around the corner, the sound of his boots muffled on the wide strip of dead grass that grew alongside the house and led to a flat, rocky yard, the deck and the detached garage.

She shifted as he came around the corner of the house, and the bright yellow of her tank top caught his attention. He stopped instantly, his anger momentarily forgotten, his eyes drawn to her almost against his will.

Had she always been so pretty? He had somehow forgotten the delicate lines of her face and the feelings that stirred deep inside him every time he saw her. He must have forgotten if he had truly believed he could come back and feel nothing.

He took a step back. He wasn't prepared for this. He wasn't ready to face her.

But he didn't turn and run, the way he wanted to. The way he'd done eight years ago. He knew already that he couldn't run fast enough or far enough to get away from her. He would have to face her sooner or later, and he'd just as soon do it without benefit of an audience. Besides, he needed to find his mother. Caitlin could tell him where she was.

The natural wood of the deck was rough and unfinished. It complemented the rough plaster of the house. Big clay pots, some filled with red-flowering plants and others with cactus, provided color among unpainted benches and chairs. The only thing out of place was the pastel-colored lounge chair where Caitlin sat, chosen for comfort rather than esthetics. An upturned clay pot next to her chair served as a table, holding a glass of tea. The ice had melted, and condensation formed a small pool around the bottom of the glass. She didn't notice that when she picked it up with long slender fingers and lifted it to her lips.

Jess watched her, part of him aching with unwelcome desire. When you went without a woman for months, he told himself, any woman could arouse that desire. It had nothing to do with Caitlin in particular.

Caitlin didn't know what it was that caught her attention—if he had made some noise as he stood there motionless, or if her inner sense realized that she was no longer alone—but suddenly she sat straighter, her muscles tensed, and she turned her head toward him.

Jess knew the very second she became aware of him. His body and mind, once so finely tuned to everything about her, had lost none of their sensitivity. He could read the tension in the lines of her body, and he smiled without humor—a bitter, twisting grimace. Had he expected her to happily welcome him?

He walked toward her, climbing the steps that led to the deck, never taking his eyes from her face. Her beauty amazed him, and her anger overwhelmed him. There was something cold, hard and unforgiving in eyes that had always laughed. Something grim and relentless in a mouth that had always smiled. She was angry, and it made him remember his own anger. What right did she have to be upset? He was the one who had been betrayed, the one who had lost everything. She'd gotten exactly what she'd wanted: her loving father. Nothing else had mattered to her. So why was she mad now?

Her inner self screamed in alarm, recognizing him before her eyes did. In the instant it took her to realize that this was Jess, the other self was already drawing in her defenses, already searching for ways to protect herself.

She rose to her feet, clenching her hands in fists behind her back, battling for control. She had known he would come—sooner or later, he would come, because Jess loved his mother as much as Caitlin did—but she hadn't prepared herself for it. She hadn't readied herself to see him, to talk to him. She didn't know what to say, how to act. One part of her wanted to scream and yell, to throw things and order him off her property and out of her life. One part wanted to show him that his presence didn't bother her, that she no longer cared about him. And one part—one tiny, insignificant part buried under years of resentment and hurt and bitterness—wanted to run to him and kiss him, to feel his arms around her, to hear him say one more time, "I love you."

She wasn't shocked by that. She knew herself well enough to know that the time when Jess couldn't affect her intensely would probably never come. But as long as he didn't know, she was all right.

Her calmer side won. She didn't throw a tantrum or anything else, and she made no move toward him. Her fingers twined so tightly together behind her back that their tips turned white, she asked him, "What do you want?"

The answer came swiftly to him: *You.* He wanted her, but he wasn't going to allow himself to have her. Caitlin, with her soft brown eyes, her dark, silky brown hair, and her gentle, sweet words, couldn't be trusted. He had learned that the hard way once before. He wouldn't forget it.

"Hello, Cait," he greeted her.

His voice was soft, but there was nothing gentle or nice about it. Coupled with the nickname that only he had used, it made her shudder. It brought back memories of a love that had been so sweet—a love that had been mostly one-sided. She wanted to cry, but instead she hardened herself. It was easy to do; she'd had plenty of practice over the last eight years. "What do you want?" she asked again.

Cold. Her voice was as cold as the December winds at the top of Sandía Peak. He remembered when its husky tones had flowed over him with all the warmth and sweetness of honey, whispering vows of love and cries of ecstasy—not terse, angry questions.

He could be just as cold. "Where is my mother?" he demanded.

Caitlin looked faintly guilty. "She's at work right now."

That answered only part of his question. "Where is she living?"

"Here." Now there was a definite look of guilt in her eyes. "Her house burned down a few months ago, so I asked her to stay here."

Jess silently cursed. Why hadn't she included that little bit of information in her letter? Why had she written the damned letter at all, if she couldn't bother to tell him everything he needed to know? "Why didn't you tell me?"

She shrugged, trying hard to look at ease and failing so miserably. "I didn't think it was important. Isabel's a small town. I knew you'd find her."

In a low, deadly voice, he said, "Not important? You thought I wouldn't care that our house had burned down? That my mother was living in Grant Pierce's house?"

She winced at the hatred he put into her father's name. There was no need to ask how he felt about the past. "All right, Jess," she admitted. "I didn't tell you because I thought you might not come back if you knew she was living here."

He walked to the rail and leaned against it, his back to the desert. His arms were crossed over his chest, pulling his shirt tight. "You flatter yourself, Cait. Do you really think I would stay away from my mother because of you?" he asked with a sneer.

Caitlin shrugged again. "You've done it for eight years."

He stiffened, but he couldn't deny the truth, so he changed the subject. "If she's so sick, why is she at work today?"

Caitlin chose a section of railing at right angles to Jess and leaned back herself. She didn't look nearly as relaxed as he did. "She can work," she replied.

"But she's sick." He clearly didn't believe her. "I want the truth, Cait. Why did you write me that letter? Why did you want me to come home? Did you decide after eight years that you miss me, or did you get tired of living your life for Daddy?"

She was trembling, and she hated it. Jess would notice, and he would use it against her. "I wrote to you for Lupe," she defended herself. "I didn't want to see you. I didn't want you to come home. But Lupe needs you."

"Just when did you become so full of concern for my mother?"

Caitlin's head jerked up, and she stared at him with wide brown eyes. "That's not fair!" she exclaimed. "I have always been concerned about Lupe. I've always loved her! *I've* been here with her, Jess, all these years while you were gone. *I'm* the one who spent Mother's Day and her birthday and Christmas and Thanksgiving with her! Don't you dare question my feelings for her!"

He was wrong and he knew it, but pride wouldn't let him apologize. Wearily, he rubbed one hand over the back of his neck. "Okay. Where's your father?"

Caitlin's anger was still there, slow to dissipate. It took her a moment to answer. "Dad's working in the Middle East. He'll be back in a few months."

"Good. Then you won't mind if I stay here."

She panicked. *Mind?* How could she possibly *not* mind having Jess in her house? Simply knowing that he was back in town was going to be hard enough. She preferred it when he was in California or Louisiana or Texas or Montana, where she knew she wouldn't see him, wouldn't hear his voice. In Isabel, she would risk running into him. In her house, she couldn't possibly avoid him. It was impossible. She couldn't let him stay in her house.

And she couldn't turn him away. She had written to him for Lupe, and this was now Lupe's home, too.

He knew Caitlin didn't want him staying in her house, and he knew that she would let him stay anyway, out of some sense of...what? Obligation to Lupe? Guilt? He left the rail and sat down in the chair she had vacated. It was still warm from her body, and the air around it smelled faintly of her perfume. He liked the smell. "Does Mom still work for Dr. Ramirez?"

"N-no, she had to quit."

"Had to? Why?"

She turned her back to him and stared out at the desert. This wasn't her responsibility. She had gotten him home; now it was up to Lupe to tell him why. No matter what feelings she still had for Jess—and, at the moment, she was so confused that she wasn't sure what they were—she wasn't going to be the one to tell him that his mother was dying.

He left the chair again and crossed to her in a few steps. His hand on her arm felt rough as he turned her to face him. "Why did she have to quit?"

She tried to ignore the warmth spreading through her from the point where his hand made contact with her skin. She tried not to notice the subtle woodsy scent of his aftershave. She tried to pretend that her heart was beating faster because it was a stressful situation, not because of Jess. And she failed at all three. "She quit because there were sick people there," she answered at last, her voice breathy and choked.

Jess looked puzzled. "There generally are sick people in a doctor's office. What does that have to do with Mom?"

"She—she couldn't be exposed to other illnesses like that. Her—her immune system..." She couldn't go on. She couldn't tell him about the disease that was killing his mother, about the chemotherapy that had made her violently ill, causing her hair to fall out and temporarily suppressing her immune system so that a common cold could be life threatening. She had stopped the therapy, and her immune system was in working order again, but she had chosen not to return to her receptionist's job in the doctor's office.

Jess started to push her, to demand a complete explanation, then decided he didn't want one. Not yet. The kind of problem she was describing had to be serious, far more serious than he had expected. He wasn't sure he could deal with it yet. "So where does she work now?"

"She's the bookkeeper in Carmen Mendez's store. It gives her something to do, but she doesn't see a lot of people."

His hand dropped from her arm, and he turned away. She watched him, unsure of what to say.

The lines of his face were hard, unforgiving. Physically he was the same, though perhaps more muscular, she thought, letting her gaze move slowly over him. But his eyes were different. They were a deep brown, darker even than hers, and they were empty. Before, there had been life and laughter and love, and now there was nothing. He reminded her of a man who had lost his purpose in living. One who had lost his soul. It made her sad.

"Would you like a glass of tea?" she offered.

He looked up, surprised, as if he had forgotten her presence. "Do you have any beer?"

She shook her head.

"Tea's fine."

She escaped into the house, taking her time about filling a large glass with ice, then tea. Through the glass-paned door, she could see him. He was sitting on a bench near her chair, his elbows on his knees, his hands clasped loosely together. He looked tired—not physically, but emotionally—and her heart went out to him. Had the last eight years been hard for him?

Frowning darkly, she cautioned herself. Jess didn't need her sympathy. He didn't need anything from her. He had taught her that a long time ago.

She carried the glass outside, setting it on the bench near him. She didn't want to touch him, not even accidentally. She picked up her own glass, sat down once more in the lounge chair and turned her gaze toward the desert. Jess turned his eyes on her.

She was intensely aware of his stare, but she won the struggle inside her. She didn't turn away, didn't run, didn't hide. She sat motionless and let him look until, having seen enough, he looked away.

She had changed. Maturity had turned her teenaged prettiness into quiet beauty, and she had gained the few pounds needed to fill out her five-foot seven-inch frame. But the biggest change, he thought, was in her eyes. Eyes that had laughed and teased and sparkled were now subdued, as if they hadn't laughed for far too long. Because of him and her father? he wondered, or was it just life in general?

How did she feel about him? Did she hate him? Love him? Not give a damn about him? He couldn't tell, but he would find out in the next few weeks.

Did she ever regret turning him away all those years ago? As much as Jess wanted to know, he knew he wouldn't ask. If she said no, even now, even after so long a time, it would hurt.

His eyes shifted to her hands. Her fingers were long and slim. The nails were cut short and bare of polish. Her hands were also bare of rings. Of course, that didn't mean that she hadn't married, or that she wasn't involved with anyone. Still, once he'd given her his ring, she had always worn it, even when she was working. Even when it infuriated Grant.

"I'll change the sheets in Dad's room."

Her voice broke into his thoughts, and he looked up as she

stood. Her legs were long and tanned, and for just an instant he couldn't shut out the picture of their lovemaking, her legs twined with his. Almost groaning, he squeezed his eyes shut. When he opened them again, Caitlin was closing the door behind her.

Lord, how could he still want her? So much had happened; so much time had passed. She had betrayed him, had let him down at a time when he needed her badly. Didn't he have enough pride to keep from wanting her like a sex-starved, adolescent virgin?

After a moment he followed her, heading through the kitchen and down the long tiled hallway to the bedroom that had been Grant's.

Caitlin was spreading a sheet over the mattress, pulling the fitted corners down. She didn't look up when Jess walked in. "I didn't tell your mom that I wrote to you."

"Why not? You knew I would come."

"I didn't even know if you would get the letter. Most of Lupe's letters got returned."

Some small knot of tension inside him dissolved. He had always wondered if his mother ever tried to contact him. Knowing that she had made the last few years seem less dark.

Then Caitlin added, "You move around too much."

He got defensive. "What I do is my business, Cait. Not yours."

She shrugged and reached for the top sheet. Jess leaned against the dresser and watched her, not offering his help. "What time will she be home?"

"About three."

She smoothed out the sheet, spread the quilted coverlet and coaxed fat pillows into cases. While she finished, Jess looked around the room, the only one in the house that he'd never been in before. It was a comfortable room, with walls of pale yellow stucco, deep-set windows on either side of the bed and a wood floor that gleamed. The furniture was heavy and sturdy, made of ponderosa pine in the northern New Mexico style. The paneled headboard was carved with miniature sunbursts and intricate swirls. The carving was repeated on each drawer of the dresser against which Jess leaned, as well as on the simply designed nightstands. Brass rings were attached to the drawers as handles, and a collection of old brass candlesticks stood on one nightstand.

A large set of plain bookshelves stood in one corner. They held a few books, a photograph of Claire before she married Grant and a collection of hand-painted glazed tiles. The picture of Claire, he was sure, was Caitlin's; there had been no love between Grant and his wife. He was also certain that the tiles and the only picture in the room, a desert sunset with a dozen different shades of red, had been painted by Caitlin.

"How long will I be here?"

Caitlin knew what he meant. She was surprised by the sudden pain she felt. Was he only planning to stay as long as Lupe needed him? Then would he disappear again, as he had done in the past? Would she never see him again after this visit?

"Caitlin?"

She lifted her shoulders in a helpless shrug. "I don't know."

It was true. Even the doctors couldn't say how much time Lupe had. She might go into a remission of sorts, but the results would eventually be the same: the disease was killing her. It might take a month, two months or two years, but she was going to die.

Fear took shape inside him. If Caitlin had found it necessary to send for him yet was so reluctant to discuss his mother with him, then the illness must be even more serious than he suspected. He couldn't imagine his mother ill; she'd never even had a cold.

When he spoke, he sounded sharp and uneasy. "What do you mean, you don't know?"

"Talk to your mother, Jess," she answered, practically pleading. With that she fled the room, closing the door with a snap behind her.

Jess sat down on the quilt that Claire's grandmother had made. All his good feelings about coming home were gone, and in their place was fear. He was losing his mother. His mother—the woman who had given birth to him when her friends had urged her to have a then-illegal abortion; the woman who had kept him and raised him, even though it meant being disowned by her family for the disgrace she had brought them; the woman who had given him so much love that he had rarely ever missed the father who had abandoned him. He was going to lose her, and there was nothing he could do to stop it. He had never felt so helpless in his life.

* * *

A soft knock at the door filtered through the layers of sleep that surrounded Jess's mind. It was down the hall, he told himself. No one ever visited his room. Then his eyes opened, and he realized he wasn't in his room, and the knock *was* at his door. Even as he looked, it swung open, and Caitlin stepped inside. "Jess?" she whispered.

"Yeah?" He rolled onto his back. He'd needed the nap, but it had left him feeling thick-headed, unbalanced. It was a dangerous time to be dealing with Caitlin.

"I'm going to fix lunch. Are you hungry?"

"Yeah."

She stayed at the door, not venturing farther into the room. Despite the rest, he still looked tired. Vulnerable. She scolded herself. She didn't need any tender feelings toward Jess. They weren't safe. "Are sandwiches okay?"

He repeated the same word. "Yeah." While his eyes were shut, the door closed. Yawning wide, he sat up, then slid his feet from the high bed to the floor. He straightened the mussed covers before leaving the room.

The kitchen had been completely remodeled since the last time he'd been there. The counters were overlaid with the same copper-colored tiles that covered the floor. A long, wide bar had been added to separate the kitchen from the small informal dining area. The dining room walls were a soft pink stucco, the kitchen walls copper-colored tile. Painted tiles of New Mexico scenes formed a border along the walls. The wood in the large room was dark, and it carried the usual ornate carving. The small table was old, with a feather pattern along the four legs and surrounded by four pueblo-styled chairs with the same feather pattern and soft fabric cushions.

Caitlin had set the table and was carrying a platter of food over when Jess walked in. "Do you want tea?" she asked when she heard his boots on the floor.

"Yeah."

She put together a thick sandwich of sliced turkey, Swiss cheese, mayonnaise and tomato, then cut it into manageable pieces.

"What is Grant doing in the Middle East?" he asked as he fixed his own sandwich.

A smile curved her lips involuntarily. The day that Jess Trujillo felt safer discussing Grant Pierce instead of a million other topics, things were in a sorry state indeed. Her father and his unreasoning hatred of Jess had been the source of every serious argument they'd ever had. "What he does best—giving advice."

"I don't remember any of his advice being particularly good," Jess said with a slow drawl.

"No, it wasn't. Not for us, at least." The extent of Grant's advice to her in the last few years with Jess had been to "get rid of that bastard before it's too late." "It's easier to break up with him now than to get a divorce later," he had counseled. "He's not good enough for you, Caitlin. He's never been anything but trouble from the moment he was conceived. How can you even consider marrying him? Having children with him? They'd grow up to be ashamed of their bastard father." That last night she had learned the reasons Grant hated Jess—for the circumstances of his birth, for who his parents were and for trying to take Caitlin from him. In some irrational manner, Grant even blamed Jess for Caitlin's illegitimacy.

"He's been over there a couple of months," she went on, shaking off old memories. "He likes it."

"I thought he liked New Mexico. Whenever you talked about moving, he always had something to say about what a wonderful place this is." His bitterness was evident in the way he talked. He couldn't help it. Grant Pierce had made his life miserable for as long as Jess could remember. He had tolerated every insult, every snide remark, every vulgar slur, and he had still lost.

"You still resent him." Caitlin offered the observation hesitantly, afraid he would erupt in anger. Instead his reply was quiet and thoughtful, and almost sad, she thought.

"I tried to be what he wanted for you."

She knew that was true. Despite his frequent fights at school, Jess had been the epitome of politeness to Grant. He had never spoken to the man without frequent sir's and the proper degree of respect in his voice. But Grant had never liked him. "That worthless bastard," he'd called him, often to his face. Jess had endured it for months, for Caitlin's sake. Then he had exploded.

She knew that most of the blame for that night belonged to her and her father. She didn't blame Jess for what he'd said—it was his leaving that had made her bitter. After all the times he'd sworn he loved her, he had left town without a word, had never called her, and never come back for her. Even now, he was here for Lupe, not Caitlin.

They finished their lunch in silence. While Caitlin put away the leftovers, Jess rinsed the dishes and stacked them in the dishwasher. She was preparing to return to her studio when he asked, "Did you ever marry?"

Her eyes widened in surprise. "No, of course not. I...I... No. I didn't." She pushed her hands into the pockets of her shorts because they felt shaky. Jess didn't need to know how uneasy the subject of marriage made her. "Did you?"

He didn't know what had prompted him to ask that question— just curiosity, he guessed. He shook his head in response. "No."

She smiled, an uncomfortable, awkward gesture. "I'll get back to work now."

He watched her go. When the door of the old garage closed behind her, he turned to leave the kitchen. He could have followed her, but he didn't. He had two hours to pass until his mother was due home from work, and he wanted to spend them alone, so he could think. So he could figure out what was happening to him, before it was too late.

Caitlin ignored the painting she had been working on and went to sit on the sofa in the corner. This huge old room that served as her studio was also her refuge, her place to hide. No one had ever been invited inside for any length of time, not Grant, not even Lupe. Inside there was peace and security, and today she needed them more than ever.

The studio could be stuffy on hot afternoons; the huge windows that let in light also let in a fair amount of heat. Caitlin didn't notice, however. She sat in front of them and looked out.

Jess had loved the desert and their little town. How hard it must have been for him to go away. In their youth, Caitlin had been the one who wanted to leave. She had wanted to see the world after they were married, and he had always protested that he loved Isabel—though not as much as he loved her, he'd added. Yet he had been the one to leave, and she had been left behind.

Stop it! she commanded silently. The first two years after Jess left had been difficult, but for the last six she had gotten by without thinking too much about him, without remembering too much. She couldn't go on like this or she would drive herself crazy—or right into Jess's arms.

Maybe she shouldn't have written to him. Then she thought of how pleased Lupe would be to see Jess again, and she was glad she had. She hoped the older woman wouldn't see the changes in him as easily as Caitlin had. Let her time with Jess be good, Caitlin prayed silently. Let her be happy.

The faint scent of cedar drifted out as Jess opened one of the dresser drawers in the master bedroom. He had unpacked his belongings, putting them in the dresser and the closet, and changed to a shirt that wasn't quite so worn. It was a few minutes before three, and his mother would be home soon.

He was filled with a longing so intense it made him ache. He felt like a child again, teased once too often by cruel neighborhood children and their sometimes-more-cruel parents, running to his mother for comfort. He desperately wanted to be held in her embrace, to hear her tell him that everything would be all right. He whispered a silent prayer to that effect. *Let it be all right.*

Soft footsteps sounded in the hall, the slap of sandals against tile. They stopped at his room; then he heard Caitlin's faint knock. She opened the door and stepped inside. "Jess, she's here."

He looked startled.

He was afraid. Caitlin wanted to touch him, to offer him reassurance, but she didn't know if he would welcome her touch. She left the room, Jess following a few steps behind.

He let Caitlin enter the living room first, and heard her say, "You have a visitor, Lupe." Then he slowly entered the room.

His mother crossed herself and murmured a quick prayer, then stood up and flung her arms around his neck. "You came back!" she cried, her tears soaking into his clean shirt. "Thank God. You came back to us!"

Chapter 2

Lupe was too tired to cook that evening, though they pretended not to notice. After watching from the corner of her eye while Lupe made a salad, Caitlin took over, shooing her from the kitchen. "But I always cook dinner," Lupe protested.

"But tonight is special," Caitlin argued. "Sit down and talk to Jess. I can cook."

Lupe asked endless questions: where he had been, what he had done. He answered them, describing places that meant nothing to him, jobs that were unimportant, people he hardly knew. He condensed eight years of his life into a few minutes of talk. Caitlin listened, saying nothing. She was aware of everything he said—and all the things he didn't say. She could feel his eyes on her as she worked, but she was careful not to look at him. That made it too easy to remember the Jess of eight years ago. The one she had loved.

When Lupe left to answer the phone, silence fell over the kitchen. Caitlin felt vulnerable now that she was alone with him again. She dropped the spoon she held, then the dish towel. While slicing the onions for the salad, she cut neatly right into her finger, then stuck it under the faucet to rinse away the blood—under hot water.

"Do I make you nervous?" he asked in a silky voice.

"Whatever gave you that idea?" she answered dryly.

"You weren't always so clumsy. Of course, things were different before, weren't they?"

They certainly were. She had been stupid before, gullible and trusting. Now she knew better than to trust him.

Jess leaned his elbows on the tile counter and watched her. She pretended not to notice him, but he didn't mind. Just looking at her was enough.

"That was Carmen Mendez," Lupe said as she returned to the kitchen.

Slowly Jess shifted his gaze from Caitlin to his mother, waiting for her to go on.

Lupe had seen the way he was watching Caitlin, and she silently rejoiced. She had prayed for years that they would work out their problems, and now she had a real reason to hope.

She had accepted that she was going to die. For herself, she didn't mind. She had lived a good life—not as long as she would have liked, but good nonetheless. She worried, though about Caitlin and Jess. They were adults, capable of living their own lives, but neither of them was happy. Though they might be too stubborn to see it, they needed each other. If only she could see them together again, happy and in love and married, as they should be, she could die without regrets.

"You remember Carmen, don't you, Jess?"

He thought of the small, slender woman who had been Lupe's best friend since Claire Pierce's death and was the mother of his own best friend. "Of course I do. I remember everything."

Caitlin shot a glance at him. He expected it, and was waiting. He was smiling cynically. His eyes held hers, and without words, he told her some of the things he remembered best of all. She blushed and turned away, her hands trembling.

"I told Carmen that you were home, and she wants to have a party. I told her I would check with you."

His dark gaze measured his mother. She looked weak. Would a party tire her too much?

"Well?"

He turned to Caitlin for guidance. "A party would be fun, wouldn't it, Lupe?" she said with a smile. It wasn't subtle, but Jess got the message.

"Tell Carmen I would be honored."

Lupe was delighted. "I'll call her right now." She got to her feet and started toward the door.

"Will it be all right for her?" he asked Caitlin in a quietly urgent voice as soon as his mother was gone.

Caitlin shrugged. Lupe's illness wasn't a subject that she wanted to discuss with Jess, but answering one question wouldn't hurt. "The doctor said she can do almost anything she wants. She gets tired easily; she doesn't have the energy she used to. But he hasn't restricted her activities yet. He said it's good for her to work because it keeps her mind occupied. It's going to be so hard for her when she has to quit."

The fear that had found root inside him earlier that day grew. She was saying that the illness, whatever it was, was progressive; Lupe was going to get worse. He'd known all along that it had to be serious, but he refused to accept that his mother was going to die. Until he heard it from her lips, he wouldn't believe it was going to happen.

Before he could ask any more questions, Lupe returned with the news that the party was set. She was more animated at dinner than Caitlin had seen her in months, full of plans for the party—listing people to call, things to buy, food to cook—until Caitlin called a halt to it. "I thought Carmen was giving this party."

Jess scowled at her. His mother was happy; why was Caitlin interfering?

"She is, but he's my son, so I'm helping."

Caitlin ignored the dark anger radiating in her direction. "It sounds like you're taking over. Carmen will regret ever accepting your help." The words were spoken lightly, but Lupe received their message: *Take it easy; slow down.*

"You're right," Lupe agreed grudgingly. She knew her own limits, even if she did sometimes pretend not to. "I'll relax and enjoy it. You and I, Caitlin, will be the guest of honor's guests of honor."

Caitlin silently jeered. Honor, she was sure, was a word that Jess didn't associate with her in any way.

Jess leaned over to kiss his mother's cheek. "I'll be the luckiest man there, with the prettiest woman in the state of New Mexico."

Lupe scoffed. "Your mother is too old to be pretty. You must be talking about Caitlin. Isn't she beautiful?"

Caitlin sat still, wondering what his answer to that would be. He looked at her, his eyes touching her with all the power of a physical caress; then he agreed. "Yes, she's very beautiful."

The words sounded like a compliment, but the look in his eyes robbed her of any pleasure she might have taken from it. They were cold, dark, bitter. He must hate her as much as he hated her father, and that hurt her. Although she no longer loved Jess, no longer felt anything at all for him, they had once been important to each other. How sad that he could forget all the good in their lives, replacing it with hate.

His voice cut into her thoughts, and she looked up. "I'm sure Caitlin won't mind doing the dishes this evening," he was saying. "Come and talk to me, Mom."

Before Lupe could protest, Caitlin quickly agreed. "Go on. You haven't seen him in a long time."

Jess pulled Lupe's chair out. Over her head, he was frowning at Caitlin. He didn't need any reminders of how long he'd been away—or of why he'd been forced to leave. Then he helped his mother to her feet, and they left Caitlin alone in the kitchen.

She loaded the dishwasher, wiped the counters and went down the hall to her room. When she passed the living room she heard the quiet murmur of their voices. She paused for a moment, then continued along the hallway.

She didn't expect to sleep well that night, but once she had showered and climbed between the cool, sweet-smelling sheets, she drifted off right away. She didn't hear the soft footsteps that stopped outside her door several hours later. She didn't hear the whispered oath before the steps continued down the hall to the master bedroom.

Sleep came easily to Jess, too, and he was disturbed only by dreams that he knew he wouldn't remember in the morning. Dreams he wouldn't allow himself to remember. Dreams of soft brown eyes and whispered words of love. Nightmares.

When Caitlin awoke Friday morning, the familiar little question was there: *Would he come today?* She stopped in mid thought. He was home. Jess had come home.

She dressed in jeans and a yellow T-shirt that bore a big red Zía sun, a circle from which four sets of four lines extended in the four directions of the compass. Underneath it, also in red, was written, New Mexico—*Tierra de Encanto.*

The kitchen was dark and silent, a sign that Lupe had had a restful night. Caitlin whispered her thanks as she reached for the light switch. Then she stopped short.

Jess was sitting at the table, a glass of milk between his hands. He wore a T-shirt that stretched across his broad chest and a pair of jeans as faded and as comfortably tight as Caitlin's. He hadn't shaved, his hair was tousled and he didn't look awake enough to be in a good mood, but she thought he looked amazingly handsome. Then she admonished herself. That was the wrong thing to be thinking about Jess Trujillo. She would have to learn to be careful.

"Good morning," she greeted him cautiously.

He got gracefully to his feet. He moved like a person at ease with his body, never clumsy or awkward. "Good morning."

"Do you want some breakfast?"

"You don't have to wait on me, Caitlin."

She shrugged off the censure in his voice. "I'm fixing my own. Eggs and bacon all right?" Her voice floated out from inside the refrigerator; then she backed out, holding a carton of eggs and a package of bacon.

He took the meat. "I'll do this." He followed her to the stove, his eyes skimming appreciatively over her body. This was something he had missed. Not Caitlin, he hastily reassured himself. Just her body and the pleasures it could give.

Caitlin got two skillets from the cabinet and handed one to Jess. As soon as the bacon was sizzling, he turned her to face him with one hand on her shoulder. "*Tierra de Encanto,*" he read aloud from her shirt. His eyes remained on the words a bit longer, moving over the curves of her breasts beneath the writing. At twenty-one she had been slim and straight, her breasts small. She was still slender, but the few pounds she had gained had given her soft, enticing curves. "Land of Enchantment," he translated.

She turned away, making his hand fall. "Guessing, or did you know?" Caitlin, who had studied Spanish in high school, had often teased Jess, both of whose parents had been born in Mexico, for his inability to speak even one sentence in Spanish.

"I spent a few months in Mexico. The people I worked with thought there was something wrong with me—a Mexican who couldn't speak Spanish."

"Did you like it there?"

He shrugged. "It was all right."

Caitlin removed the cooked eggs from the skillet, then fixed a pitcher of orange juice while Jess finished the bacon. "What did you do in all those places you lived?" The topic of his years away seemed safe enough, as long as he was willing to talk, and she admitted to a certain curiosity about what he'd done.

"Worked."

The night before he had explained away eight years of his life in fifteen minutes. This morning it took him one word.

She suggested that they eat their breakfast outside on the deck. As soon as they were settled at the rough-hewn table, facing each other in the early morning sunlight, she said, "You must have done something besides work. You had friends, didn't you?"

He shook his head.

"Women? Surely there were women." The thought of Jess with another woman stung, even though she had no right to be jealous. She'd given up her rights to him the night she had refused to go away with him.

Jess just looked at her for a long time, his eyes narrowed slits. "Of course there were women," he bluntly agreed. "Did you think I would give up sex forever because you weren't in my bed?"

Sex. Was that all it had been to him? It was such a cold word. It meant no feelings, no commitment, no love. Could he really classify their intensely passionate, incredibly gentle lovemaking as sex?

"What about you, Cait? Did you give up men after I left?" His harsh laugh indicated his opinion of the subject. He was positive that she hadn't.

"The men in my life are none of your business," she replied stiffly. It wasn't a real lie, but it was close enough to make the blood rush to her face. She hated even hinting at such a lie, but she hated even more the thought of telling him that she hadn't been with a man in eight years. He wouldn't believe her, anyway.

Jess had been certain that she'd had other lovers, but hearing her as much as admit it was like a blow to his gut. Jealousy, ugly and vicious, rushed through him. He wanted to leave, to run off by himself and scream his anger and pain to the world, but he remained in his chair, with Caitlin beyond reach.

It took him several minutes to regain his self-control. He didn't own Caitlin. He had once before—and that was the only reason the idea of her in another man's bed disturbed him so much, he told himself. She wasn't his anymore, and her life was none of his business. Not even her love life.

But he kept probing. "The *men* in your life, Cait? You mean Grant finally relaxed his hold on you long enough for you to find more than one?"

"That's enough, Jess." It was too much. Too close to the truth. She had always known that her father's love was demanding, restrictive, almost possessive. He had never wanted her to date, or even to talk about marriage. None of the young men in Isabel was good enough for her, he'd told her, and a man from somewhere else might take her away from her father and her home. He had been afraid of losing her.

He needn't have worried. Once Jess had gone, there had been little chance that she would get involved with another man. She simply hadn't cared.

"So what do you do now?" He sounded as if he couldn't care less, but he couldn't sit there in silence until his mother woke up.

"I paint." She said it as if it were obvious; then she forgot that he'd gone away before her paintings started selling.

"Do you make a living at it, or does Daddy support you?"

Caitlin winced, and Jess's forehead wrinkled into a frown. It seemed he just wasn't capable of carrying on any kind of a conversation without working Grant into it.

"I make a living at it. I imagine I make more with one painting than you do in several years." There, that made her feel better. Most men's egos couldn't handle women who made more than they did.

It didn't bother Jess in the least. He was glad she had become successful because he knew how much her art meant to her, but he couldn't find the grace that would allow him to say so. "Then why do you still live here? Why haven't you found a place of your own?''

She pushed her chair back from the table and crossed her legs. "This is my home."

That was a concept he understood. Home. All those years he'd been gone, he had never found a home. None of the towns or cities where he'd lived had been able to fill the place in his heart that belonged to Isabel. This dusty little town was home.

"And, of course, Daddy's here." Dammit, he'd done it again. Why couldn't he keep from mentioning Grant Pierce? Merely the man's name was sure to anger one or both of them, yet he couldn't stop the sarcastic remarks from coming.

Caitlin got to her feet and picked up her untouched breakfast plate and glass. She walked to the door, then looked back at him. "Maybe you wouldn't be so obsessed with my father if you had one of your own, Jess." Sure that her barb had hit its mark, she turned and went inside.

Jess sat frozen. In his thirty-one years he had heard a lot of insults about his illegitimacy, but never from Caitlin. She was the only person besides his mother who had never, ever commented on that fact. It was surprising how much it hurt.

Caitlin dumped the food from her plate into the garbage disposal, then put the dishes in the dishwasher. She was ashamed of her petty remark, but she'd be damned if she'd go out there and apologize to him.

And there was a cruel irony to what she had said. If life had worked out the way Grant had planned when he was younger, he would have had a son, and not another man's daughter. Jess would have been that son. Lupe had been Grant's great love, but she had refused to end her relationship with Roberto for him. She had preferred the shameful position of being a married man's lover over the offer of marriage that Grant had made. Even when Roberto had broken up with her when she got pregnant and Grant had offered again to marry her and raise Jess as his own, she had still refused. He had never been able to forgive her for it, and he had hated Jess for being the bastard of the man who had, in his eyes, stolen Lupe from him.

Caitlin tried to picture her father with Lupe, but she couldn't. Lupe was such a giving, loving, gentle woman, and Grant—Grant had been a good father, but at times he'd been cold and selfish.

He'd found it difficult to give of himself. No wonder Lupe had chosen to raise her son alone rather than expose him to Grant. Life with Grant had sometimes been difficult for Caitlin, but she was certain that, for a son, it would have been impossible.

Just as she was turning away from the sink, Lupe entered the room. She looked rested, and she was smiling brilliantly. "Good morning, Caitlin." She gave the younger woman a hug and kissed her cheek.

Caitlin didn't need to ask what had brought about this change. She firmly believed in the power of the mind to fight illness, at least up to a certain point. Jess's return home had definitely given Lupe a reason to fight. "Did you sleep well?"

"Yes, I did. Better than I have in months." She got a bowl from the counter and filled it with cereal. Caitlin handed the milk to her. "Did you and Jess have breakfast together?"

Caitlin thought of the food she had thrown away without tasting, but answered yes anyway. She wouldn't let Lupe know how much his presence disturbed her.

"How does he seem to you, Caitlin? Yesterday he looked so...tired. Unhappy. Do you think he's all right?"

Caitlin looked through the glass doors to Jess, who was staring out over the desert, not shading his eyes against the bright sun. "He's fine, Lupe. He's home."

"And what about you? Are you all right?"

Her smile was forced, and it looked it. "Of course I am. It was a long time ago, Lupe. It doesn't still hurt. Excuse me. I'm going to get an early start today."

More lies. Lord, she had told more lies in the last hour than she had in the last five years. Having Jess around *did* hurt. It shouldn't, not after eight years. That had been plenty of time to accept that Jess didn't love her. She had told herself that she was over him, that he would never be able to hurt her again, that her feelings for him had died the night he left Isabel. Foolishly, she had believed herself. Until now.

Somehow she still cared for him. Somehow he could still hurt her. Somehow some feelings had survived. But as long as she kept them to herself, she would be all right.

She had to go past him to get to her studio. He watched her walk by, but neither of them spoke. When she reached the door, she heard Lupe greet him as she stepped out onto the deck.

The studio was her own private place, off-limits to everyone without an invitation. It was where she went when she wanted to work and when she needed to be alone. She was safe there.

The garage was large. Built originally for two cars, there was plenty of room for all of Caitlin's supplies, plus a small bathroom, a dormitory-sized refrigerator, a desk and a sofa. The north and east walls had been replaced with glass, flooding the room with light. It was a perfect place to work.

Although she could use oils or pastels skillfully if the subject demanded it, she worked primarily in watercolors. She preferred the brilliance of the transparent paints over the heavy, denser oils.

She chose a sheet of heavy paper, set it up on the easel, then began to prepare her paints. The tubes were arranged in no particular order in the small cases. She looked them over quickly, picking up one, discarding it for another, until she had the selection of colors she wanted.

She had a picture in her mind of exactly what she wanted to create, as detailed and correct as a photograph. A few weeks earlier she had visited one of the pueblos for a feast-day dance. Taking photographs was forbidden in that particular pueblo, but she had been able to sketch the dancers and their elaborate costumes. Now she was ready to do the painting.

She used a slab of glass, sitting on a table next to her easel, as a palette, squeezing small dabs of paint onto it as she needed them. The red sable brush she used was her favorite, its bristles soft and pointed. Like the paints and papers she used, her brushes were top quality—and she paid dearly for them. But what was the use in painting anything at all with less than perfect equipment?

Her strokes were smooth and sure, picking up the paint from the glass and laying it down in a transparent wash. She worked without regard for time, her hand never faltering.

She worked until her back and shoulders ached; then she took a break, lying down on the sofa near the east wall. She lay on her back, her hands propped beneath her head, and studied her unfinished painting with critical eyes.

Her style had changed in the last eight years. There was a maturity to her work that had been missing before. With bitter humor, she thought that she could easily classify her work into two periods: Before Jess and After Jess. Before he left, she hadn't been confident enough to attempt to paint people, so she had concentrated on inanimate objects. Mountains, deserts, mesas, canyons, buttes—as long as it didn't have life, she would paint it. After he left, she put all her energy into her studies and had gained the skill, technique and confidence to paint anything that caught her eye. Now the majority of her work teemed with life, particularly Indian life.

That was probably the only good thing that had come from Jess's revelation that night. The knowledge that her father had been Indian, that she herself was part Indian, had spurred an interest in her father's people: their history, their culture, their life today. She had spent hours in the Albuquerque library; she had visited each of the pueblos that were open to the public, as well as the Cultural Center in the city; she had gone to every historical site in the state that dealt with the Pueblos. She knew as much about her father's people as she could learn, but she could never know her father, not even his name.

Had Claire loved him? According to Lupe, she had—enough to have his baby, even though there was no way she could pass it off to Grant as his, since they had separate rooms. She had even tried to leave Grant once, to run away with her lover, but he had stopped her. Then her father had died, and, soon after, so had Claire. Of a broken heart, Lupe had insisted. When she was in a romantic mood, Caitlin was inclined to agree.

The opening of the door startled her so much that she couldn't move. No one had ever entered her studio while she was working—not once in the eight years she had used it. Who would dare...?

Jess, of course. A closed door wouldn't keep him out. A sign saying Do Not Disturb wouldn't keep him out if he wanted to go in. She scowled darkly at him.

"I thought you'd be hard at work, and here you are, lying down on the job."

"I've been working," she pointed out unnecessarily, because he had stopped in front of the easel to look at her painting. She steeled herself for his response, for some sarcastic comment. She found herself hoping that he liked it, yet afraid that he wouldn't.

Jess couldn't have been sarcastic if his life depended on it. He stared at the unfinished work, amazed by what he saw. He had always believed in Caitlin's talent; as teenagers, it had been Jess

who encouraged her to make a career of art, even when Grant
had done his best to dissuade her. But the paintings she had done
then were insignificant compared to this. It seemed so real that
he could almost believe he was there.

She waited, and the silence dragged on. At last she said
crossly, "Haven't you stared long enough?"

He turned and smiled slightly. "This is really good, Cait."

It was the first time he'd spoken to her without sarcasm, without the wary, bitter look in his eyes. The simple compliment,
along with his smile and the warmth of his voice, pleased her
far more than it should have. She almost smiled back, but he had
already turned away to look at her studio.

"Grant must have spent a fortune redoing this place for you,"
he observed. The sarcasm was back.

She said nothing.

"How long ago did he do it?"

"A few years."

He looked at her again. "A few years? How many is that?
Two? Three? *Eight?*"

A deep flush colored her cheeks. Quickly she looked away,
but he saw her guilt.

"Eight years ago. Not a bad reward for staying behind, was
it?"

At last he had brought up that night. Caitlin had known it
would happen; sooner or later, they would have to talk. There
were too many loose ends, too much unfinished business. They
had to settle the past. "We both made choices that night," she
said quietly.

"Yeah, and you chose to stay with Daddy." He leaned against
the wall, his hands in his jean pockets, one ankle crossed over
the other. In any other person, she knew, the posture would have
been easy and relaxed. Not with Jess. He was as tense and coiled
as a man could get.

"No," she corrected. "I chose not to let you run my life."

"Asking you to go away with me is running your life?" He
laughed harshly. "You've lived your entire life with the most
dominating man I've ever known, and you say *I* was trying to
run your life?"

"You didn't ask anything, Jess; you *demanded*. You insisted
that I go with you. You wanted me to turn away from my father,

to pretend that he no longer existed. The way your father pretends that you don't exist.''

Twice in one morning she had hit him with insults about his father, but he'd be damned if he'd let her see how they hurt. "You made a bad choice, Cait," he said in a low, malicious voice.

"I never regretted my choice." Yet another lie, she thought wearily. *Lord, help me.*

It just proved what Jess had believed all along: Caitlin hadn't loved him enough, not with the love of a woman for a man. In the end, the lasting pain had been his. He had struck out in anger, only to find that the woman he'd worshiped didn't exist, that the love he'd lived for wasn't real. Knowing that hurt far more than anything else he had ever suffered. Eight years later, he didn't think he could forgive her for it.

But it shouldn't hurt now. He didn't care about Caitlin. Eight years of hard work, constant moving, strange cities and lonely nights had convinced him of that. His love had died, gone in the pain of losing her. Yet there *was* pain, somewhere so deep inside him that he couldn't touch it. He couldn't love her, but he couldn't stop hurting for her. And he couldn't stop wanting her.

She couldn't read anything in the harsh, set lines of his face. If he was angry—or hurt or relieved or happy—it didn't show. His face was a handsomely carved mask, revealing nothing of his thoughts or his emotions. But his voice...When he spoke, his voice vibrated with every violent emotion he had ever experienced.

"Why should you have regrets, Cait?" he demanded. "You lost nothing. You gave up nothing. You stayed here in your cozy little house. You had your fancy studio and your precious Daddy, and you even had *my* mother. You didn't lose anything. You didn't need anything."

I needed you!

Shocked by the traitorous words, Caitlin clenched her jaw to keep them from escaping. He didn't need to know how desperately she had missed him; how she had cried herself to sleep every night for the first few weeks; how, even months later, she had still woken in the middle of the night, her pillow soaked with tears. He didn't need to know that she would have sold her soul to have him back.

"Why are you here, Jess?" She sounded weary, tired of dealing with him.

"You should know. You sent for me."

"Did you come because I sent for you, or because Lupe is sick?"

He made an impatient gesture. "Because of Mom, of course." How could she possibly believe anything else? his tone asked.

She grew a little sadder. He had come home because Lupe was sick. Well, dammit, she had been sick, too—sick at heart for months after he left, slowly losing herself in the ache—but he had never come back for her. He had said he loved her, had made tender love to her; then he had cut her completely out of his life. If he had really loved her, he couldn't have done it. If he had really loved her...

"You have friends here," she said. "Why don't you stay with one of them?"

He smiled slowly, coldly. "Because I'd rather stay here. I like the idea of living in Grant Pierce's house, of sleeping in his bed. I like knowing how outraged he'll be when he finds out. But, by then, there won't be anything he can do about it."

He sounded bitter, like a man out for revenge.... Caitlin lifted her eyes to him. Revenge? Was Jess capable of that? One look into the icy depths of his dark eyes told her the answer. Yes, he was capable. Without doubt.

"That's it, isn't it? You want to repay my father and me. You want to avenge whatever wrongs we committed, and that's why you're here in this house."

He opened his mouth to deny it. He was too smart to believe in the practice of vengeance. Any time you set out to deliberately hurt someone else, you always got hurt more, and he'd been hurt enough to last a lifetime. He didn't want to hurt Caitlin, anyway. He would like to see Grant punished, he admitted, but not her. He had loved her too much once to want to destroy her like that.

He denied only part of her accusation. "Not you. In some ways you were as much Grant's victim as I was." But that was all he said. Let her believe he wanted to hurt Grant. Then he could do anything he wanted and hide behind her theory of revenge. He could even seduce her, he realized with a traitorous rush of feeling, and she would never guess that it was because he wanted her; she would make the obvious connection that the easiest way to hurt Grant was through her.

And, Lord, how he wanted to seduce her. He wanted to make love to her more than he had ever wanted anything in his life. Every time he saw her, he remembered the times they'd made love before. Different ways, different places, different times—they all had one thing in common: they had all been perfect. He had never experienced another woman like Caitlin, not before, and definitely not after.

But when he took her to bed, it would be just sex. He'd have to remember that. It wasn't just a question of semantics. For Jess, there was a definite distinction between having sex and making love. Sex took place on a completely physical level; making love involved emotions. If he allowed himself to make love to her, he would end up falling in love with her all over again, and he couldn't do that. He could want her—he could even need her—but he would never, ever love her again.

Caitlin felt sick. He said he didn't want to hurt her, but he had to know there was no way he could take revenge on her father without hurting her, too. "Please," she said, and her voice was a mere whisper. "Go away."

He shook his head. "We're having lunch with Mom."

The thought of food made her stomach queasy. She shook her head. "I can't."

"Mom wants you and me—both of us—to meet her for lunch," he said stubbornly. "You're going, Cait, and you're going to pretend to have a good time. You're not going to let her down." He placed his hands on his hips, his fists clenched. "Now, do you go willingly, or do I carry you out of here?"

She got to her feet reluctantly. Just as Jess had come home only for Lupe, she was going with him only for Lupe. Her friend had so little time left, and Caitlin was willing to do anything to make it happy.

She cleaned her brush and set it aside to dry, then rinsed the glass palette. When she was finished, she left the studio, stopping as soon as Jess followed her out to lock the door. He trailed her into the house, and when she went into her bedroom, he continued down the hall to his room.

Caitlin took her hair down and brushed it out, then pulled it into a ponytail. She took a handful of colored elastic bands and slid them into place, an inch or two apart, capturing her hair and holding it together in one smooth, round tube that dangled almost to her waist. She sprayed cologne over her wrists and on her throat, then left her room.

Jess had changed into a white western-styled shirt, rolling the sleeves to his elbows while he waited for Caitlin. When she came out, her purse tucked under her arm, they left the house.

His truck was at least twenty years old and looked even more battered than Caitlin remembered. They'd had some good times in that old truck, but that day they sat in silence as Jess drove it down the long hill into town.

The windows were down, but it was still hot. The faint breeze created by their motion lifted Jess's black hair, ruffling it lightly. It also carried the scent of Caitlin's cologne through the cab. It smelled...exotic. Wild. Erotic. He smiled faintly. It was perfect for her.

"Isabel hasn't changed much."

Caitlin glanced at him. Idle conversation? The Jess of the past had never felt the need for it, had never minded silence. But the silences of the past had been comfortable. Peaceful. "I doubt that Isabel has changed much since Amos's days."

She knew the story well. Other children received fairy tales as bedtime stories; Grant had told her the Pierce family history. Amos and his wife Isabel had been part of a wagon train on their way to California. The war in the South was over, and he was going to make his fortune in the gold fields. But Isabel had become pregnant, and in this spot, a few days' journey from Albuquerque, they had made camp so that she could give birth to a son named John. He was born April 25, 1868, and Isabel died the next day. Amos lost interest in gold and California. Though the desert was a harsh, lonely place, he couldn't bring himself to leave his wife, so he and John, along with a couple of other families who were tired from the long trip, stayed there, building the town and naming it after the dead Isabel.

"I missed it." He was staring straight ahead when he said the quiet, heartfelt words. The dusty little town was as much a part of him as Lupe was, as Caitlin had once been. He couldn't leave it again.

Caitlin hesitantly reached across the seat and touched his hand as it gripped the steering wheel. "Welcome home," she said softly.

The desire to turn his hand over and take hers before she could pull back was almost more than he could stand. He squeezed his fingers tighter around the plastic and metal in an effort not to, and then, in a moment, her hand was gone.

"Is Carmen's store still on Main?" He was relieved that he sounded almost normal.

"Yes, but it's a couple of buildings down from the old place— next to the town offices."

He turned onto Main, then parked in the middle of the block. It was only a few yards to the store. As soon as the truck came to a stop, Caitlin slid to the ground. She started quickly toward the shop, but Jess easily caught up with her.

Carmen Mendez's shop was the only place in Isabel to buy women's and children's clothing. Her stock was reasonably priced, well made, and came in all styles and sizes. Along with Lupe, Carmen's eldest daughter Amelia helped run the store.

Caitlin watched from a position near the counter as first Carmen, then Amelia, greeted Jess. He had hugs and smiles for them both. She turned away, disgusted with the jealousy that flared inside. What did she care who Jess hugged? Who he smiled for? He meant nothing to her, and to him she was only a way to hurt her father. Let him happily greet every single woman in town except her. She didn't care.

"Did you have a good morning?"

She turned to face Lupe. "Yes, I did. I got a lot of work done."

Lupe grimaced. That wasn't the kind of good morning she'd meant. "Did you and Jess talk?"

"A little."

"Did you settle anything?"

Just his reason, other than Lupe, for being there. How far would he go to get back at Grant? she wondered. "Oh, I guess we did. Where do you want to go for lunch?"

"Do the Goldmans still have that restaurant on the north side of town?" Jess asked, joining them.

"Yes, they do. Would you like to go there?"

That agreed on, they left the store and walked to Jess's truck. Caitlin purposely lagged behind, maneuvering Lupe so that she got into the truck first. That left Caitlin sitting next to the door, safe from Jess.

Lupe did most of the talking over lunch. Caitlin ate her food without tasting it and answered the few questions directed to her without thinking. All her attention was on Jess, across the table from her, close enough to touch. When she looked up, she saw him. When she shifted on the vinyl bench, her legs bumped his. And whether she looked at him or touched him or remained perfectly still with her eyes lowered, she felt his presence.

Caitlin's relief when the meal was finished was short-lived. When they reached the truck, Lupe quietly insisted that Caitlin sit in the middle, next to Jess. She protested until she saw the faintly sarcastic, knowing grin he wore. Cutting off her complaint in mid word, she climbed in and slid across the seat toward him.

His thigh was hard and warm against hers. She swore that Lupe was deliberately taking up more of the seat than usual, forcing her to sit so close to Jess that she could feel his leg muscles tighten when he moved his foot from the accelerator to the brake. Each time he reached for the gearshift his hand brushed her. It was intentional, she knew, so she bit the inside of her lip to keep from reacting to it.

As soon as Lupe got out of the truck to return to work, Caitlin started to move across the seat. Jess caught her arm. "What's wrong?"

"Nothing."

"Then why don't you stay where you are? You always used to sit right here next to me."

"That was when we were kids, Jess," she replied through clenched teeth. She was beginning to get an idea of what form his revenge might take.

"I was twenty-three, Cait. I wasn't a kid." Then his voice deepened and became husky instead of harsh. "And neither were you. You stopped being a kid the first time I made love to you."

She struggled free of his hand and moved so far away that she was all but out the door.

"I make you nervous, don't I?"

"Yes."

"Why?"

"Because I'm not as naive as I used to be. Now I know better than to trust you."

His grin was broad and white and mocking. "You're the one who's not trustworthy," he disagreed. "I should know. I found out the hard way."

Caitlin turned to stare at him for a long, silent moment; then she swung her gaze ahead again. Realizing they were headed north, back in the direction of the restaurant where they had eaten, she said sharply, "I want to go home."

"I'll take you home. Soon."

They left the town behind. The paved road narrowed, turned to gravel, then gave way to rutted, hard-packed dirt. When they were several miles from town, Jess pulled off the road, found a secluded spot and stopped. He pocketed the keys before turning sideways in the seat to face Caitlin.

Maybe if she weren't so beautiful... No, that wouldn't matter. Whatever attracted him to her came from inside. It couldn't be explained as easily as beauty. His hands ached to touch her. He kept one on the steering wheel and rested the other on the back of the seat, only a few inches from her shoulder.

Caitlin kept her head lowered. She wished she had left her hair down; it would have provided a sheltering curtain from his unrelenting gaze. Her hands were clasped together in her lap, her fingers tightly twined. Whatever Jess's reasons for bringing her out here, she didn't like them. Not one bit. She wanted to go home.

"Tell me about the men, Cait."

That jerked her head up, made her look at him. "What?" she gasped.

"You said there had been other men. Who were they? Anyone I know?"

"I...I... It's none of your business, Jess."

He tilted his head in acknowledgement. "But I'm making it my business. Where did you meet them? Where did you sleep with them? In Grant's house? In their cars? Out here in the desert?"

Her face burned. He hadn't chosen those three places at random. They were all places where she and Jess had made love. She didn't need the reminder.

"Well? Can't you answer me? Or were there so many you've forgotten?"

She couldn't answer; she couldn't explain a lie with more lies.

For her, there had never been anyone but Jess. "I'm not going to answer, Jess. The day you left town, you lost all right to question me about any part of my life," she said with a quiet, sad dignity.

He had never given up any rights, he thought. He had left because there was no reason for him to stay. Caitlin had preferred to be Grant's daughter instead of Jess's wife, and so he had gone. But he hadn't given up his rights.

It was hot in the truck under the midday sun. Perspiration beaded on her forehead, and her yellow T-shirt clung uncomfortably to her. That was what drew Jess's gaze. The fabric lifted and fell with each breath she took and molded softly to her breasts. The Zía sun was directly above her left breast. Jess leaned forward slowly and touched his outstretched fingers to its rays, tracing along those on top. When they moved to the ones on the right, she caught her breath, and when they reached those on the bottom, brushing over her sensitive nipple, she gasped.

Before she could stop him, he stopped himself. He drew back and turned in the seat to face forward. Playing with Caitlin was a lot like playing with fire. It was exhilarating and exciting, but if he wasn't careful, it could destroy him. He wasn't ready for this yet.

Years of longing and denial threatened to explode inside Caitlin. His touch had been so brief, but it had made her want so much more. She would have been angry with him if he continued, yet now she was angry with herself for being disappointed that he'd stopped. If he had been able to seduce her so easily, so quickly, then he'd know that she wasn't as unaffected by him as she wanted to be. He would know that she had lied about the other men, and that he was right in believing she wasn't trustworthy.

When the silence grew so loud that she wanted to scream, Jess spoke. "What's wrong with my mother?"

Her fingers were starting to ache from the lack of circulation, so she forced them apart, laying them flat on her thighs. "That's not for me to say."

"I have a right to know."

"So ask Lupe."

"I did. I asked her last night, but she wouldn't tell me."

"She has rights, too."

His temper slipped loose. "You like it that you know something important about my mother that she won't tell me, don't you?" he accused. "She's *my* mother, Cait. All your life you've tried to make her take the place of *your* mother, who didn't care enough about you to stick around and take care of you. Well, she isn't yours, Cait; she's *mine*."

"I know that. As for knowing secrets about each other's mothers, you kept a secret about my mother from me for years. You kept it so you could use it against Dad and me, to hurt us. I'm not going to tell you what's wrong with Lupe. I don't have that right. If she wants you to know, she'll tell you."

"I wasn't trying to hurt anyone," he denied. "I just wanted him to stop calling me 'bastard' all the time. I wanted him to get off my back. I wanted—" His voice softened, and he gave a shake of his head. "I wanted to hurt him. I wanted to humiliate him, and I wanted to take you away from him."

Grant's biggest fear, one that had plagued him since Caitlin's birth, had been that the townspeople would find out that she wasn't his daughter, that her father had been Claire's Indian lover. He didn't want anyone to know that his wife had turned to another man for the love and comfort and affection that he couldn't give her, and he certainly didn't want anyone to know that the daughter he was raising, the child who would carry on the Pierce name, wasn't a Pierce at all, but a half-Indian bastard. Finding out that Jess knew not only about that, but also about Lupe's rejection of him, had terrified him.

Again the heavy silence was broken by Jess. "Is she dying?"

A lump formed in Caitlin's throat. She tried to stop them, but tears rolled down her cheeks anyway. That was answer enough for Jess.

He slumped back against the seat. His suspicions yesterday hadn't been wrong. He could pretend all he wanted that it wasn't true, but that wouldn't change the facts. His mother was dying. Whether he accepted it or not, she was dying.

"Can they do anything?"

She shook her head.

Jess tried to imagine life without his mother. The last eight years had been hard and bleak, but he'd always known that Lupe was in Isabel; she would be there whenever he needed her. How could he stand knowing that she was gone? That she was dead?

She was the only family he had—the only friend he had. He couldn't let her go, dammit!

Blindly he reached out to Caitlin, his hand connecting with her shoulder. "Don't cry," he said emotionlessly. "There's no sense in crying. It gives you a headache."

She wiped her cheeks with a tissue she found in her purse. "I'm sorry, Jess," she whispered.

His sigh was desolate. "Lord, so am I."

Chapter 3

The party at Carmen Mendez's house was in full swing by the time Lupe, Jess and Caitlin arrived. People filled the small house and spilled out onto the patio—old friends, old neighbors and a few new faces. All of Jess's friends were there, accompanied by their wives and children.

It seemed odd, seeing his best friend, Tom Mendez, with a wife and two children, and every other friend from his high school days married, some with as many as five kids. Jess had been the first of their group to get engaged; he was going to be the first married, the first with children. Instead, all of them were married, and he was still single. Not for the first time in the past years, he felt left out. Alone.

Caitlin carefully avoided looking at Jess. Her gaze strayed to him occasionally, but fear that he would catch her watching him made her look away quickly.

She didn't miss the speculative glances she received from the other guests. She knew Jess was the reason. He'd been home for three days; by now, everyone in town knew he was back and staying at her house. The more romantic of them probably expected to hear a wedding announcement any day. The more vicious probably hoped for the worst for them—like Grant returning to Isabel eight months early. Whatever they said or thought, she didn't like it. She didn't like being the subject of their gossip. But there was little she could do about it. It was part of the price she paid for being Grant Pierce's daughter.

She spent most of the evening with the few people she considered friends: Lupe, Carmen, Amelia and Tom's wife, Bonny. Jess was surrounded by his buddies and their wives, and even some of Lupe's friends. They bombarded him with questions about the places he had lived, the work he had done and his plans for the future. Caitlin strained to hear his answer to that last question, but there was too much noise in the room.

It shouldn't matter to her what he did after Lupe was gone. He could go back to traveling, working and living his life the way he pleased, and it shouldn't make one bit of difference to her.

But it did.

She was confused by the emotions churning inside her. She should never want to see Jess again—but she was glad he was home. She should hate him—but she didn't. She should do her best to avoid him while he was here—but she almost enjoyed his company. When he wasn't being sarcastic, he could be very pleasant. And they shared their love and concern for Lupe.

"So how's it going?" Bonny asked when they had a few minutes alone.

Caitlin shrugged. "Okay, I guess."

"Are you glad he's back?"

"Of course I am. Lupe needs him now."

Bonny looked skeptical. "Oh, so you're glad for Lupe's sake that he's come home. Come on, Caitlin. You two dated for three years. You were engaged to be married. You must still feel something for the man."

Caitlin leveled her gaze on the other woman. "He left me, Bonny. He left, and he never wrote, he never called, and he never came back to see me. He forgot I even existed."

"He wrote to Lupe," Bonny pointed out.

"Sure, once every six months." And every one of those letters had hurt Caitlin, because there was nothing—not even one word—for her. "Yes, Bonny, I feel something for him now, but it's nothing you'd want to know about."

Bonny paled at her vehement reply and suddenly got to her feet. "I—I'll be back in a minute."

"It's something I'd want to know about," a silky voice said from behind Caitlin.

She stiffened in her seat. How had he gotten so close without her feeling his presence? Then she said a silent prayer of thanks that she hadn't been voicing her earlier thoughts, about being glad he was home or enjoying his company when he sneaked up on her.

He stayed behind her. She'd worn her hair down, and he slid his fingers beneath it, gathering the heavy weight into his hands. "Tell me what you feel for me, Cait," he invited. He was hardly breathing; his chest was tight with anticipation. Did she remember the good times they'd had together? Had she missed him? Had she been lonely for him? Was she glad he had returned?

She tried to move forward, but his grip on her hair stopped her. "Right this minute I can't stand you," she hissed in a low voice.

"What about other minutes? What about Thursday, when you first saw me? What about yesterday in the truck, when I touched you? What did you feel for me then?"

Caitlin panicked and pulled away. He released her hair immediately, but it still pulled at her tender scalp. "Leave me alone, Jess," she whispered. "Go ahead and punish my father if it will make you happy, but leave me out of it."

It took him a moment after she'd fled the room to realize what she'd meant by that remark. So she really did believe he was out for revenge. The decent part of him wanted to tell her that it wasn't true. He wasn't going to risk getting hurt again just to play out some ridiculous game with Grant. But the part of him that wanted her, that wanted to make love to her again and again, until she couldn't remember a time without him, needed the excuse of revenge to touch her.

Tom called him from his thoughts, and he went out to join his friend on the patio. It was getting late, and most of the guests were leaving. They were alone outside.

"Are you going to try to get her back?"

Jess merely stared at Tom for a moment. He liked his privacy, and he resented attempts to take it from him. Then he remembered that this was Tom, his best friend since he was a kid. "I don't know," he replied. "I hadn't made any plans beyond coming here."

"She never saw anyone else, not the whole time you were gone."

His eyes narrowed. "She told me she had."

"If she has, she managed to keep it one hell of a secret, and you can't keep secrets in Isabel. I know she hasn't been out with anyone here in town, and I don't think she's seen anyone from the city. It would have gotten out if she had."

Jess sat down and rocked the chair onto its back legs. It was too hard to believe that Caitlin hadn't had at least one date, at least one affair. Maybe Tom was wrong...but, Lord, how he hoped he was right!

He grimaced. It didn't matter to him if she'd had one affair, a dozen, or none. He didn't care about her. Emotions had no place in dealing with a woman like Caitlin. Everything he felt was strictly sexual. Desire. Pure animal lust.

And if he told himself that often enough, he just might begin to believe it.

Caitlin bade Lupe good-night when they arrived home, then went to her bedroom to change from her dress into shorts and an oversized T-shirt. Assuming that Jess was in his room, she moved quietly through the darkened house to the kitchen, intending to go out to the deck. It was her favorite place to sit at night, when the day's heat was replaced by coolness and the stars shone overhead like jewels, blinking down on the tiny town. It was peaceful, and some of that peace seeped into her, flowing through her with her blood.

She sat on a rough bench, her knees drawn to her chest, her hands clasped around them. She loved the desert, and she loved the nighttime. Together, they were perfect.

"Do you want to be alone?"

She glanced over her shoulder to see Jess standing in the door leading to the kitchen.

He waited for an answer, but when none came, he started to leave. As soon as he turned, Caitlin knew she didn't want to be alone, not now. There would be time for that later. "Come on out," she invited.

He walked silently across the deck to the railing. His feet were bare, and the pale blue shirt he wore was unbuttoned. The tails fluttered in the slight breeze.

Jess stared off into the distance. There was a faint glow in the sky to the northeast that he imagined to be the lights of Albuquerque reflected from the sky. He didn't know if the lights could really be seen fifty miles away, but he liked to think so.

Why had he come out here? He had gone to his room to get undressed for bed. After a long day and a half-dozen beers at the party, he was ready for sleep. Then he'd heard the kitchen door open and close, and he'd known Caitlin was out there on the deck. He forgot about sleep. He wanted to see her.

He was a fool for coming around. She didn't want to get involved with him, and the last thing he needed was an affair with her that was bound to bring trouble with Grant. But what he needed and what he wanted weren't always the same, and what he wanted tonight was Caitlin.

"How do you sell your paintings?"

"Do you remember Melly Wilkins?"

Without turning he nodded. She had been one of Caitlin's instructors at the University of New Mexico during her sophomore year.

"She owns a gallery in Old Town. She sells everything there. I also do some work on commission, mostly for people who own other pieces of mine."

"You must be pretty pleased with the way things have worked out."

Pleased? She shrugged. She had achieved most of what she had wanted with her life. She had a secure position among New Mexico's numerous artists, a satisfactory relationship with her father and a loving friendship with Lupe. But there were things she missed, too: Jess's companionship, their incredible lovemaking, the children they would have had if their marriage had taken place as planned. She had never planned to be twenty-nine and single and childless. She had never planned for painting to be the great love of her life.

"It's been all right."

If his life without her had been all right, he would have been thankful as hell. But it hadn't been all right; it had been miserable.

"Do you ever regret leaving?" she asked hesitantly.

Jess gave a short, bitter laugh. "Every single day."

"Why didn't you come back?"

"To what? There was nothing here for me."

Nothing but me. She bit her lip to keep the words inside. If he had wanted her, he could have come back at any time, and she would have welcomed him.

"How long have Tom and Bonny been married?"

"Carla's four-and-a-half, so they've been married almost five years."

"She was pregnant when they got married?"

Caitlin made a soft sound of agreement. It wasn't that unusual in their small town for brides to be several months pregnant when they got married. It was frowned on but accepted nonetheless. It was the illegitimate babies the townspeople found difficult to accept. She and Jess were the only ones that she knew of, although the circumstances of her own birth were still a closely kept secret.

"When did they start dating?" When Jess left Isabel, Tom had been determined to stay single the rest of his life; there were too many beautiful women to tie himself down to only one, he'd claimed.

"I don't really know. A year or so before they got married, I guess."

Slowly he turned around to face her, and she looked closely at him, taking stock. On Thursday she'd thought he had changed very little physically, but now she could see subtle differences. At six foot two inches, he had always been lean. Now, his shoulders were a bit broader, and inside his open shirt she could see well-defined muscles that hadn't been noticeable in the younger man she'd known.

His hair was longer than it had been, thick and dull black. It covered the collar of his shirt, its ends too heavy to curl. Caitlin remembered its texture, soft and springy, and her fingers itched to touch it. To keep her hands from reaching out to him, she clasped them even tighter.

"What is your father doing overseas?"

"He's working for one of the oil companies." Grant was an energy consultant. During his long career he had worked under contract for nearly every major oil company in the world. He was sought after for his vast knowledge of the business, and companies were willing to pay whatever price he asked. He enjoyed his job, but Caitlin had always believed privately that he did it for the attention. He liked the power he held.

That was about the extent of safe conversation, Jess thought bitterly. There had been a time when he and Caitlin could discuss anything for hours—from the weather to their friends to their plans for the future. Now they had little in common, and there was no future for them.

She had been his friend, his lover, the woman he wanted for his wife, and he had lost all of that. Tonight he thought he missed the friend most of all.

He lowered his head, his eyes shut tight. For a long time he seemed to forget that Caitlin was there; then he looked at her and smiled. It wasn't much as smiles went, she thought, but the corners of his mouth curved up a bit. "So...we've run out of things to say," he said quietly.

Caitlin shifted uncomfortably. There was nothing she could add to that. At one time they had been important to each other, but that had been so long ago. So much of their lives had been lived separately.

"How much time does Mom have?"

Her discomfort grew. "Jess, you have to ask her that."

He nodded once. "If she won't tell me, will you?"

Lupe was stubborn enough to refuse; they both knew that. Still, that was her right. But how could Caitlin be cruel enough to let Jess watch his mother die without knowing why? It was Lupe's choice to make, but she was responsible for bringing Jess home. Didn't she owe him something? "If she won't tell you," she said reluctantly, "then I will. But give her a chance."

"How many chances? Until she's on her deathbed?"

"Talk to her again, but not right away. Jess, she's missed you terribly. Let her enjoy having you home for a while without thinking about dying."

He left his position at the railing and walked to stand beside her bench. He reached out one hand to her cheek. His touch was so gentle, so brief, that she almost thought she imagined it. "What about you, Cait! Did you miss me?"

She almost said yes, she had missed him horribly. But she didn't want him to know how long it had taken her to get past the hurt and the tears. She didn't want him to know how much of the desire and tender feelings still existed. But he seemed so sad, emotionally exhausted, that she couldn't be cruel and lie outright. "Yes, I did, at first," she said, her voice a husky murmur.

That was better than he had expected. He chose not to ask her how long "at first" was. He didn't want to know. "Good night, Cait." He touched her quickly again, then went inside the house, closing the door quietly behind him.

A few minutes later Caitlin went to bed, too. Last week her life had been simple, even boring—she painted her pictures and spent her free time with Lupe. There had been no confusion, no tangled emotions to sort through. Tonight her mind was in such turmoil that it would take forever for her to fall asleep.

Frankly, she preferred being bored.

On Sunday morning Lupe was surprised to find both Jess and Caitlin dressed for church. Though Caitlin wasn't Catholic, it wasn't unusual for her to accompany Lupe, but neither of them had expected Jess to join them.

It was the first time Jess had been inside a church in years. This was the church he had attended as a child, the church where he and Caitlin had planned to be married. The building was old, built in the late eighteen-hundreds of mud-and-sand bricks. Stained glass windows made by Lupe's grandfather filtered the sunlight into faintly colored shafts that did little to light the sanctuary. It was a quiet, solemn place, fitting to Jess's mood that morning.

He had lain in bed for hours last night, considering Caitlin's advice. She was right, he'd finally concluded. As much as he wanted to know what was wrong with Lupe, knowing wouldn't change anything. It wouldn't hurt to let her wait a while before pressing for an explanation.

The church wasn't air-conditioned, but the thick adobe walls served to keep it relatively cool. Leaving it and walking into the blazing midday sun after mass was a shock to the system. Jess blinked a couple of times at the brilliance of the sun, then took Lupe's arm and walked with her to his truck.

She wasn't able to eat much of the light lunch Caitlin prepared.

Claiming a headache, she went to her room after the meal and lay down.

"Is she all right?"

Caitlin nodded. "Loss of appetite and headaches are two of the symptoms."

Symptoms of *what*? he wanted to demand, but he didn't. Instead he helped Caitlin clear the dishes from the table. While he loaded the dishwasher, she went to check on his mother, coming back with the report that she was sleeping soundly.

"Will you go out with me?" Jess asked quietly.

He sounded almost as if he were asking for a date. Caitlin looked at him warily. "Where?"

"I want to show you something. It won't take very long."

"All right, but I want to change first."

"I'll wait."

While she was gone, he walked restlessly around the living room. He had reached another decision last night in his room, and he wasn't sure whether Caitlin would approve. It didn't matter because he was determined to go through with it, no matter what she thought. But, for reasons he didn't care to examine too closely, he wanted her approval. He wanted her support.

Caitlin came back wearing a pair of yellow shorts with a yellow-and-white striped tank top. She left a note for Lupe, locked the door behind them and slipped her keys into her pocket.

Jess drove to a piece of land about a half mile north of Isabel. "This is it."

She looked around questioningly. There was nothing there to show her, just rocks, dirt, brush and a few lizards basking in the hot sun. "This is what?"

"This land belonged to Mom's father. He gave it to her years ago—to salve his conscience. I've been thinking about building a house for her. This is where I want to do it."

She got out of the truck and moved forward to lean against the fender. Lupe had lived with her less than three months, but she had become an integral part of Caitlin's home. She would miss her if she moved out. "She's welcome to stay with me," she said softly.

Jess leaned against the opposite fender, facing her across the hood. "My mother isn't going to die in Grant Pierce's house." His cold tone left no room for argument.

"Okay. When are you going to start?"

"Tomorrow."

"Alone?"

He shook his head. "Tom offered me a job in his construction company. That's what I've done most of the past eight years, anyway. He'll get the subcontractors, and I'll oversee the work. When it's finished, I'll work full-time for him."

"Will it be adobe?"

He shook his head. "Takes too long. I'd have to make all those bricks, then let them dry. I don't have time for that. It's not going to be anything fancy. Do you think she'll like it?"

"I'm sure she will. It was really hard on her when the old house burned." She cleared her throat, gathering courage for her next question. She didn't want to offend him. "Do you...need any money?"

For an instant he bristled; then he visibly relaxed. "I made pretty good money while I was gone. I didn't have many expenses, so most of it went into savings. It's just been sitting in various banks earning interest. I'll have enough to pay for this, and then I'll have my job with Tom." He paused. "Thanks anyway."

They walked around the front portion of the land. Jess showed her where he would put the house and the driveway, discussed the styles of architecture that he liked and the pros and cons of planting grass, turning the yard into a rock garden or leaving it as it was.

Caitlin looked around, absorbing the view. To the south slightly below them, was the town of Isabel. Great mesas, rocky and rugged, spread in all directions, and far off in the east were the Sandía Mountains, rising majestically above the Río Grande Valley. She would like to paint it someday.

"Will you help?"

She looked back at him. He stood straight and tall, his shoulders back and his head lifted, but he looked almost embarrassed to be asking for her help. He had always been a proud man, but not with her. It was just one more reminder of how much things had changed. "What do you want me to do?"

He moved closer to her, stopping only a few feet away. "Nothing, until we're ready to finish the inside. I'd like you to choose the floors, paint, wallpaper, do the kitchen—that sort of thing."

"Don't you trust your own taste?" she asked lightly. The re- alization that she was teasing him made her uncomfortable. Jess thought his nearness was responsible for her sudden stiffening, and he took a few steps back.

"I've lived in boardinghouses most of the last eight years. They were pretty shabby. No, I don't trust my own taste."

"There's nothing I wouldn't do for Lupe," she said with a smile. "I'd be glad to help."

Her eyes were so soft looking, Jess thought, studying her sol- emnly. When her desire was aroused and immediately after it was satisfied, her eyes were liquid brown, a color he couldn't describe with any words other than beautiful. *She* was beautiful.

Maybe he'd been wrong to make her choose that night. Maybe he should have let things stay the same. He could have tolerated Grant's abuse awhile longer. He could have kept the truth about Grant and Claire and Caitlin's father to himself. There had been no need for her to know, and if such a need had ever arisen, he could have told her properly, gently.

He looked away. He could have tolerated Grant's abuse awhile longer—but only awhile. No, if he hadn't done it that night, it would have happened eventually. He didn't doubt that at all. The closer their wedding date drew, the more hostile Grant had be- come. He would never have allowed Jess to marry her. He had sworn that, as long as he lived, Jess would never have Caitlin.

There was no sense in regretting the past. Caitlin didn't, so why should he? Regret couldn't change anything.

"Are you ready to go back?"

"In a minute." There was one other thing he wanted to discuss with her before they returned to the house. He tilted his head to one side. "Tom told me that you hadn't dated anyone since I left here."

She swallowed hard. She should have known that was a stupid lie. There were too many people who could verify that it wasn't true: Lupe, Carmen, Bonny and, apparently, Tom. "Do you sup- pose Tom knows every detail of my life?"

"Have you been out with another man?"

"We were talking about lovers, not dates. Where is it written that you have to go out with a man before you can go to bed with him?" Lord, she was digging a deeper hole for herself. One more lie and the sides were liable to cave in on her.

"Why didn't you tell me the truth?"

"My sex life is none of your business."

"Your sex life? You don't have one, do you?"

She looked down at her feet. Her cheeks were burning with shame, but her deep tan hid it. "It's none of your business," she insisted stubbornly.

He laid his hands on her shoulders, and she shivered. He pulled, gently, steadily, until her body was pressed against his. "Why did you lie to me, Cait?" he murmured. "You don't have any lovers. You would never make love with a man you didn't care for, and you've never cared for any man but me."

His head came slowly down. Caitlin closed her eyes before his lips reached hers. His mouth was gentle, his hunger under tight restraint. He teased her with slow lazy kisses that covered her mouth from corner to corner; then his tongue licked along the length of her lips, encouraging her to open to him. She allowed him entry, and his tongue followed familiar paths into the moist warmth of her mouth.

She shouldn't be doing this, she thought wildly. There was too much wrong between them. He was kissing her and making her want him, but he didn't want her; he wanted only to hurt her father. He was using her to punish Grant, and she couldn't let him do it.

But she didn't push him away. Instead her hands moved to his waist, settling over the soft waistband of his faded jeans.

He was right, he thought with satisfaction. She had lied about the men. She'd had no lovers in a very long time—possibly years. That knowledge elated him, though he knew it didn't matter. He couldn't let it matter.

With his right arm cradling her, he raised his left hand to her breast. It fit snugly in his palm. Rubbing back and forth, his hand teased her nipple into an aching peak, rousing a need for more. She whimpered softly, the sound passing from her mouth into his.

He'd been too long without a woman. That was why his body was burning with fever, he insisted silently. That was why he responded so quickly and so fiercely to the feel and touch and the taste of her. Any woman he kissed who kissed him back so willingly would do this to him.

Any woman.

Carefully he set her away from him. He avoided her eyes, so he didn't see her confusion at his sudden withdrawal, and she didn't see his desire. "Let's go home," he said shortly, walking back to the truck with long strides.

Caitlin was silent for the short drive home. The next few weeks or months—however long his plan took—were going to be hard. She was already bewildered by her own feelings, and being part of Jess's game was going to make things worse. She was going to have to see him and hear him and be with him, and know that everything he did and said was calculated to cause Grant the most harm, and her heart, which had finally almost mended, was going to break all over again.

And it *would* break. She cursed her own weakness. Back there in the desert she had known what he was doing—laying the foundation for his vengeance—but she hadn't been able to stop him. She had wanted him to go on kissing her, to never let her go. It had been so long since she'd been kissed, so long since she'd felt so alive. Even knowing he couldn't be trusted, she had trusted him.

When they got home, Jess went to his room, Caitlin to her studio. He pulled off his boots and let them fall with a clatter to the floor. He pulled his shirt off and tossed it to the floor, too, then lay back on the bed. He sure as hell wasn't in a good mood, he decided crossly. He knew what would have happened if he hadn't pushed her away out there. He could have seduced her— he was sure of it—right there under the hot sun. He could have stripped her clothes off and taken her, and she wouldn't have made so much as a whimper of protest. But he hadn't, and he couldn't figure out why. He must be a bigger fool than he'd thought.

Caitlin's mood was just as dark. When she reached the studio she locked the door behind her. She usually found comfort in the bright airy room, surrounded by her paints and brushes, canvasses and papers, finished paintings and tentative sketches, but not this time. She chose a prepared canvas of pure, closely woven linen that had been primed with two coats of white oil paint and went to work.

It was late when she finished. The painting before her was dark and angry, the stormy scene full of violence and unleashed fury. It was done in oil instead of the softer, gentler watercolors

that she preferred, and it completely lacked the sense of serenity
that characterized her work. But that was all right, she acknowledged, because when she had started it, she'd felt anything but
serene.

The sagebrush trembled, and sand and dirt and tumbleweeds
were swept along before a fierce wind that she could almost feel.
The lone structure in the scene, an old wooden shack, leaned
under the force of the gale, and black, angry clouds filled the
sky, illuminated by jagged forks of lightning. It accurately reflected the turbulent, agitated whirl of emotions inside her. She
liked it.

Whistling softly, she cleaned her brushes and the glass palette,
then washed her hands in the small bathroom. Now she felt better. Now she could deal with Jess again.

Dinner wasn't bad. Lupe was well rested, though she still had
little appetite, and Jess wasn't in the mood to talk. Caitlin didn't
mind at all.

After dinner she sat on the sofa in the living room while Jess
told his mother about his plans for the house. She was delighted
with his ideas, more for his sake than her own. A house represented a sense of permanence, and she couldn't help but hope
that even after she was dead, Jess would continue to live there.
The longer he stayed, the better the chances that he and Caitlin
would get back together. Anyone could see they were meant for
each other: anyone except them and Grant, she added somberly.
But Grant was out of the way, for the time being, at least. Maybe
it would be long enough.

Caitlin got some paper for Jess, and he drew rough sketches
for Lupe. The older woman slowly broke into a smile. "You
remembered."

He nodded. They had planned the house together, room by
room, when he was only a child. Lupe had called it her dream
house—not because it would be perfect, but because she had
known it would never exist except in her dreams. But now he
could make it real.

It was going to be a large house, Caitlin noticed—too large
for only two people. She counted at least four bedrooms, plus a
room in the northeast corner that seemed to have no particular

purpose. When she asked what it would be, Jess lifted his shoulders. He really couldn't say; he had added it as an afterthought.

Her attention returned to the bedrooms. Why did Jess and Lupe need four bedrooms? She could think of only two reasons, and she didn't like either of them: either Jess was planning to marry one day and wanted rooms for his children, or he was looking ahead to the time when Lupe was gone, adding the extra rooms to make it a more attractive home to the family he would sell it to. She wouldn't even consider the possibility of another woman having his children; the day that happened, she would leave Isabel and New Mexico forever. But she didn't like the idea of him selling out and moving away any better.

"This is wonderful," Lupe said, giving her son a hug. She smiled apologetically at Caitlin. "I've loved living here with you, but...well, your father will be back in January, so I'll have to move out before then. This will work out perfectly." After a pause she added, "I'll miss you."

Caitlin squeezed her hand. "We'll be able to see each other every day. It's not far."

Jess thought of Caitlin being at his house every day. The idea had a certain appeal. After all, if they had gotten married, she would have been with him every day and every night. But they hadn't gotten married, he sternly reminded himself. She had chosen to stay with her father instead. She had left him, and he wasn't going to forgive her for it.

Over the next week they fell into an easy routine. Jess left the house as soon as breakfast was over, going to the building site, to the various offices for permits and information, to conferences with Tom Mendez. Lupe went to work at Carmen's shop, and Caitlin cleaned house before going to her studio. Lupe returned home shortly after three, but Jess's hours varied. Sometimes he got home at five or six, but other times he didn't make it in until eight or nine o'clock, and he was always tired. He and Caitlin rarely talked, though Lupe gave them plenty of time alone. He studied plans, made lists and generally ignored her.

Work was a good way to avoid her, Jess decided by the third day. He drove himself hard during the day—to finish the house before it was too late for Lupe, he told himself. It was convenient, though, that it left him too tired to talk to Caitlin in the evenings and much too tired to do anything else to her. But it didn't stop him from thinking about her, and it certainly didn't stop him from wanting her.

By the fifth day he'd forgotten about avoiding her. Instead of leaving after breakfast, as usual, he stayed around until Lupe was gone. "I have to go into Albuquerque today to buy some supplies. Will you go with me?" He didn't ask if she wanted to go; he could think of no reason why she should. But he hoped she would say yes.

Caitlin couldn't think of anything pressing to stop her from going. She had no projects that needed her attention right away; in fact, she'd spent the better part of the last two days lying on her stomach on the couch in her studio, daydreaming. Add to that the fact that this was the first time Jess had sought her company since Sunday, and she became even more willing to go.

"How's the house going?" she asked after they were on the interstate.

"Pretty good."

"How long will it take?"

"Three, four months. Tom's schedule is pretty full, so he's got to work me in when he can. There's only so much I can do alone."

"I can help."

He glanced at her from the corners of his eyes. "What do you know about building houses?" he asked dryly.

"Nothing. But I know a lot about following instructions."

Unbidden, an image of Grant appeared in his mind. "You should," he retorted. "You've been doing it all your life."

She had left herself open for that one. Frowning, she turned her head to look out the window. That was the last time she would ever offer him help.

He knew he could leave it there, and she wouldn't bring it up again. Still, he added, "It's hot out there."

"It's the desert. Of course it's hot." She was glad to find that she could be as sarcastic as he was.

"Why would you want to work out there?"

"Because the sooner *that* house is finished, the sooner you'll be out of mine."

Jess's eyes were almost black, and his mouth was a tight,

angry line. He stared at her for a long time, until the blare of a horn warned him that the truck was drifting across the line between the lanes. He looked back at the road and jerked the steering wheel to the right, guiding the truck back into the proper lane. "I'll move out tonight."

"No, Jess...I didn't mean... Please..." She scooted across the seat until she could touch him, but he shrugged her hand off. "Jess."

Suddenly he swerved onto the shoulder of the road, bringing the truck to a stop with a squeal of rubber. Shutting off the engine, he turned in the seat to face her. "Just what the hell do you want from me, Cait?" he demanded.

She was too close to him. She could feel the heat of his body, mixed with the heat of his anger. She knew she had to move away or she would get burned, but she was frozen in place. She couldn't move.

Jess grabbed her shoulders and gave her a shake. "Answer me, dammit!" he shouted. "What do you want?"

She was trembling. "I don't know," she whispered. "I want you to forget my father. I want you to leave him alone. And I don't want you to hurt me."

His eyes closed, shutting out her face. She was afraid. Sometimes he liked her anger, and he was amused by her nervousness and aroused by her softness, but he didn't like seeing her scared, especially not of him. With a low groan, he pulled her to him. "For God's sake, Cait, don't you know I wouldn't hurt you?" he asked in a ragged voice.

You did before, she silently replied. But she said nothing out loud. Instead, she let him hold her; she turned her face against his chest and drew strength from the presence that surrounded her.

She didn't know when the comforting changed, but when his fingertips tilted her face up to receive his kiss, she let it happen. She had accepted his kiss Sunday; this time she took control from him. Her hand slid up to cup his jaw, smooth and hard, and her tongue blocked entry to his. She explored his mouth as she had done so many times in the past, savoring the texture and taste of him.

He couldn't breathe. His lungs wouldn't expand, wouldn't accept the air he tried to force into them. He was losing himself in her kiss. He was excited, aroused and thoroughly intoxicated. His hands adjusted her across his hips, letting her feel him grow heavy with desire. He pushed her head back and caught her lower lip between his teeth, gently sucking at it. "Caitlin," he muttered hoarsely. "We've got to stop. This isn't the place."

"I don't care," she whispered.

"I do. Just let me hold you. Just for a minute." His hands slid from her face to her shoulders, then her back. His arms surrounded her, warm and strong and gentle. His hands rubbed over her spine, making small, pressing, circular motions, easing the kinks caused by tension. When she was absorbed by her painting, Caitlin could work for hours at a time without rest, and Jess had often pampered her with a sensuous massage. Her soft moan told him that she remembered.

What else did she remember? he wondered. Did she ever think about their lovemaking? Did she remember how it felt when he filled her? Too many years and too few women later, he remembered. He remembered every detail of every time they had ever made love. Sometimes, late at night, in a strange city and a lonely bed he had tortured himself with those memories. Never had it hurt worse or felt better than it did right then.

"Put your arms around me, Cait," he whispered hoarsely.

She mindlessly obeyed, and the action pressed her closer to him, against the jutting ridge of flesh that nudged her thigh. She moved again, and he made a small sound of pleasure.

Her hair smelled so sweet. He pressed his face against it, testing its softness. He was suffering the most exquisite pain all through his body, and he didn't want it to end. But a rushing eighteen-wheeler, with a blast of its air horn, set the pickup to rocking, and Jess repeated his admonition to himself: this wasn't the place for seduction. Reluctantly, he lifted Caitlin off his lap, set her on the seat and turned around.

She was embarrassed. All it took was a little attention from him, and she repeatedly threw herself into his arms. He must think she was incredibly desperate for a man.

He started the engine and pulled onto the highway. Once the truck reached its maximum speed, he reached across and lifted Caitlin's face with one finger under her chin. "I won't move out yet, okay?" he offered. She nodded, and he smiled. "Have I told you lately that you're beautiful?"

"Not in eight years or so." She cleared her throat to get rid of the hoarseness that betrayed how strongly those few minutes in his arms had affected her.

"You are beautiful."

Her blush deepened, and she murmured a thank-you before looking out the window again.

In Albuquerque, Jess was reluctant to go straight to the store for his supplies. That was his reason for coming, and when it was done, he would have no excuse for keeping her with him. "Let's go to Old Town," he suggested when he saw the sign along the freeway.

He parked in a lot at the edge of the historical district, and they walked along the narrow street side by side. It was crowded with summer tourists, but he didn't mind. The crowds kept him close to her.

"Where's Melly's gallery?" he asked when they reached the plaza.

"A half block down that street."

He took her hand and tugged. "Come on. I want to see some of your work."

Caitlin let him keep her hand. It felt nice, enclosed in his bigger, rougher palm. She directed him to the gallery in an adobe house said to be over a hundred and sixty years old. Only one customer and Melly's assistant were inside. Caitlin's paintings, along with the works of the few other artists the gallery represented, were too expensive for casual browsers to buy.

She left Jess to look while she chatted with Melly's assistant. "Hi, Caitlin, who's the hunk?" the young woman asked with a grin.

"Hi, Tanya. He's a friend. Where's Melly?"

"She's not coming in until this afternoon. She'll be sorry she missed you. Is this friend married, engaged or otherwise attached?"

Although Tanya was pretty and attracted more than her share of men, Caitlin didn't mind her interest in Jess. The other woman liked all men: tall or short, heavy or thin, handsome or plain. She wasn't about to settle on one and give up the others. "Not at the moment."

"Are you working on it?" Without waiting for an answer,

Tanya continued, "If he's yours, I'll keep my hands off and just look, okay?"

Caitlin nodded vaguely—this wasn't a subject she cared to go into at the moment—and walked away. She didn't care that she was being rude to Tanya. She was too aware of Jess for that.

He studied the seven originals of Caitlin's that hung on the far wall of the gallery, then looked over the signed and numbered prints available of her other works. The paintings had no prices on them, but the prints did, and they cost far more than he would have imagined. If people would pay three hundred dollars and up for a print of which one hundred to four hundred copies existed—and apparently they would, since several were marked as sold out—the original paintings must be worth a fortune. It left him a little in awe.

"See anything you like?" Tanya asked when he joined them at the counter.

"I like them all. I apologize for doubting your talent, Cait."

She remembered his sarcastic question about earning a living with her painting and smiled. "I think you're the only one who didn't doubt it. Tanya, this is Jess Trujillo. Tanya is Melly's assistant."

"Which is a fancy way of saying 'go-fer.' How do you do, Jess?"

"I do all right," he said with a genuine smile.

She leaned forward a little and looked him over from head to toe. "I bet you do. How'd you get tied up with Caitlin?"

Caitlin nervously edged back. "We've known each other a long time."

"Hmm." Tanya examined him again. "Are you married, Jess?"

"No."

If Tanya noticed that his voice was a little less friendly, she didn't show it. "Ever been married?"

"No."

"Ever been engaged?"

"Once."

"Perfect. You might be just the one to entice Caitlin here into marriage. If she doesn't find a man soon, she's going to be too old to have kids. We don't want anyone who's been married and divorced, but then again, we don't want anyone who's reached the age of thirty without a serious relationship, either. What do you think, Caitlin?''

Tanya didn't know it, but her teasing wasn't funny. Caitlin was staring at her, her eyes wide and sad and hurt. "I think we'd better be going," she said in a voice that shook. She started toward the door without looking to see if Jess was following.

Tanya sobered instantly. "What did I say?" she asked in dismay.

Jess's smile was without pleasure. "The woman I was once engaged to," he said slowly, "was Caitlin. It was nice meeting you, Tanya."

He found Caitlin standing outside, staring unseeingly at a display of silver-and-turquoise jewelry in a shop window. "Do you want to go anyplace in particular?" he asked quietly.

She shook her head. "Let's just walk."

At last they ended up back at the parking lot. She got inside the truck and waited for Jess to start the engine before breaking the silence. "I'm sorry."

"It was eight years ago."

"Is that supposed to matter? I'm not supposed to care just because it was eight years ago."

"That isn't what I meant." He rubbed his hand over his eyes. He didn't even know what he meant. "Do you like me, Cait?"

"I—I—"

"I like you. I don't mean the way I remember you. I like the woman you've become. I like being with you, looking at you, talking with you—and God, I like kissing you and holding you."

The coldness inside was starting to thaw. His words sent a heat rushing through her that she felt all the way to her toes. "I like you, too," she admitted in a whisper.

He smiled at her, and she felt like the luckiest woman in the world. She knew she was a damned fool, but she couldn't help it. She knew she couldn't trust him, but she did. And she knew she'd be crazy to fall in love with him again, but she was very much afraid that that was exactly what was happening.

"How about some lunch?" he suggested, and she nodded numbly. He could have suggested jumping from the top of Sandía Peak, and she probably would have agreed just as quickly.

They went to a fast-food restaurant down the street. Caitlin loved small-town life, but greasy fast-food hamburgers were one of her weaknesses, and Isabel was too small to attract one of the major chains.

After lunch they went to the building supply store. Caitlin wandered up and down the aisles while Jess filled his order from the list he and Tom had put together. When he was finished and the supplies had been loaded in his truck, they headed home to Isabel.

She expected him to drop her off at her house, but instead he drove straight through town to the site. She looked questioningly at him, and he grinned. "You wanted to help."

Grateful that she had worn jeans and a T-shirt, she climbed into the back of the truck and went to work. Within minutes she was soaked with sweat. "It isn't fair," she said, tugging at the tail of her shirt to wipe her face.

"What isn't?"

She pointed at his shirt, discarded as soon as they'd started working. "You can take your shirt off and be at least a little cooler."

He was standing on the ground, looking up at her. He could tell that she was braless beneath her shirt, because it was so wet that it clung to her. "You can take yours off," he invited. "I wouldn't object."

Caitlin scowled at him, wiped her forehead again and grabbed a hammer, swinging it menacingly. He picked up a load of lumber and started toward the small shed he and Tom had built a few days earlier. His laughter floated back to her.

It was a good sound, she thought, watching him until he disappeared inside. He hadn't had too many reasons to laugh in too many years. Neither had she, come to think of it. Maybe things were going to change for both of them.

Caitlin sank down on the open tailgate, crossed her legs and bent over at the waist. "I thought I was in good shape," she said with a groan.

Jess sat at the opposite end. He didn't see anything wrong with her shape, but he didn't dare say so. The hammer she had threatened him with had been put away, but there was still a hefty two-by-four within easy reach. "Tired?"

"Sore."

He took his shirt and put it on again. "Thanks for the help."

Slowly she sat up, keeping her spine straight. "I think it probably would have gone just as fast without me."

"Not as fast," he denied with a shake of his head. "And it definitely wouldn't have been as pleasant." He offered her a hand and pulled her to the ground, then closed the tailgate. While he double-checked the lock on the shed, she walked over to the place where the house was going to be. The site had been graded, and they were going to pour the foundation on Monday. Markers had been set out for the subcontractors, outlining the house. She walked around the area, trying to imagine how it would look when it was finished. Then she came to the room that had drawn her interest in Jess's sketches. It was at the very back of the house, with three walls facing out. She had heard him tell Lupe that those three walls were probably going to be glass, and Tom had suggested putting in a skylight. It would be a wonderful room to work in, with all that light and three marvelous views.

Her thoughts made her wistful. It was foolish to think of herself in this house, in that room. Even if Jess proposed to her, she would be stupid to accept, because such a proposal could never come from his heart. His biggest interest in her was as a tool: an easy, effective way to punish Grant. A means to an end.

Despite the warm sun, she shivered and wrapped her arms across her chest. He must really hate Grant if he could stoop this low. He had to know he would destroy her if he pursued her only to avenge himself on her father, but that was just what he was going to do. Oh sure, he might really think she was pretty, but it was revenge that really drove him. What other reason could he have for kissing and holding her the way he had that morning? For smiling at her as if she were the most special thing in his life? What other reason could he have for asking her to spend the day with him?

She sighed, and her shoulders slumped. She wished that she could tell him to leave her alone and mean it. She wished she could stop herself from falling in love with him again, could stop her heart from breaking. She wished he could forget the past, forget Grant and want only her. But most of all, more than anything, she wished he could want her and need her and love her. Dear God, she wished he could love her.

Chapter 4

Carmen Mendez brought Lupe home from work shortly after lunch on Tuesday afternoon. Caitlin was in her studio doing a sketch for her latest painting, but she came out immediately at Carmen's call. "Is Lupe all right?" she asked when she climbed the steps to the deck.

"She's going to lie down." Carmen looked tense. "She's sicker this time than ever before. Caitlin, I'm so worried."

Caitlin put her arm around the smaller woman's shoulder and went inside with her. "It's going to get worse, Carmen," she said gently. "We just have to do what we can to help."

"She doesn't deserve this. Dear God, I wish it had never happened."

"So do I. Can you stay awhile, or do you need to get back to the store?"

"I've got to go back. Amelia's there now, but her little boy has a doctor's appointment in half an hour. Call me later and let me know how she is."

"Thanks for bringing her home. Jess will bring me by tonight to pick up her car." She closed the door, then went to Lupe's room.

Lupe's room was on the opposite side of the house from the

other bedrooms. It had originally been intended as a servant's room, but Lupe had preferred it over the other rooms because of its location. She often had restless nights, and she didn't want to disturb Caitlin.

Now Caitlin knocked at the door, and Lupe called out an invitation to come in. "Hello. Can I get you anything?" Caitlin offered.

She shook her head wearily. "I just have a headache."

And a fever, too, if her flushed face meant anything. She looked so tired, Caitlin thought. She regretted that she had been less than attentive to her friend in the days since Jess's return. The weight loss that had first prompted Lupe to let Dr. Ramirez examine her was continuing, as he had warned it would. Her skin seemed to hang from her bones, and even careful dressing could no longer disguise the fact that she was wasting away.

"You don't have to sit with me."

Caitlin went to the window to draw the heavy drapes. "Unless you're telling me to get out, I'm staying. I don't have anything to do right now." She pulled a straight-backed chair over to the bed and sat down.

"Thank you, Caitlin," Lupe said with a tired smile.

Leaning over, Caitlin smoothed her hand over Lupe's forehead. The other woman's skin was warm. She did have a fever. The doctor had warned them about that, too. He had told them about all the symptoms—the itching, the headaches, the breathing difficulties, the fatigue, the loss of appetite—but he hadn't told them how to save her, because there was no way, and he hadn't told them how much time she had, because no one knew.

Another thing he hadn't told Caitlin was how to deal with it. How could she sit by and watch the woman who was like a mother to her die? Watch the disease eat away at her, killing her an inch at a time? How could she accept that she was going to lose one of the most important people in her life? And how in the world was Jess going to accept it?

Lupe slept, her breathing heavy and labored, and Caitlin sat in the darkened room and watched her. Her work was forgotten—everything was forgotten except the love that she felt for this woman. She would give anything if she could help her.

The afternoon was over when Lupe finally awoke. She felt better. Now she only had a headache instead of the pounding throb she had gone to bed with. Her fever was down, too, for the time being. She opened her eyes and brought Caitlin into focus. "You didn't need to stay here all afternoon," she gently admonished.

Caitlin sat straighter in the chair and smiled. "I wanted to."

"I'm glad you're here. There's something I want to ask you." Lupe shifted in the bed, pulling the covers closer. The subject was one she hated to bring up—not because it bothered her to talk about her own death, but because it bothered Caitlin. She had found that in the two months since her disease had been diagnosed that the prospect of her death didn't frighten her, but most people couldn't face it. She understood, in a way. It was much easier for her to know that she was dying than it would be to know that Jess was dying, God forbid.

"You know I'd do anything for you, Lupe," Caitlin said with a smile.

"You haven't heard it yet. You may change your tune." She sat up in bed, and Caitlin helped her fix the pillows behind her back for support. "Caitlin, I want you to tell Jess about me. He already knows I'm dying—I can see it in his eyes—but he doesn't know the details. I want you to tell him."

Caitlin stared at her, a sickly paleness stealing over her face. She couldn't do that. She couldn't be the one to tell him in brutally hopeless terms that his mother was dying and nothing could change that.

"I know it's not fair. I'm asking you to do something that I don't have the courage to do myself. But he's got to know, Caitlin, and if you can't tell him, I'll have to ask the doctor to do it. Please. It would be better for him to find out from someone who knows and cares for him."

Slowly the color returned to Caitlin's face, and the tightness in her chest eased. Lupe had given her so much—starting with her unconditional love—and she had rarely asked for anything in return. How could she turn her down now, when it was so important to her? "All right, Lupe. Do you want me to tell him today?"

"Could you, please? And tomorrow evening, after he's had time to understand it, I'd like to talk to him. Will you tell him that?"

She nodded. The lump in her throat kept her from speaking.

With a satisfied smile, Lupe reached for her Bible on the night-stand. "I'd like to be alone now," she requested. "I'm going to read."

Caitlin kissed her forehead, turned on the bedside lamp and left the room. Then she went down the hall to her own room, where she lay across the bed and cried. She cried for Lupe and she cried for Jess, but most of all she cried for herself. She was losing a woman who had been an important part of her life, and she was certain that a part of herself would die with Lupe. Lupe's death would leave a void that no one could fill, not even Jess.

When she heard his truck in the driveway, she went into the bathroom and splashed her face with cool water. It didn't wash away all traces of her tears: her nose was red and her eyes were puffy, but she didn't think he would notice.

She was wrong. As soon as he saw her, he knew something had happened. "What's wrong?" he demanded.

Caitlin took a step back from him. She couldn't do this! But she had promised Lupe that she would. "After you take a shower, can I talk to you?"

"Talk to me now." He took hold of her arm and pulled her down the hall to his room. Inside, with the door closed, he let go of her. "What's wrong?"

"Your mother asked me to talk to you. She wants me to tell you what's wrong with her."

Jess stared at her for a long moment, then headed toward the master bath. "I'm going to clean up first."

She knew what he was doing. As much as he said he wanted to know, he didn't, not really. He would avoid it as long as he could; then he would let her tell him. She wasn't going to force him to listen until he was ready.

He stayed in the shower a long time, scrubbing the dirt and sweat from his body, washing his hair, letting the cool water beat down on him until he was cool, then chilled. At last he got out and dried off, then went into the bedroom, a soft towel knotted around his hips.

Caitlin was sitting on the bed, waiting for him. Now that she was ready to tell him, she wasn't going to give him a chance to put it off.

Jess scowled at her. "You could have waited in the living room."

She got to her feet.

"Never mind. I'll be ready in a minute." He got his clothing from the dresser and returned to the bathroom to put it on. When he returned, wearing only a pair of white cotton running shorts, Caitlin decided that she preferred him in the towel. It was less revealing.

There were no chairs in the room, so he leaned against the dresser. It was safer than sitting on the bed with her. "All right," he said quietly. "Talk to me."

She took a deep breath. Once the disease had been diagnosed, she had spent hours with doctors and complex medical texts, researching it. She could talk intelligently about it with the doctors—in fact, she was better informed than many of them. But when it came to discussing it with Jess, with someone who didn't care about statistics or causes, someone who cared only that his mother was dying because of this disease—that was hard.

"A few months ago, Lupe asked Dr. Ramirez to give her a checkup. She was losing weight, got tired easily, and she itched for no reason that she knew of. He did an exam and some blood tests, then sent her to a doctor in the city. He did the same tests and a biopsy, and he diagnosed it as Hodgkin's disease."

Jess raised his head to look at her. He'd heard of that disease, but he knew nothing about it, except... "Isn't that always fatal?"

"No. If it's diagnosed early enough, in Stages I and II, there's a pretty good survival rate with radiation therapy. But in Stages III and IV, survival rates drop. Chemotherapy helps, but..." She shrugged.

"And Mom?" He forced the words through a closed throat and clenched teeth.

"Lupe was in Stage IV when it was diagnosed. She underwent chemotherapy for a while, but she chose to discontinue it."

"Why?" he demanded. "Why did she stop it? Why did you let her?"

"It's a treatment, Jess, not a cure. For some people it has terrible side effects, and Lupe is one of those people. Her hair fell out. The nausea and vomiting were so severe that she had to be sedated. She was so sick that she used to pray to die. When it was over, she swore she would never go through it again, and I wouldn't make her if I could. I was there, Jess. I practically lived at the hospital while she was undergoing chemotherapy. I saw what she went through."

"If it can save her life—"

"But it can't. Nothing can. She takes medication that helps relieve the symptoms, but it does nothing for the disease itself. The purpose is to make her as comfortable as possible until she dies."

"When will that be?" He sounded as if he were choking.

"No one knows. It could be a few months or a few years."

He pushed himself away from the dresser and paced restlessly across the tiled floor. There was anger in his jerky movements and anguish in his face. She understood both emotions because she had often experienced them herself. Suddenly he stopped and turned toward her. "It's not right, Cait," he said harshly.

"No, it isn't."

"I want her to see a doctor someplace else. There are some big cancer research centers back east. I'll take her to one of them."

She shook her head. "Her doctor in Albuquerque is an oncologist—a cancer specialist. The doctors back east can't do anything for her that Dr. Carson can't do. There is no cure, Jess."

"Then she has to start the chemotherapy again." He held up his hands when she started to protest. "So it won't cure her—it will prolong her life, won't it?"

"Maybe," she answered reluctantly. She wished he would just accept it; fighting wasn't going to make a difference. And she was glad that she was telling him instead of Lupe. She was able to deal with his anger better than Lupe could. Her friend was too weary. "Don't do this, Jess. She went through it with the hospital staff. They tried to convince her to continue the treatment, and when that didn't work, they badgered her until she couldn't stand it anymore. They're doctors—they're used to saving people's lives, not standing by and doing nothing while they die. But Lupe has to do what's best for her. Not you and me and all the people who love her, but *her*."

He was staring at her as if she were some kind of insect. "Just let her die—that's what you think we should do?"

She left the bed and went to him. She wanted to shake him until he understood, but she simply laid her hands on his arms.

"Jess, she *is* dying, and there's nothing in the world that anyone can do to save her!"

He shrugged her off. "No. I don't believe you. I *won't* believe you! I'm not going to let her die, do you understand? I'm not going to let her die!"

The door slammed behind him, making Caitlin jump. She hadn't expected it to be easy, but Lord, she hadn't expected it to be so hard, either.

When she finally left his room to look for him, she discovered that his truck was gone. She checked on Lupe and found her dozing, her Bible in her lap. She set it on the nightstand, shut off the lamp and pulled the covers over her.

It wasn't a long walk to Carmen's store, and the cool evening air might help clear her mind. She put on tennis shoes, got the spare set of keys to Lupe's car and set out down the hill.

Across the street and down a block from the store was Rusty's Bar, one of only two in Isabel, and parked out front was Jess's truck. Caitlin hesitated only a moment before crossing the street and going inside. The bar was dark and smelled of stale smoke and beer. The few women inside were strangers to her, but she knew most of the men by sight or reputation. They looked up with interest as she came in, but she ignored them while she searched for Jess.

He was at the far end of the bar, a half-empty bottle in front of him. Her mouth thinned into an angry line, she went to him. "What the hell are you doing?"

He didn't look at her. "Get out."

"If you want to get drunk, do it at home. Come on."

Then he did look at her, and his eyes were black and angry and nasty. "I said get out, Caitlin. You don't belong here."

"And neither do you."

"Where I belong, and what I do, is none of your damned business," he snarled. He took a long drink from the glass in front of him, emptying it, then refilled it from the bottle.

She could plead with him, but it wouldn't do any good, and she wasn't about to throw away her pride for nothing. "All right," she said coldly. "But when you leave—*if* you leave here—you leave that truck parked out front and walk home. You're in no condition to drive, and you're not going to do a damned thing that might hurt your mother. Do you understand?"

She spun around and sailed across the room, carried by anger that masked a deeper worry.

Jess watched her go, took another drink and stared after her. He reached the door in time to see her head into the alley that led to a parking lot behind Carmen's store. Some part of his brain that was still functioning realized that she'd come after Lupe's car, not him, and it angered him.

Caitlin dug the keys from her pocket and tried to stick the wrong one in the door lock. She swore softly and tried again. Just as the lock turned, a strong hand wrapped around her arm. She screamed, but another hand covered her mouth as she was turned around.

She sagged with relief. It was Jess. But it was a drunken Jess: ill-tempered, disagreeable and downright ugly. She shoved his hand away from her mouth and demanded that he let her go.

"What's wrong, Cait? Just a minute ago you were full of concern that I might not get home all right. I thought you wanted me to come with you." He sounded all innocence, but there was a hardness to his voice that made her shiver.

"You made it clear that you didn't want my concern."

"Oh, but I do." He pulled her closer against him and lowered his head until his mouth was only an inch above her ear. "I wasn't thinking too straight in there. I do want your concern, Cait. Show me how worried you are."

When he tried to kiss her, she turned her head. He shoved her against the car and held her with his body, then used both hands to hold her head still. The taste of liquor was strong, and it sickened Caitlin. She struggled with him, managing at last to free her mouth, but only for a moment. "Jess, stop—"

He kissed her again, and his hand moved beneath her shirt to grasp her breast roughly. Tears rolled down her cheeks, and her stomach churned; she thought for an instant that she was going to be ill. Then his fingers gentled, and so did his mouth, and he relaxed the pressure of his body so that she could move.

He was drunk, but not so drunk that he could force himself on her. When he made love with her, he promised himself, she was going to cry because she wanted him so damned much, not because he was hurting or scaring her. He released her face and wrapped his arms around her. "I'm sorry, Cait," he whispered. "I'm sorry."

She tried to push him away, but he held her tighter. He knew she was disgusted with him, but he needed the contact with her for just a moment longer.

She was trembling. "You hurt me," she accused, her voice quavering, but it wasn't a physical ache. Somewhere inside she was shocked that Jess could ever use force against her.

He groaned. "Oh, honey, I wasn't going to rape you, I swear to God. I didn't mean to hurt you. I'd never take you like that. I'm sorry, Cait."

She didn't feel like being forgiving, not tonight. "Let me go."

He did. He backed away from her and watched, his hands at his sides. She got into the car and pushed the key into the ignition; then he spoke again. "Can I get a ride home with you?"

"Go to hell."

He winced. "Please, Cait. Don't leave me alone. I don't want to be alone."

He looked so lost and forlorn that she couldn't stay angry. "Get in," she invited with a sigh.

Just before they reached the house, he began talking in a low, emotional voice, almost as if he'd forgotten that he had an audience. Caitlin parked the car, shut off the engine and listened.

"My grandparents used to live out on that piece of land where we're building the house—not right there, but farther back, way off the road. When Mom got pregnant with me, they kicked her out, and she went to live with Carmen's family. Her mother used to sneak out to see her sometimes, but her father wouldn't have anything to do with her. He said she had shamed the family by getting pregnant—by a married man, no less. He cut her off completely. None of her brothers or sisters would have anything to do with her, and before I was born, her mother stopped coming around, too."

Caitlin was surprised; she hadn't known that Lupe had had relatives in town. When he continued, Jess explained why she hadn't known.

"When I was about a year old, her father went to see her. He told her that she had dishonored their family name, that he could no longer bear the disgrace. He was taking the family and leaving New Mexico. As of the day I was born, he told her, his daughter Guadalupe was dead." He looked at her, the moonlight showing the despair on his face. "She gave up so much for me, Cait—

her family, her reputation. It was hard for her in this town, raising an illegitimate son, but she did it, and she did a pretty good job.'' He smiled crookedly. ''Cait—'' His voice broke, and a sob shook his shoulders. ''My mother's dying, Cait, and I feel so damned helpless! I love her, and I want to do something for her, but there's nothing I can do! God, I hate this!''

She moved across the seat to put her arms around him and pulled his head onto her shoulders. ''I know, Jess,'' she said softly. ''It's all right. I understand.''

She didn't know how long they sat there, how many times she said the soft, comforting words that meant nothing. When at last he raised his head, her arm was numb, and her legs were starting to cramp from being in the same position too long.

''I never thanked you for taking care of her while I was gone,'' he said after clearing his throat.

She simply nodded.

He looked at her a moment longer. He could kiss her now, if he tried. This time she wouldn't pull away. This time she wouldn't be frightened. So this time *he* was going to pull away. ''I—I've got to get some sleep. Thanks for bringing me home.''

After she unlocked the door, he added one more thing. ''Cait, thanks for telling me. I know it wasn't easy for you.'' He bent and kissed her forehead, then walked away.

He undressed in his darkened room and lay down, but he couldn't relax. There was too much tension inside him. Emotional. Sexual. He could have seduced her so easily with just a kiss, but for reasons he couldn't explain to himself, he had refused. He lay in his lonely bed, hard, his need for her still achingly evident. Only Caitlin could make the ache go away. Only Caitlin could satisfy his hunger. But not yet. He couldn't go to her yet.

She was disappointed. She wanted more than that brief impersonal kiss. After holding him so close like that, she wanted so much more, but he wasn't willing to give it. She locked the front door behind her and went to her bedroom.

She should be grateful that he was giving her time. An affair with Jess wasn't a decision to make lightly. He'd been right that day when he told her that she could never make love with a man she didn't care for. Her willingness—even eagerness—to go to bed with him meant only one thing. Her love for him had never died. All those years, when she had told herself that she was over him, she had lied. She still wanted him; she still loved him, and she was willing to take him any way she could get him.

Where was the stiff-necked pride that had gotten her through those awful weeks when he'd first left? Her heart had been broken, but she had managed to survive with her head held high. She needed that pride now to keep her from doing something as foolish as having an affair with him—an affair that guaranteed heartache—but she didn't care. If he wanted her, she wouldn't tell him no.

At breakfast the next morning Jess had little appetite. When Caitlin told him about Lupe's request to see him that evening, he simply nodded. After Lupe joined them, Caitlin offered him a ride to his truck, but he shook his head. He didn't want to be alone in the close confines of the Jeep with her. It had taken a long time last night for his desire to subside, and even a few minutes alone with her would stir it up again. He would walk the short distance, as she had done last night. He could use the fresh air.

All day he dreaded the talk with Lupe. When he got home Caitlin had dinner ready—trays for him and Lupe, who was resting in her room, and a single setting at the kitchen table for herself.

When Jess entered her room, Lupe knew that Caitlin had done as she had requested, because he wouldn't look at her. He had avoided her eyes that morning, and he avoided them now, staring at the floor, the wall and the painting Caitlin had done for her that hung next to the bed.

She was relieved that he knew the truth. It had been cowardly of her to ask Caitlin to tell him, but she hadn't been able to face the task herself. In the last two months she had become dependent on the younger woman—for a home, for friendship, for love. Caitlin had done a lot for her, and all she could offer in return was her own love.

After the meal was finished, Jess took their dishes to the kitchen. "Sit down, Jesus," Lupe invited when he returned. She gave his name the Spanish pronunciation, a smooth flow of soft sounds, "Hay-soos." When he moved toward the nearby chair, she stopped him. "Sit here, next to me. Are you glad to be home?"

He nodded. "Of course I am. I missed you."

"Did you miss Caitlin, too?"

After a moment's hesitation, he nodded. "I guess I did."

"Do you think you two might get together again?"

The tension in his shoulders didn't go unnoticed. "I don't know. It was a long time ago, Mom. People change."

She pooh-poohed that. "Neither of you has changed that much. There's *un dicho*, an old saying, that goes, *Amor que ha sido brasa de repente vuelve a arder.* A love that still flickers can easily reignite."

Not without trust, Jess hoped. He intended to become Caitlin's lover again, but he was never again going to trust her with his love. "There's another old saying: *Donde hay amor, hay dolor.* Where there's love, there's pain."

Lupe was delighted by his flawless pronunciation of the language he had always refused to study when he was younger. "It's about time you learned some Spanish," she admonished. "I suppose love always brings some pain, but Caitlin can forgive you for that. She's not the sort to hold a grudge."

Jess stared at her, not certain he understood. What did Caitlin have to forgive him for? He had been talking about his own pain. Who knew whether Caitlin had ever cared enough to be hurt when he left? She had missed him, or so she claimed, "at first." He had never stopped missing her, never stopped wanting her, needing her, lov—

He grew rigid with dismay. He would not love her. God help him, he would *not* love her!

How had it happened that his own mother took Caitlin's side? Didn't she know that he was the one who had been betrayed? That Caitlin, who had claimed to love him passionately, fiercely, for all time, had chosen to stay with her father rather than support him? How could Lupe disregard the fact that *he* was the one who had been wronged, the one who had been hurt, the one who wasn't going to forgive?

He didn't respond to Lupe's observation. Once again he turned his attention to the painting on the wall. Seeing the stubborn set of his jaw, Lupe let the subject drop. "That's *Nuestra Señora de Guadalupe.* Caitlin did it."

He took note of the details of the painting before him, of the beautiful young woman wearing a fur-trimmed robe, a mantilla filled with stars and a cross around her neck. She stood in front of the sun's rays, on top of the moon, and was supported by an angel whose wings contained the colors of the rainbow. He was familiar with the painting. He had grown up with images of Our Lady of Guadalupe in his home.

"Do you remember the story?" She had told it to him often enough that she knew he couldn't have forgotten, and she wanted him to talk. These silences of his were unnerving.

He lifted his shoulders in a shrug. "Over four hundred years ago she appeared to an Indian in Mexico. She was beautiful, young, dark and pregnant. She told him to ask the Bishop to build a church for her so she could tend to her children, but the Bishop didn't believe him. He had to return to the spot to ask her to give him a sign from Heaven as proof for the Bishop, which she did."

It was a brief version, told in the unemotional tones of one who cared little for old legends. Lupe smiled, understanding in her eyes. Jess had little use for religion or saints or miracles, but she herself loved the story of Guadalupe, for whom she was named. "Do you remember what the cross symbolizes?"

He shrugged again. "Life in death."

"And also death in life."

Then he looked at her, and his throat tightened. He wasn't ready to talk about death, not so soon after finding out that she was dying.

"*La Guadalupana.* She speaks to those who struggle, to those who suffer." Lupe sighed, then turned away from the painting to look at her son. "She has been a great comfort to me—during the problems with your father and my family, and even more so now."

"Do you ever regret not getting married?" Jess knew that his father had chosen not to leave his wife for the mother of his child, but Lupe had been a very pretty young woman, and there had been others—including Grant Pierce—who had been willing to take her illegitimate son in order to get her.

It had been many years since Lupe had discussed Jess's father with him. As a teenager, the mere mention of the man who had, in his eyes, rejected them had been enough to send Jess into a quiet rage; then he had gotten so involved with Caitlin, and then he had disappeared. "No, I don't regret it. I loved your father, Jess."

"Mom..."

She raised her hand to silence his protest. "He never lied to me. I knew from the beginning that he couldn't marry me. The Church wouldn't have recognized a marriage between us, anyway. But I knew that, and I still saw him, and I still fell in love with him."

"You gave him everything, and you got nothing in return."

"That's not true. He gave me the most precious gift of all—you."

He flushed uncomfortably. "He didn't deserve you, Mom."

"I loved him, Jess, and he loved me. That's why I never married. If I couldn't have Roberto, I didn't want any man."

Jess couldn't understand how any man could turn away from the woman he claimed to love, how any man could father a child and never want to see or know him, or how any woman could love a man like that. It wasn't rational. But who said love was rational? He was a good example of that himself. For months after he'd left Caitlin, if he'd had the slightest indication that she would take him back, he would gladly have returned. Thank God he was beyond that now.

"The only regrets I have are for you, Jess. Because you had no father to teach you. Because children can be cruel with their name-calling, and often their parents are no better. Because life hasn't been easy for you. But you grew into a strong, good man anyway, and you've made me very proud." She was silent for a few minutes; then she held her arms out to him. "I'm tired now," she said while she hugged him. "I'll see you tomorrow." With a loving kiss, she dismissed him.

When he closed the bedroom door behind him, he stood still for a moment in the hallway. He could go to his room, try to get some sleep to make up for last night's restlessness. He could go out on the deck and sit in the peaceful quiet. Or he could go into the living room where the soft murmur of voices from the television meant Caitlin was still up. He chose the living room and Caitlin.

She was lying on the sofa, reading a book and half-watching a detective show. She looked up when he walked in, her gaze measuring. When he didn't speak, neither did she, and she went back to reading the book.

He settled into the upholstered recliner, the only piece of furniture in the room that wasn't made in the northern New Mexico style. It was a large chair, bought because it could accommodate the large frame of Grant Pierce.

It was a cozy scene, he thought. Caitlin looked sleepily comfortable on the sofa, and he felt relaxed and at ease a few feet away.

The show didn't interest him; how could it, when Caitlin was so close? So he watched her instead of the television, and he considered his conversation with Lupe. Had he hurt Caitlin when he left that night? He wanted to believe he had, because that would mean that she *had* loved him, but he'd spent too many years convincing himself that she hadn't for him to easily believe otherwise now.

That night had been a nightmare. Grant had yelled and screamed at him, and Caitlin had looked like a frightened, traumatized child. Jess had hardly recognized himself as he taunted Grant with his failings as a suitor and a husband. He had been so angry, so filled with hatred, that all he had been able to think of was destroying the man who had brought him so much pain. But he had miscalculated; he had depended too much on Caitlin and her love, and he had been the one to be destroyed. If he could go back to that night and change everything he'd said, everything he'd done... In the long run, it wouldn't have mattered. He still would have lost Caitlin.

She ignored his stare for as long as she could, but at last she closed the book and raised her eyes to meet his. Neither spoke; they just looked.

That dark smoky look in his eyes: she recognized it as the same one she'd seen dozens of times in the past. Desire. He wanted her. But would he take her if she offered? Could she bear it if he rejected her?

Jess knew she wanted him to make love to her. That was what he wanted, too, so why didn't he speak to her, hold his hand out to her—do anything that would make her leave the couch and come to him? Because it wasn't time. He wasn't ready. Then, to dispute that, under her steady, hungry gaze, his body responded, swelling, stretching, his need becoming embarrassingly obvious.

Caitlin couldn't understand. He wanted her, but he didn't intend to take her—not now, at least. Something was holding him back, stopping him from accepting her silent invitation. Guilt? Maybe Jess wasn't as cold as he thought he was. Maybe planning to use her to hurt her father was easier than actually doing it. She could tell him that she didn't care what his reasons were, that she wanted him anyway. But when it was over, she would have nothing because she would have given it all to him, even her pride. She couldn't do that.

Guilt didn't enter into Jess's thoughts. Grant played no role, either. He couldn't explain it, couldn't put it into words, but he knew that if he took her now he would regret it later. He wanted to wait. To spend more time with her. To get to know her better. To savor the anticipation. To get the past out of the way. When they made love, there would be no ghosts from the past intruding. It would be just the two of them, him and Caitlin. When they made love, nothing else would exist.

He got out of the chair, moving cautiously. He stopped at the door and smiled back at her. "Good night, Cait," he whispered. "I'll see you tomorrow."

Ruefully, she smiled, too. "Good night, Jess." And silently she hoped that he had as much trouble sleeping tonight as she knew she would.

A call from Melly Wilkins the next morning brought Caitlin wide awake. She stared blankly at her clock for a moment before the time registered. Good Lord, she had not only slept well the night before, she had slept half the day away; it was almost noon. She grabbed for the phone on the third shrill ring and croaked a greeting.

"Hi, Caitlin, it's Melly. Am I disturbing you?"

A grunt was the best she could offer.

"Tanya told me you were in last week with some gorgeous guy. I'm sorry I missed you. Listen, remember Christopher Morgan, the man who bought that series of paintings you did on Pueblo dances?"

"How could I forget?" she asked dryly. It was the biggest sale she'd ever made.

"He called this morning and said he'd like some more—another four, if you can do them—and he's willing to pay even more than he did for the first four. Are you interested?''

"I'm interested. Does he have any specific dances in mind?"

"I don't know. Can you come into town and meet with him Saturday morning? He'll be at the gallery around ten."

"Okay, I'll see you then. Thanks, Melly." She replaced the phone and rolled onto her back. Maybe this was what she needed to get her mind off Jess. Four dances would mean research: reading, studying photographs, if any existed, and finding pueblos where the dances would be performed so she could see them firsthand. That should keep her busy enough to keep Jess out of her thoughts.

And that left her puzzled Saturday morning as she sped along the interstate toward Albuquerque. If these paintings were such a good chance to get Jess out of her mind, just why had she invited him to come along? He was sitting quietly in the passenger seat of the Jeep, his head back, his eyes closed.

She'd had no intention of inviting him when she got up that morning, but the words had just popped out before she could stop them. And Lupe had immediately begun encouraging him to go, so she'd been unable to call them back. Once he'd accepted, there was no way she could back out, and, foolishly, she hadn't wanted to. She was glad he'd said yes.

"Are these paintings important to you?"

Four paintings weren't going to make or break her, but she answered yes anyway. "The man already has four. He bought them at a time when I really needed the sale to keep from getting discouraged. I want to keep him happy."

A little twinge of jealousy made him shift uncomfortably. He knew it was stupid to feel jealous of this guy. He was probably old enough to be her father, with gray hair, a wife, three kids and six grandkids. There weren't that many young people who could easily afford even one Caitlin Pierce original, much less four. Still, curiosity made him accompany her to Melly's gallery. He had planned to do some shopping while she kept her appointment; now he told himself that he just wanted to see the man she was meeting before running his own errands.

A half hour later, as he wandered the crowded streets of Old Town, he wished he hadn't gone in with her. The man, who'd been introduced as Christopher Morgan, had a little gray hair, but it was premature; the rest was black. Jess judged him to be in his mid-thirties. He was handsome, charming, wealthy—"real estate," Tanya had whispered to Jess—and single. He was also interested in more than Caitlin's talent, Jess had noted sourly as the man put his arm around her and led her back into Melly's private office.

He bought a necklace for his mother, then began searching for the other gift he needed. Caitlin's birthday was a few weeks away; Lupe had reminded him—as if he could forget. After browsing through numerous stores, he found what he wanted in the display of one of the sidewalk vendors.

The earrings were made of silver. Tiny fine strands of silver chain were woven together to form an intricate pattern with a diamond-shaped pink mussel shell suspended in the center; then the chains were allowed to dangle. At the end each chain was weighted with a small but perfect piece of mussel shell. They were large earrings, but delicately made, and they would look perfect on Caitlin. He paid the man and waited patiently while they were wrapped.

"Your friend's late coming back," Christopher Morgan observed. Jess had agreed to return in an hour, and it was fifteen minutes past that.

Caitlin smiled at him. "He had to buy a gift."

"For you?"

She shook her head. "His mother." She walked to the front of the gallery to look at the sand paintings there. It also gave her a view of the sidewalk, so she could watch for Jess.

Morgan followed her. "How long have you been in love with him?"

Her denial was ready, but she couldn't force the lie past her lips. Why deny something that was so obvious? "A long time."

"And he's done nothing about it? He must be either a fool or blind."

"We've had...problems."

"Problems can be overcome if you try hard enough."

She saw Jess as he sidestepped a group of tourists. "Not if only one's trying," she murmured softly.

There was a soft chime as Jess came into the gallery. He saw

Morgan extend his hand to Caitlin, saw her take it, and his jaw tightened.

"I'll look forward to hearing from you," Christopher said. "Mr. Trujillo, nice meeting you."

He responded with a curt nod. "Are you ready, Cait?"

"Sure. See you, Melly, Tanya."

Instead of going to the Jeep, Jess steered Caitlin toward a bench in the plaza. They sat in silence, watching the tourists.

He was disturbed by something, Caitlin realized, and she waited for him to bring it up. She half suspected it was Christopher Morgan who was bothering him; she'd seen the searching look he'd given the older man, and he'd been almost rude to him when he had returned from his shopping.

A tiny bird landed in the grass in front of their bench, and a small girl dressed in a lavender sunsuit ran toward it as fast as her chubby legs could carry her. In her excitement, her feet got tangled together, and she fell with a plop onto her heavily padded bottom. Her lower lip trembled, and tears welled in her big blue eyes. With a laugh, Caitlin got up and helped her to her feet. "You're all right, aren't you sweetheart?" she asked in a soft, warm voice that earned her a sunny smile.

Jess watched her brush the dirt from the girl's clothes and legs; then he suddenly turned away. It hurt too much to see her fussing over someone else's child.

She walked back and sat sideways on the bench, facing him. "I'm waiting."

"For what?"

She took a gamble. "Your questions about Christopher."

Was his jealousy that obvious? He decided it must be, so he didn't try to deny it. "How long have you known him?"

"I met him once when he bought the first series. That was about four years ago."

"You like him?"

She carefully considered her answer, her head tilted to the side. "He's nice." Then, with a throaty laugh, she corrected that. "He's perfect. Everything about him is so precise—his hair, his clothes, the things he says and the way he says them. It's like he never makes a mistake, never does anything wrong. He makes me feel...awkward."

That didn't lighten his mood. Back there in the gallery he had compared himself, in jeans and a T-shirt, to Morgan, with his expensively tailored suit and the aura of wealth that clung to him, and he had wondered what in the world she could possibly see in him when Christopher Morgan was available. "He likes you," he offered uncertainly.

She grinned. "Everyone likes me. That's because I'm a nice person."

"That's not what I mean." He didn't dare put into words exactly what he did mean: that Christopher Morgan liked her the way Jess himself liked her. A lot. A hell of a lot. They both wanted her. They both desired her. If it was a contest between the two of them, he wasn't sure which of them Caitlin would choose, despite her wary feelings about the other man, and that worried him. "How closely will you be working with him?"

"Not at all. He told me what he wanted, and that's what I'll do. Jess, Christopher doesn't matter," she said gently. "It takes two to make a relationship. It doesn't matter how much one person loves another if the other person doesn't want his love." She paused for a moment. They were a perfect illustration of that point. She loved Jess, but in spite of his apparent jealousy, she wasn't sure yet if he wanted her love. If he didn't, then it meant nothing.

She swallowed hard and continued in a slightly shaky voice. "Morgan is a nice man—a client. That's all. He means no more to me than anyone else who's bought one of my paintings." She waited for another question, but none came, so she assumed it was safe to change the subject.

"Did you find what you wanted for your mother?"

He reached inside the paper bag on the bench beside him and pulled out the small white box that held the necklace. His fingers brushed against the earring box, but he left it alone, then took the necklace out and let it dangle from his fingers.

"Oh, Jess, that's pretty. Lupe will love it. She loves turquoise." She touched the stone that hung from a silver chain and set it swinging. "What do you want to do now? Do you need to get home?"

He had planned to work on the house that afternoon, but if Caitlin had something better to suggest—and anything that included her company qualified as better—he was willing. It wouldn't hurt to take one day off. "What do you have in mind?"

"Lunch at the Indian Pueblo Cultural Center, then we could go through the museum. It's not far from here, on the other side of the interstate. Is that okay?"

At his nod, she got up from the bench and extended her hand to him. They walked together to the Jeep; twenty minutes later they were pulling into the parking lot of the crescent-shaped complex. "It's modeled after Pueblo Bonito at Chaco Canyon," Caitlin said as they approached the main building. "Pueblo Bonito was the largest and most advanced of the ancient southwest cities. The people lived in multi-storied, walled buildings, had elaborate irrigation systems and even a road system that crisscrossed the desert."

"Chaco Canyon is northwest of here, isn't it? Have you been there?"

She nodded as they stopped to pay the entrance fee. "It's really impressive. Do you want to see the museum first, or eat lunch?"

He didn't even have to consider it. "Lunch," he voted, and she led the way across the hall to the restaurant.

There were tables down the center of the dining room, but the waiter led them to one of the high-backed booths along the wall. Caitlin sank into the thick cushion and leaned back while Jess studied the menu.

"Do you come here often?" he asked after they'd given their orders to the waiter.

She laughed. "That sounds like some corny pick-up line."

He looked offended. "I know the right words to say if I want to pick you up," he said with a grin.

Slowly her smile faded. That was the truth. He knew her so well. He knew exactly what to say, how to look at her, how to touch her, to get what he wanted. It made his job so much easier. All he had to do to get back at Grant was have an affair with her. He was close to succeeding, and, so far, he'd hardly even had to try. He knew his victim well.

Her sudden solemnity erased Jess's grin. He knew what she was thinking; he could see it in her soft brown eyes. She still half believed he was using her. He didn't want to use her—that would only hurt her. He'd been foolish to let her think that for even a minute, but he had needed the excuse to be with her, to touch her. Now he needed no excuses. Wanting was enough. He could want without loving; he could even need without loving. As long as he didn't allow himself to make the mistake of loving her again, he would be all right. He could spend time with her, talk with her, laugh with her and make love with her, but he wouldn't lose himself in her. He wouldn't love her.

"I don't want to hurt you," he said quietly.

She cleared her throat. "I believe that. But I also believe that you didn't want to hurt me the first time. Whether it's deliberate or accidental, Jess, it hurts all the same."

So Lupe had been right. Caitlin had been hurt when he left all those years ago. "Do you trust me, Cait?" he asked seriously.

"I'm not sure if I should." But, heaven help her, she did. "Do you trust me?"

He knew he shouldn't; he knew he should be wary. He had far more to lose than she did. He drank some ice water, then smiled tightly. "I haven't trusted anyone for a long time, but I'm willing to learn. Will you give me time?"

Her gaze held his for a long moment; then she smiled calmly, serenely. "I don't have any choice, do I?" The simple act of loving him took away many of her choices. She would do whatever she had to do. For him.

He laid his hands, palms up, on the table, waiting for her to place hers in them. When she did, he leaned forward and placed a kiss on the back of each of her hands. "It'll be all right this time, Cait," he assured her. "I won't hurt you."

Not "I don't want to hurt you," but "I *won't* hurt you." It was a promise. A promise that he was going to do his damnedest to keep.

Chapter 5

The atmosphere at the building site the following Saturday was more like a party than work. Jess, Tom and several of Tom's employees were working on the house, but they had invited Caitlin and Bonny and the other wives, along with their children, to join them. They had erected a canvas canopy to provide shade from the bright sun, and that was where the women stored their picnic lunches and coolers, along with Bonny's sleeping baby. They set their lawn chairs in the sun, watched the men work and the children play, and talked. Music blasted from the radio one of the men had brought, mingling with the laughter and cries of the kids and the sounds of hammers against wood.

Caitlin leaned back in her lounge chair, her legs stretched out in front of her. Khaki shorts and a yellow blouse left plenty of skin exposed to the warmth of the sun. She had pulled her hair into a pony tail, then braided it loosely and allowed it to hang over the back of her chair to keep its bulk out from under her head.

She rubbed sunscreen over her face and arms; her legs had already received a liberal coating. With her sunglasses in place again, she relaxed and looked around her.

She was glad Jess had invited her. She rarely took the time to socialize; she occasionally saw Carmen and Amelia and Bonny, but it had been months since she'd spent an entire day doing nothing but chatting with old friends. It felt good. Almost like old times, when she and Jess had been together and had spent much of their time with these people. Some of the couples had changed—Bonny had dated Matt then, and Pete had dated Donna; Bonny was married to Tom now, Donna had married Matt, and Pete had married Susan—but it was the same circle that had been friends since high school.

She had thought she had become relatively self-sufficient in those eight years without Jess. She had needed no one in her life but her father and Lupe. When Jess left, their friends had still called her, still tried to include her in their group, but she had refused all invitations until finally the calls stopped coming. The fewer people she got involved with, she had reasoned, the fewer the chances of getting hurt. But she had been lonely. She had missed them without even realizing it, until today. She had missed eight years with their friends: sharing their lives, knowing their children, celebrating their joys and mourning their sorrows. Whatever happened between her and Jess, she didn't want to give up her friends again.

Along with her thoughts, her gaze strayed to Jess. Like the other men, he had taken off his shirt, and his bronze skin gleamed with sweat. His jeans, once blue, had faded to white and rode low on his narrow hips. He was incredibly handsome. Were other women as devastated by the sight of him as she was? Someday she would like to paint him, in the desert, without clothes to hide the perfection of his body. It would be difficult to capture his power, his force, but she was confident she could do it. The painting would be a masterpiece—after all, so was the subject.

She would use oils. The background wouldn't matter, as long as it was the desert that he loved so much. It would be a pleasure researching the painting, because the only research possible was watching him—watching him move and stretch, seeing him at work and at rest, learning his body and his movements better than she knew her own—and she could start now. She could study the long smooth line of his back, the broad shoulders, the muscular arms. When he turned, he gave her a view of his strong chest and a glimpse of his hard, flat abdomen. His hips were slim, and his legs were long, long, never seeming to end. Yes, she thought with a secretive smile, it would be a pleasure.

Jess felt her gaze on him, steady, unwavering. He resisted looking at her as long as he could, because he knew what he would see when he did look, and he knew how he would respond. At last he put his hammer down, leaned against a post for support and raised his eyes.

She was incredibly beautiful. Did other men feel the same pain when they looked at her that he felt inside? Did they ache to hold her, to kiss her, to touch her? To fill her? To satisfy her? Were they overcome at the same time with an indescribable tenderness and an uncontrollably savage yearning, as he was?

The desire that he had known he would see was there in that little smile that played over her lips, in her eyes behind tinted sunglasses. The response that he had known he would feel surged, swelling inside him. Dear Lord, how he wanted her! She haunted his dreams at night, made his waking hours a living hell. No matter what he did, he could smell her, taste her, feel her. He wanted her. He needed her.

"Hey, Jess, give me a hand here, will you?" Matt asked.

Slowly he straightened from the post. His eyes held Caitlin's eyes as he turned; then at last he broke contact and turned his back to her. He could still feel her.

Caitlin turned onto her stomach. With her face down, he was hidden from view. So was the faint evidence of her arousal: the flush of her cheeks, the hardened peaks of her breasts. *He* knew she wanted him. *He* knew she was hungry for him. No one else needed to know.

When the men broke for lunch, everyone ate under the canopy, sitting on quilts spread in the shade. Caitlin deliberately sat down in the corner, slightly separated from the others. She needed space, time to recover, to keep from embarrassing herself with her desire. Jess deliberately sat down next to her, bridging the gap. He needed to touch her, to feed the wild demand in him enough to keep from embarrassing himself with his need. Just a brief touch, casual, nothing intimate.

Later she could remember nothing of the meal: what she ate, who she spoke to, what she said. All she was conscious of was the heat radiating from the man beside her, spreading into her through the small contact of his knee against her thigh. It was a potent heat that blocked everything else from her mind.

After lunch the men returned to work, and Caitlin accepted Carla Mendez's request to play with the kids. Playing would keep her busy, she hoped, too busy to notice Jess. They chose to play around the supply shed, where the small building more often than not kept Jess out of her sight.

"Aunt Caitlin, Travis is in the shed," Carla said in her soft, little-girl's voice. "Dad said to stay out of there." At four, she was too young to call her parents' friends by their first names, but Miss Pierce and Mr. Trujillo were more than she could handle. With her permission they had become Aunt Caitlin and Uncle Jess.

"Okay, you stay here, and I'll get him." Caitlin circled the small building and stepped inside. It was stifling hot and the darkness made her blink. There were piles of lumber, shingles and concrete blocks, along with nails, hammers, saws, rolls of insulation and other supplies. Climbing along the top of blocks was six-year-old Travis, Matt and Donna's oldest son. "Okay, Travis, come on down," she commanded.

He grinned. "I like it up here."

Caitlin placed her palms on the stack of lumber in front of her and leaned her weight on them. "You don't want me to come up there, do you?"

"You couldn't. You're a girl."

"Girls can do anything," Carla said from the doorway. "My mom said so."

"Come down, Travis," Caitlin said sternly. "You were told not to play in—"

He leaped then, jumping onto the wood, then to the ground. The force of his jump caused the blocks to teeter, then as if in slow motion, they began to fall sideways, onto the lumber Caitlin was leaning against.

Travis and Carla watched the blocks fall, watched them catch Caitlin before she could move. One landed on her hand; the others fell to the floor, tumbling against her body and scraping against her legs on the way down. Travis stared in horror at the accident he had caused. Carla raced toward the house screaming, "Uncle Jess, Uncle Jess!"

Bonny reached out to grab her daughter as she ran by. "Carla, what's wrong?" she demanded.

Jess looked at the distraught girl, then saw Travis run out of the shed. There was no sign of Caitlin. He jumped down from the foundation and ran toward the rickety building. A moment later Tom and Matt followed.

Caitlin was trying with her left hand to free her right, but the block was heavy. With a curse, Jess kicked the blocks on the floor out of his way and jerked the other one off her hand, tossing it into the corner. "My God, are you all right?" he demanded, his voice harsh.

The tears that had filled her eyes disappeared when he lifted her into his arms and carried her through the crowd to his pickup. Bonny opened the passenger door, and Jess set Caitlin on the seat, then reached for her hand.

It was her right hand. Jess felt sick way down inside. He could taste his fear. Caitlin was right-handed. She painted with her right hand.

It was already swollen, darkening with bruises. God, it must hurt, and that made him hurt. Dammit, he shouldn't have asked her to come. If he hadn't, this wouldn't have happened. Those blocks could have broken her fingers, or the bones in her hand, could have crushed the tendons and nerves. He never should have let her come!

Caitlin avoided looking at her hand, gently cradled in Jess's bigger ones. She knew it would be a miracle if something wasn't broken. She focused on his face and saw his fear. "Jess?" she whispered.

He gave her a sickly grin. "It's all right," he said in a ragged voice. "You'll be all right." He raised one hand to her neck and pulled her head against his chest. He wasn't sure who needed comforting more—her or him. He just knew he needed to hold her.

"You'd better take her to the doctor, Jess," Donna suggested. "And be sure he cleans those scrapes on her leg."

For the first time Jess saw the ugly red scratches that extended the length of her leg. He gave a quiet curse, turned her in the seat and fastened her seat belt. "I'll be back later."

"You don't need to come back," Tom said.

Carla was excitedly telling her mother, Donna and Susan how

Travis had caused the blocks to fall. As Jess swung into the truck, they heard Matt bellow his son's name.

"I wouldn't want to be Travis right now," Caitlin said with a feeble smile.

Looking carefully behind him, Jess backed the truck away from the crowd. "I'd beat him senseless if he were my kid." His scowl lent ferocity to his threat.

Caitlin knew he wouldn't. Jess would be a good father, if he ever chose to settle down and have children. He would be firm, offering discipline tempered with respect and love, and his children would love him dearly in return.

Dr. Ramirez lived next door to his office. It took only a moment to rouse him from an afternoon nap, then he was leading them into an examining room. He didn't bother to tell Jess to wait outside; he could tell from the stubborn look in his eyes that he was expecting just such an order and was ready to fight it. "Have a seat on this stool, Caitlin. Stick your hand up here on the table."

He poked and prodded, not apologizing for the twinges of pain he caused. He wasn't insensitive to others' pain, but he couldn't help making it worse with his exam. "Come on down the hall, and I'll get some pictures of it," he suggested gruffly. "You wait here, Jess. You can't be in the room while I X-ray it."

When she returned alone a few minutes later, Jess knelt on the floor in front of her stool. "Are you all right?"

She nodded.

"God, Cait, I'm sorry."

"It's not your fault. I never thought a kid as skinny as Travis could knock over a stack of blocks like that."

Dr. Ramirez returned, and Jess had to move away from her. "You've got a hairline crack in your middle finger, but at least it's not really broken. You're lucky—it could have been a lot worse. I'm going to splint that, and then we'll clean those cuts on your hand and leg. Watch me, Jess. You or your mother will need to do this every morning for about four weeks."

He took a long foam-lined aluminum splint from a cabinet and measured it against the middle finger of her left hand. He bent her finger into the proper position, then bent the splint to fit. Next he applied the splint to the same finger of her right hand and taped it into place. "You'll need to wear this every day for about four weeks, but take it off at night. I'll look at it again then. Now, let's see those cuts."

Using squares of gauze saturated with an antiseptic cleansing solution, the doctor cleaned the cuts and scrapes on the back of her hand and her leg. None of them was bad enough to need stitches, or even a bandage. When he was finished, he pronounced her fit to leave.

Jess's arm was around her shoulders when they left the office. "I'll take you home now," he said firmly.

"I don't want to go home. I'd rather go back out to the house."

He helped her into the truck, closed the door and leaned his arms in the open window. "Wouldn't you be more comfortable at home lying down?"

"No."

"Cait—"

"*You* would be more comfortable if I was home lying down. I wouldn't. I'll stay out of trouble, Jess. I promise."

He gave in gracefully. Besides, he knew that if he insisted on taking her home, as soon as he was gone she would drive herself back to the house.

Travis was tearfully apologetic when they arrived. Caitlin accepted his apology with a hug, then sent him off to play while she joined her friends again.

It was shortly after four when work stopped for the day. The site was cleaned up—garbage loaded into the trucks, supplies securely locked in the shed. Caitlin and Jess were the last to go.

"How's your hand?"

She smiled. "Okay. It feels funny, with my finger bent like this."

He studied her face, then reached up to brush a strand of her hair back. "It hurts." He could see the pain in the lines of her face, in her eyes.

"Not too badly." She gestured toward the house. "It's taking shape."

He nodded. "It's coming along faster than I expected. We should be able to move in in a couple of months."

With some of the walls up, she was able to tell more about it than she could from the drawings and blueprints she'd seen. "It's going to be a lovely house, Jess. Lupe will be happy here."

He looked down at her, intending to simply nod in agreement, but when his eyes met hers, the action was arrested. His desire, forgotten in the shock of her injury, returned to life with a vengeance, overwhelming him. With just a look, heat spread through him. With just a look, she was making him burn.

He touched her cheek and made a soft, hoarse noise that sounded like her name. For a long moment she forgot to breathe, and when she remembered, she had difficulty filling her lungs. Her heart seemed to expand until it filled her chest, leaving her light-headed.

He watched desire overcome her, and his body tightened. Her lips parted, unconsciously inviting his kiss, and her breath whispered out in tiny puffs. Her breasts swelled, her nipples pressing tautly against her shirt.

In silence he took her left hand in his. He paused to pick up the quilt he had folded and set on the hood of the truck; then he led her around to the back of the house. Still without speaking, he dropped her hand and spread out the quilt, smoothing its edges with long, roughened fingers, then moved her into the center of it. Softly, gently, he touched her face, his fingers tracing over it as if it were some delicate treasure. "I need you, Cait," he whispered. "Today. Now." Then he kissed her.

Together, without pulling apart, they lowered themselves to the ground. The quilt was still sun-warmed, comforting against Caitlin's bare legs. She was hardly aware of moving; slowly she came to the realization that she was now lying on her side, only inches separating her from Jess. Without words he encouraged her to roll onto her back, and she did so without effort, an easy, floating movement. There was a small stone beneath the quilt that pressed into her back, but it was a minor irritation, not worth breaking the spell around them.

Jess leaned on one arm for support and stared down at her with an intensity that turned his already dark eyes black. He moved just the tips of his fingers over her face, slowly, tenderly. Into his mind came memories of other times when they had made love—always perfect, she had claimed—and his hand trembled. It had been so long for both of them. So much could go wrong. He could disappoint her; after eight years, he could hurt her; it could end so quickly for him that she'd have little time to enjoy it. He felt like a virgin again: his body aroused and hungry for the satisfaction he could find, yet his mind unsure and frightened by the possibility of failure. It was even worse this time, because the girl who had initiated him had been a friend, nothing more. This was Caitlin.

She saw his hand shake as it reached her lips, and she parted her teeth to nip lightly at his fingers. Startled, he looked down and saw her smile, gently, reassuringly. She understood. Desire welled through him, leaving no room for indecision or nervousness.

He bent his head to kiss her once more. His tongue found its place deep within her mouth, while his hand slid, bit by bit, along her throat, then down to her breast. Eight years had passed, but he remembered vividly how her breast had fit so perfectly in his palm. Though slightly larger now, it still fit. He remembered how she liked to be caressed, how her nipples were sensitive to his slightest touch, how his lips on her breast could make her writhe and moan with mindless pleasure.

Her blouse was her favorite lemon yellow, a perfect color for the dull coppery shade of her skin. Its buttons were small and closely spaced, but Jess had no difficulty undoing them, slowly, one at a time, folding back the fabric, revealing the soft curves of her breasts and the flat plane of her stomach. When he reached the waistband of her shorts, he pulled the shirt free and unfastened the last button.

For a long time he didn't touch her. He forced himself to breathe deeply while he merely looked at the wide strip of flesh he had exposed. His body was reacting violently: his heart pounding, his chest tightening, his sex surging and swelling. At that rate he'd be lucky to get her undressed before he exploded inside the faded denim that was uncomfortably cradling him.

When he felt reasonably certain that he could control his body's response, he reached out to her again. He hooked one finger beneath the edge of her shirt and, not touching her, lifted that side of the fabric away, leaving her breast uncovered. His muscles tightened, and he slowly repeated the procedure with the other half of her shirt. He swal lowed hard. How had he forgotten how beautiful she was?

Caitlin's teeth were clenched. Every time his eyes moved slowly over her, shivers rushed along her nerves. When his fingers brushed against her, lightly, almost imperceptibly, her flesh, hot and fevered, chilled with the shock of it. She wet her lips with her tongue and raised her good hand toward his face, but it fell back to the quilt before reaching him.

"Jess."

He laid his palm flat against her chest, in the valley between her breasts. He could feel the frenzied beating of her heart. It seemed almost painful.

"Touch my breasts, Jess," she whispered in a heavy voice.

"I will." But he didn't move his hand. Her skin was as dark as his. The size of his hand made her look small. Fragile. So easily broken, he thought. So easily hurt. But he wasn't going to hurt her. He had given his promise that he wouldn't hurt her.

When Caitlin thought she might cry in frustration, he moved his hand. His palm glided over the small mound of her breast to cup it entirely beneath his hand. Despite his rough calluses, he could feel the different textures: the satiny smoothness of her breast, the hard, heated peak that pressed against his palm, and the pebbly dark circle that surrounded it. He couldn't resist any longer. He moved his hand to cover her other breast, then lowered his head and dragged his tongue with agonizing slowness over her nipple.

Sensation coiled in the pit of her stomach, spiraling up and out, spreading heat and need and hunger through her body. She felt the dampness between her legs, which ached to enclose him, to welcome him back to her, and she whimpered softly.

The sound gentled Jess's touch even more. He wanted it to be perfect for her, without pain, without fear.

But the strength of her unsatisfied yearning brought its own pain. "It's been so long," she whispered. "Please, Jess. It's been so long since I've felt you."

He pushed himself away from her and stripped off his clothing. His faded green T-shirt joined the faded jeans on the ground. One limp hand shading her eyes against the setting sun, she looked at him as he lowered his body to the quilt again. The perfection she had envisioned that morning hadn't been colored by time and memory. His body *was* perfect. The hard, lean muscles that lined his arms, chest and legs were more pronounced, made visible by the tension that threaded through his body. He was the same lovely, warm shade from head to toe, and the color was enhanced by a light sprinkling of dark curling hair that grew thicker as her gaze traveled lower.

Awkwardly, with her left hand, she touched him, her fingers brushing over the tangle of hair until she held him, long and hot and hard, within her gentle caress. Her smile was loving. She wasn't afraid. She knew she was risking heartbreak by making love with him; once it was done, she would be his, to do with whatever he wanted. But she couldn't stop him, couldn't say no, couldn't deny herself what she had wanted for so very long.

He finished undressing her and knelt between her thighs, supporting his weight on his hands and knees. The muscles in his chest and arms strained with the pressure put on them, but he didn't notice. "Do you want me, Cait?" he whispered.

In reply, she pulled him to her, tugging insistently until he relaxed his arms and let her win. She kissed his chin. "I want you."

His entry was slow and controlled. She was hot and ready and moist, but tight. Eight years was such a very long time, and she was so fragile, so delicate. If he hurt her...

She raised her hips, taking control from him, and completed the movement, taking him, all of him, within herself. For long moments they remained still, each fighting for self-control, each overwhelmed by the surge of powerful emotion that swept through them. At last Jess opened his dark eyes, and his gaze locked with Caitlin's. She smiled slowly, sweetly, dazedly, and Jess knew that this longing between them, this loving, was all right; it was good.

It was perfect.

Jess was in danger. The air was still and quiet, his body was tired and sated, and Caitlin was sleepily soft at his side, her hair spilling over his arm and his chest. He should be relaxed and at peace, but he felt as if the slightest sound could make him jump out of his skin.

He had cried her name, over and over, like a prayer that could save him. He had used the word loving—only in his mind, but he had used it nonetheless. It didn't mean anything, he told himself. A lot of people referred to making love as loving. It had nothing to do with love. Nothing.

He had been overwhelmed, out of control. Nothing in his life had ever been so good, so heartachingly right. For eight years he had never wanted another woman the way he had wanted Caitlin. For the rest of his life he would never want another woman. Period.

She was so still. He was afraid to look at her. Afraid that he would see it hadn't meant as much to her. Afraid that she would see how much it had meant to him. Was she disappointed? Was she hurt? He had tried to be so careful, but she had taken control from him and had forcefully completed his entry.

She had lied to him about the other men. He didn't know why, unless she had been embarrassed to tell him at the beginning that she had waited for him. As surely as he lived, there'd been no one else. She had been so tight, had fitted him so perfectly. There had been no one but him.

Caitlin left his arms, getting carefully to her knees. Her hands were folded primly in her lap, and her eyes were clear and trusting. He hadn't disappointed her, and if he had hurt her, she had forgiven him for it. God, she was beautiful!

"Are you all right?" she asked softly.

He nodded.

"Do you regret it?"

His eyes widened; then he laughed. "Regret it?" His laughter grew richer and deeper.

Caitlin knew he wasn't laughing at her, so she wasn't offended. She enjoyed his mirth. It was good to see him laugh.

Jess sat up and lifted her into his arms. "For a moment, when I was deep inside you, it felt so exquisite that I thought I was going to die. For God's sake, Cait, how could I possibly regret it?"

Then his smile faded slowly. He didn't know how she did it. How did she make him want her without doing anything? How could just the feel of her satiny skin make him grow hard and hungry for her again? How could one look from her warm, soft eyes send flames licking through his veins, setting his body on fire to have her again, to be a part of her once more?

Caitlin uttered a husky moan as he lowered her gently to the quilt. His body blanketed hers, and he slid slowly inside her, sure of his welcome. "How could I possibly regret this?" he repeated in a voice that was husky with need.

* * *

The clouds overhead were thick and fluffy, tinged pink and purple from the setting sun. They seemed as lazy as Caitlin felt, slowly drifting across a sky so blue that she knew she could never duplicate it on canvas if she tried forever. It didn't matter. The sky was always there, and it was often this incredible color, and she had much, much better things to do with forever than paint.

The stone beneath her back became more than a minor annoyance. As much as she hated to, she had to find it and toss it away, or else change positions. Since she was lying in the snug warmth of Jess's arms, she opted for finding the stone. She sat up and folded back the quilt until it came into sight, then threw it into the bushes.

Jess lay on his back, his face turned upward, his eyes closed. Complete satisfaction had left him lazy and tired and drowsy. Endless months of celibacy were ended, forgotten, his hunger sated by Caitlin—for now, at least. He knew that a look, a touch, was liable to drive him back to her, but for now he was at peace. She had been a healing for his soul.

Caitlin lay on her side, her right hand carefully propped between them, and looked at him. A lock of hair fell into a curl across his forehead. His eyes remained closed, his lashes shadowing his cheekbones in a delicately tangled web. His nose was straight and flawless, perfectly proportioned to the rest of his face. That he had managed to reach adulthood without his nose being broken at least once, considering the number of fights he'd been in as a teenager, amazed her.

By the time her solemn study had reached his mouth, he was smiling. He was so aware of her presence next to him that he could feel her gaze as it brushed over him. "Don't you know it's not polite to stare?" he asked in a husky voice.

"Sorry," she answered softly, but she didn't mean it, and she didn't turn her eyes away.

He rolled onto his side, so that they faced each other. "I didn't ask you if you enjoyed it."

She smiled fleetingly.

"But I don't need to ask. I could tell. Do you have any regrets?"

"Not about this."

He wondered what she did regret, but he didn't want to talk

about it. "We'd better go home, or Mom will will wonder where we are."

Caitlin sat up. Her hair had come loose from the braid during their lovemaking, so she removed the band and shook the thick dark mass loose. She was going to rebraid it, but found that the splint on her finger made it impossible. "I don't suppose you can braid."

He shook his head. "Leave it down. I like it that way." Reaching out, he smoothed his hand over her hair, from the crown to the ends. He brushed over first one breast, then the other. "I do like it."

Dressing was awkward for her. She managed to get her clothes on, but even her good fingers found buttoning and zipping difficult. With a good-natured chuckle, Jess pushed her hands aside and fastened everything for her. "Do I get to dress you every morning and undress you every night for the next four weeks?" he teased, his mouth brushing over her ear.

"I suppose that's up to you," she replied. If he wanted to share her bed, to be with her in the morning and at night, she wasn't going to complain.

Jess shook out his clothes, then stepped into them with quick but graceful movements. After helping Caitlin to her feet, he shook the quilt to remove the sand and dirt before they started around the house to his truck.

"What are you going to do about your work for the next month?" he asked.

"I can do the reading and maybe see some of the dances," she replied with a shrug. "I don't think I'll be doing much sketching, though."

He grinned at her, his brows raised in a lcer. "I bet I can think of ways to keep you busy," he said.

Caitlin gave him a cynical smile. "You work days. You won't be able to keep me too busy."

"I could keep you busy enough at night that you wouldn't have the strength for anything but sleeping during the day," he boasted.

Caitlin began to laugh, helpless to stop herself. "Yes," she agreed. "I'm sure you could. We'd better get back before your mom starts to worry."

"She won't worry," Jess said confidently. "She knows you're with me."

It was dark when they got home. Lupe was in the kitchen, humming softly to herself while she stirred something in a pot. "Hello," she greeted them. She looked from Jess to Caitlin, then back to Jess again. What she saw satisfied her. "You have half an hour before dinner is—Caitlin, what happened to your hand?"

While she explained the accident, Jess excused himself to take a shower. As soon as Lupe was convinced that the injury wasn't serious, Caitlin went to her own bathroom to shower.

She picked up a pair of scissors and tried to cut the tape holding the splint in place, but she couldn't get the right angle. She was about to get help from Lupe when her bedroom door opened and Jess strolled in. He left a pile of clothes on her bed and walked into the bathroom as if he belonged there, taking the scissors from her and carefully removing the splint.

"What are you doing?" she asked suspiciously as he began undressing her.

"You said I could do this if I wanted to." He dropped her clothes into the hamper and swept back the shower curtain to turn on the water. Then he began removing his clothes.

"Jess, your mother is in the kitchen!" she hissed.

"And we're in the bathroom. She's not going to walk in on us." He practically lifted her into the bathtub; then he got in behind her and closed the curtain.

"I don't need your help taking a shower!"

"I know that," he calmly replied. "But you do need it to wash your hair." He pushed her head under the water and lifted the heavy weight of her hair in his hands. "So much hair. So pretty. So soft."

He squeezed his eyes shut. Lord, he wanted her again, right here, right now. He had to get his desire under control. If he could go all those months without a woman, surely he could make it a few days at a time without one.

But Caitlin wasn't just any woman. She was the woman he had fallen in love with when he was barely sixteen. The one who had made his life worth living. The one who had betrayed him.

"You're drowning me!" Caitlin complained.

He let her step back while he reached for the shampoo. He clenched his jaw and gritted his teeth, willing himself not to respond to her while he lathered and rinsed her hair, while he worked conditioner through its length with a wide-toothed comb, while he rinsed it clean. Then he brusquely traded places with her, washed and rinsed himself and got out.

He was angry with her, Caitlin thought. Why? What had she done to deserve his anger?

She suddenly felt chilled. She had made love with him. That was all he'd needed. She had been expecting an affair, but he didn't have to continue sleeping with her to hurt Grant. Just once would be enough to enrage her father. He'd only had to make love to her once—and they had done it twice.

Maybe he had realized that he didn't have to continue the game. Maybe their lovemaking hadn't been as good, as special, for him as it had been for her, so he didn't want to bother with her anymore. Maybe he just didn't want her anymore.

She shut off the water and stepped from the tub. She was tired suddenly: too tired to face dinner with Jess sitting across from her. Too tired to do anything but curl up in bed. Alone.

He was furious with himself. He almost rubbed his skin raw when he dried off, punishing his body for reacting to her. Wanting was all right, and so was needing. He could handle those. He didn't mind wanting, he didn't like needing, but he could live with them both. But obsession—he wouldn't allow himself to become obsessed with Caitlin. So their lovemaking had been unlike anything he had ever experienced: better, wilder, more wonderful; so it had touched not only his heart but also his soul. He couldn't allow desire to control him. He couldn't go around getting hard every time he looked at her...or heard her...or thought of her. He wouldn't allow it.

He knew he couldn't trust her. He knew she had betrayed him once before, and, given the chance, she would do it again. He knew that what she called love paled into nothingness next to his idea of love. He knew that if he became obsessed with her, he would fall in love with her, and if he fell in love with her, she would destroy him. Just like before.

He steeled himself to ignore her at dinner, but when he joined Lupe in the kitchen, she told him that Caitlin's hand was hurting, so she wouldn't be eating with them. Reversing their usual roles, Lupe had taken Caitlin a tray in her room.

The information made him bitter. Was she hiding from him?

Had she lied about not having any regrets? Was she ashamed of the way she had responded to him? Had her response even been real, or had it been faked, too, like her so-called love so many years ago?

The questions made Jess poor company for the evening. Soon after dinner Lupe went to bed. He tried watching television, but nothing could hold his interest. He tried reading, but his mind drifted too often to the quiet bedroom down the hall. He went out on the deck, hoping to find peace there, but the questions still nagged at him.

He didn't know if she was ashamed of what they had done, but he knew how to find out if her response had been genuine. He quickly locked up, then headed purposefully toward her room.

The room was lit by only a small lamp in the corner. Its light fell softly on Caitlin, who was standing near the French doors in her nightgown. It was white satin and fell to mid-thigh, shimmering against her dark skin. Wearing it always made her feel pretty and sexy, and she liked it.

Jess liked it, too. He stood in the open doorway, leaning one shoulder against the wall, his gaze drinking her in. He had come to prove a point: that he could make her want him as much as, or more than, he wanted her. But only seconds after seeing her, challenges were forgotten. He was hard and hungry and aching to feel her holding him tight. Standing there looking out, she brought back memories of other nights in this room, powerfully intimate memories that sent heat racing through his blood until his entire body was burning.

A shiver raised goosebumps on her exposed skin, and her nipples grew hard in anticipation. Caitlin knew Jess was behind her, watching her. She could feel his eyes glide over her body to her feet, then back again, and she shivered. Slowly she turned and faced him. She didn't know what to expect. Anger? Desire—or was it better described as lust?

He wasn't prepared for her sadness. Of all the emotions she could possibly feel, he hadn't expected sadness. It hit him hard. She did regret what they had shared. She was sorry she had made love to him. God, how could that hurt so much?

"Cait?" He hardly recognized his voice; it was husky and raspy, sounding as if he rarely used it.

He wasn't angry, and he hadn't come to mock her, she thought.

That must mean he wanted her. As long as he wanted her, whatever his reasons, whatever his goals, his wanting was enough for her. She didn't think he would ever give her anything else.

She sent him a lazy smile. "Yes?"

Her smile was inviting, and it soothed the ache in his heart. He moved away from the wall and closed the door behind him. It seemed to take him forever to cross the room, but at last he was standing in front of her.

"Tell me that you want me," he commanded.

"I want you."

"Tell me you'll always want me. The way I'll always want you."

Not love, but want. It would have to be enough. "Yes, Jess," she whispered. "I'll always want you."

He lifted his hands to hold her face. "Show me you don't regret making love to me today. Show me that it was good for you. Undress me and show me."

She lifted her right hand. The splint was gone, but her finger was still useless. "You'll have to undress yourself; then I'll show you."

He raised his hands to his shirt, slipping the buttons through the holes, pulling the garment off and dropping it to the floor. His hands moved to the fastening of his jeans, releasing the round metal buttons with deliberate slowness, then sliding the denim over his hips so he could step out of it.

When he was naked, Caitlin stepped into his embrace. She wrapped her arms around his neck and gave him a kiss that left him breathless. With the gentle pressure of her hands, she molded their bodies together. Only a thin layer of cool satin separated his heated, pulsing arousal from her, and when she moved, that satin rubbed teasingly, tormentingly against him.

Restraint ebbed away, replaced by desire growing out of control. Muttering a thick curse, Jess reached for her gown. She laughed softly. "I'm showing you," she reminded. "Be patient."

Her mouth moved over him with moist, hot kisses, touching his jaw, throat, chest, shoulders, nipples. At the same time her hands touched him, gliding down his bare hips and around to his buttocks. Her satin gown rubbed against him, and her silken hair brushed him first here, now there.

Jess sucked in as much air as his lungs could hold, then slowly let it out. Control. He needed to retain his self-control. Retain? Hell, he'd already lost it. Caitlin's sometimes gentle, sometimes rough exploration of his body was painful. Exciting. Heavenly. Months without a woman, years without *this* woman, were made worthwhile by her loving.

She eased him onto the bed, guiding him into position with gentle touches, then continued the trail of kisses along lean hips, muscular thighs, long hard calves. Jess was torn between desire to let his head fall back and his eyes close and simply enjoy, and the desire to watch Caitlin as she loved him. When her hair fell in a silky tangle around his hips, and her mouth touched him in an open, wet kiss, he chose to watch her.

His eyes were smoky, almost dazed; hers were clear. He tried to touch her, but she had taken his strength. He was weak, unable to do anything but feel and respond to those feelings. His heart was racing, his blood pulsing. His hips arched, and he groaned, a deep, low, tortured cry of release. Caitlin kissed him, held him, stroked him, soothed him, calmed him, until the tension left his body.

At last the rushing in his ears settled to a low hum. He found the strength to smile at her, and she sweetly smiled back. Now it was his turn to make it good for her.

He reached out to her, but she ignored his hands. Smiling like a smugly satisfied little cat, she swung her leg over his to sit astride his hips; then she removed her nightgown, letting it fall to the floor. She wasn't going to give in easily. If he wanted to take control, he would have to do just that—take it. She wasn't going to offer it.

"Playing games, Cait?" he asked softly. His eyes glinted, black in the dim light. Hers were liquid brown. "You're greedy. It's my turn now."

She smiled wickedly. "Your turn for what?"

"I'm going to make you feel incredibly alive. I'm going to make love to you, Cait, until you're on fire, until you think you'll die if I stop. I'm going to make you need me so badly you'll cry my name. I'm going to make you feel so good."

Mindful of her injured hand and leg, Jess grasped her wrists in his and forced her over and onto her back. Her laugh was husky, fading away as he moved over her. He teased and taunted her as long as he could stand it, longer than she could stand it;

then he leaned over her, searching, finding, sinking deep into her softness.

His kisses were drugging and dark and sweet; his hands were gentle and warm and sure; and his thrusts were deep and strong and powerful. He carried her with him, demanding responses that she was all too willing to give, answering her pleas with his own.

He had promised to make her feel alive, and she did. He had said she would burn, and the fire spread from his body to hers. He had sworn to make her feel good, and she felt better than she ever had in her life. He had told her that her need for him would be so great that she would cry his name. And she did call his name, but her voice mingled with his. In the dimly lit warmth of the room, it was Jess who needed most. It was Jess who cried.

He slept in her bed, beside her. He didn't hold her in his arms, but he kept her close so that he could touch her when the need arose. It was the first time, in all the years they'd been together, that they'd spent an entire night together. The first time Jess had been able to wake in the morning to the rising sun and find Caitlin lying next to him.

He wasn't going to touch her. She was sleeping soundly, and if he touched her, he might wake her. He was just going to lie there beside her and look at her.

It hadn't been faked. Her response, both last night and the afternoon before, had been as real and as natural as his own. Caitlin could never fake that kind of passion. That was important for him to know.

Lightly, carefully, he lifted the sheet away from her breasts. She was beautiful: the perfect combination of softness and strength. She was soft enough to make him ache, strong enough to ease that ache. If he never had anything more in his life than this, he would still be luckier than most men.

Forgetting his decision not to touch, he laid his hand on her stomach. So flat. He tried to imagine her stomach rounded and full with a baby—with his baby. She would be one of those women who flourished during pregnancy. She would be lovely and graceful and serene, no matter how difficult the pregnancy, no matter how awkward and big her body became.

Once, long ago, he had decided that Caitlin would be the

mother of his children. He suspected that was one decision that hadn't changed, even if his feelings for her had. Never in his life had he made love to—or had sex with, he cynically corrected—a woman without taking precautions against pregnancy, not even with Caitlin when they were younger. He hadn't cared this time. He had had plenty of chances to stop by the local drugstore—he had decided weeks ago to make love to her. But he had chosen not to protect her.

Maybe he wanted her to get pregnant. If she were carrying his child, there would be a bond between them, one that even Grant would find it difficult to break.

It made so much sense it was almost frightening. Jess wanted Caitlin more than he had imagined possible, and he wanted children. She could be the one to give them to him. He knew he couldn't love her, but he could enjoy being with her; he could especially enjoy making love with her. And he would love their children. There were many marriages based on less.

He jerked his hand from her stomach as if he'd been burned. Marriage? To Caitlin? Good God, he must be mad! A few hours of pleasure in her bed and he was willing to forget everything and propose marriage.

Marriage to Caitlin would be a living hell, wondering day to day if he could trust her, if he could believe her. Fearing every time they fought that she'd leave and go back to her father, that she would once again choose her father over him. He'd have to be a fool to even consider such a thing!

But once the idea had taken hold, Jess couldn't shake it. He wouldn't love her, so what would it matter if one day she chose her father over him? As long as she left their children with him, why should he care if she left him?

Because he *would* care, dammit! he argued. He didn't love her anymore, but if she disappeared from his life again, it would hurt. And what made him think that she would ever allow him to raise their children? What made him think that Grant would let him raise his grandchildren?

He could fight Grant, and, if he had to, he could fight Caitlin. He hadn't fought hard enough before, but he had been young, only twenty-three. He was older and harder and more dangerous now. If his children were at stake, he could fight damned hard, and he would win.

But would Caitlin even agree to marry him?

He looked down at her, and his expression softened. He thought she would. She cared for him. He knew how easily he could seduce her, because he knew how much she wanted him. She had waited eight years for him without taking a lover. He also knew she wanted marriage, kids, a family. A husband to give her babies, to share in her life, to stand at her side, to make her happy, to comfort her when she was sad, and to make her cry and moan and plead in the middle of the long, dark, loving nights. She would take him without love, because she knew he would give her affection and respect and children. She would be satisfied without love, just as Jess would be.

But what if he was wrong? What if he wouldn't be satisfied without love? If someday, sometime, he needed more than affection and respect? He had fallen in love with her so easily the first time. It could happen again. He could love her again, and he could lose her again. Could he survive that?

He would still have his children. If he needed love, they would love him. When he gave love, he would give it to them. He wouldn't need to love Caitlin.

He lay back in the bed, his hands under his head. It would be nice to wake up next to her every morning. It would be even nicer going to bed with her every night, he thought with a grin, remembering last night. He would finally have a home of his own, a wife, a family. Even after his mother was gone, he wouldn't be alone anymore.

Caitlin rolled onto her stomach, pillowing her head on his chest. Her breath came out warm and moist between parted lips onto his flat nipple, only inches from her mouth. It hardened in response.

His grin widened. He would definitely enjoy going to bed with her every night. His mind was made up. Now he had just one problem.

How did he get *her* to agree?

Chapter 6

Caitlin awoke alone in bed, but the sound of water running in the bathroom told her that she wasn't really alone. She rolled over sleepily and reached for her nightgown, which lay crumpled on the floor beside the bed.

"Good morning." Jess filled the bathroom door, wearing a pair of good blue jeans and a towel around his neck.

She smiled drowsily and sank back onto the pillows. "Hmm," was her only reply.

"Come on and brush your teeth, and I'll put your splint on, then help you dress. Are you going to church with Mom this morning?"

She shook her head. "You go ahead."

"We could go together. It doesn't have to be one or the other."

She shook her head again, then swung her feet to the floor. As she stood up, her gown settled around her thighs. Jess shook his head at his predictable response to the sight of her. Maybe he should go to church and pray for the strength to stop wanting her every time he saw her.

She brushed her teeth and washed her face, wincing every time she moved her right hand. While she did that, Jess got the scissors, a roll of adhesive tape and the metal splint.

Her hand was swollen and discolored. He lifted it to his mouth for a kiss so light she barely felt it; then he taped the splint in place. "Does that hurt?"

She shook her head. When he was so gentle, her chest grew tight with love. He would be that way with his children. Although he had never known his own father, and so had had no one to set an example, he would be a wonderful father himself. But who would be the mother of his children?

She didn't bother denying that she wanted that position herself. Jess didn't love her, but she had enough love for both of them. He was a good man, and he would be a good husband. But the chances that he would propose to her were so slim they were nonexistent. He would have only one reason for wanting to marry her—to prove to Grant that he could do it—but he wouldn't carry his revenge that far. He wasn't that bitter, or that willing to sacrifice himself without love.

"Today's the Fourth," he announced, still holding her hand. "There's a rodeo this afternoon out at the arena, and a fireworks display tonight. Will you go with me?"

"I'd like that. Is your mom going, too?"

He grinned. "I don't think she's ever missed it—at least, not when I've been around. We can have a picnic lunch at the park next to the rodeo grounds."

"Okay, I'll fix it while you and Lupe are at church."

"With this?" He touched his finger lightly to her splint. "I'll help you when we get back. Come on now, let me dress you before Mom leaves without me."

There was something embarrassing about him putting her clothes on, she found, though she hadn't minded him taking them off the night before. He refrained from commenting on the clothes she'd chosen until he reached the underwear on the bottom of the pile. He discarded the bra, declaring it unnecessary, then picked up the tiny silk panties. "Nice," was all he said, but his eyes twinkled mischievously.

She reached for them, but he held them away. "I can handle this," she said crossly.

He pulled the nightgown over her head and avoided looking at her. "I took your clothes off yesterday—twice. It's only fair that I get to put them back on." His touch was light and easy as he slid the silk panties, followed by a pair of gray shorts, slowly over her legs and hips. While he was on his knees, he examined the scrapes on her leg, touching his mouth to the ones just below her hip before rising to his feet again. He was standing right in front of her, and when she took a deep breath, her breasts grazed his chest. He swallowed hard. "Raise your arms."

She obeyed him, and he guided her right hand through the sleeve of her pale pink T-shirt. He pulled it over her head and other arm, tugged it down to her waist, then tucked it smoothly inside her shorts. His hands lingered over the soft, firm curve of her buttocks; then he quickly pulled up the zipper and fastened the snap.

He had tried to act and feel impersonal, but his breathing was ragged when he finished. "Shoes?" he asked, and his voice was soft and shaky.

Mutely she pointed to the pink socks and gray tennis shoes on the floor next to the bed.

She sat down, and he knelt on the floor again. He finished the job of shoes and socks as quickly as he could and got to his feet. "I've got to go," he said in a rush. He kissed her forehead, then fled the room.

Caitlin let her breathing settle. She had known that being undressed by a man could be an erotic experience, but she had never guessed that being dressed by a man could be equally erotic. If Jess hadn't left when he did, she would have asked him to remove the clothes he had just put on and make love to her. And if he hadn't felt the same way, she was sure he wouldn't have left when he did.

She was foolish to get so involved with him. What would she do when his vengeance on her father was complete? She could hope and pray that, while his plan was in effect, he would learn to care for her, but if he didn't, what would happen to her when it ended? She should hold back some part of herself, so that she wouldn't lose everything when it was over.

But she couldn't. She loved Jess so much that she just couldn't help giving him everything that he wanted to take. She hadn't made a conscious decision to become his lover—she'd had no choice. Her heart had made the decision for her. She couldn't turn away from him now, even if loving him meant only pain and heartache. She belonged to him now.

Now. She smiled sadly. Her heart had always belonged to him—to the quiet, friendly child who had been her playmate; to the fun-loving, hell-raising teenager who had been her friend; to the lighthearted, high-spirited young man who had been her lover; and now to the impassioned, intense man who was her love.

What exactly was his goal? When would he be satisfied that he had done enough to hurt Grant? Would merely seducing her a few times be enough, or did he want an affair with her? Maybe he wanted her to love him, so he could prove to Grant how much power he held over her. Maybe he even wanted marriage, she thought with dismay.

She got up from the bed and made a halfhearted effort at straightening the covers. As much as she would like to be his wife, she said a fervent prayer that he wouldn't propose to her. She couldn't bear knowing that he'd chosen her as his wife only because she was his best weapon against her father.

Before Lupe left for church, she took the time to fashion Caitlin's hair into an intricate French braid, securing the ends with a bright-pink band. She repeated Jess's instructions not to try to fix the picnic lunch, gave Caitlin a kiss on the cheek and left the house with her son.

It took most of the morning, but Caitlin fixed the lunch anyway. Her finger made her clumsy, but there was no one around to see. By the time they returned, she had fried chicken, made potato salad, sliced a tray of fruits and vegetables and had even fixed pecan brownies. After surveying the food, Jess wrapped his arm around her and hugged her to his chest. "You don't obey too well anymore, do you?"

The vague reference to her father made her stiffen, but his grin was so engaging that *she* finally smiled, too. "No, not very often. You two get changed so we can go. The park will be crowded today."

Her prediction was correct, but the Mendez family had saved a place for them. After Caitlin finished eating, she took Tommy from Bonny, giving the other woman a chance to finish her meal. She cooed to him softly and bounced him on her lap, giving him all her attention. For the first time since he'd returned, she was unaware of Jess at her side, of his eyes on her.

The decision he'd made that morning was reinforced in those few minutes. He wanted her for his wife; he wanted to be with her every morning and every night; he wanted to make love to her until she cried because it was so sweet; he wanted to see her holding their child, smiling down at their son the way she was smiling at Tom's son; and, when he died, he wanted to die with her at his side. He wanted to marry her.

If those wants, those desires, sounded too much like love for comfort, Jess chose to ignore it. He chose to think of it as friendship, as caring. Not love. Never again love.

"Isn't he adorable?" Caitlin asked of no one in particular.

Jess leaned forward, laying his long fingers across her hand, to see the baby. Tommy was about five months old, as dark as his father, but with Bonny's blue eyes, which peered up at Jess over fat, rounded cheeks. The baby looked as solemn and wise as any respected grandfather, and with that quiet, accepting stare, he captured Jess's heart. "Can I hold him?"

Knowing what he was feeling—the awe and reverence that love had created this life—she put the small child in his arms. He leaned back against the tree, settling Tommy in the cradle of his lap, the fat little legs extending up Jess's chest. For a long time they looked at each other, serious brown eyes locked with sober blue.

They could do this—he and Caitlin. They could create a child like this: small, delicate, perfectly formed. At that moment, it was something he wanted with all his heart.

When he talked to the boy, it wasn't in the soft, delighted voice that Caitlin used, but in his regular voice, low, soothing, relaxing. He talked about things a baby couldn't possibly understand, but he never lost Tommy's attention, not until the clear blue eyes were closed by drifting eyelids.

"Time for the rodeo," Tom said, taking the baby from Jess. Carmen and Lupe had decided to remain in the shady park with Tommy, while the younger people went to the arena. Tom handed the baby to his grandmother, then pulled Bonny to her feet.

Jess walked at Caitlin's side, but he made no move to touch her until he noticed the admiring looks that were sent her way by several unattached cowboys. Scowling fiercely, he put his arm around her shoulders and pulled her to his side.

"He's staking his claim," Bonny teased in a whisper meant for Caitlin's ears only. "Men do that a lot." She held up her hand, captured firmly in Tom's.

Caitlin smiled. Whether he claimed her or not, she was his. Other men held no interest for her. She wasn't going to tell him that, of course—she kind of liked his jealousy. Besides, if he knew that she was in love with him, he might decide that was all he needed to accomplish his job; then he might move on. He didn't need to actually see Grant to be satisfied that he'd succeeded in punishing him. If he left Caitlin now, she wouldn't be able to hide her pain from Grant; her father would know everything. Jess would triumph, whether he was there to see it or not.

Caitlin generally enjoyed the Fourth of July rodeo, but today her mind wandered, comparing her situation to that of her friends. Amelia and Paul, sitting next to Jess, and Bonny and Tom, on her side, were two of the happiest married couples she'd known. Both couples had had problems, but they had solved them and made successful marriages out of the messes.

Amelia had been married to another man, her high school sweetheart, when she met Paul. Her marriage had been unhappy; falling in love with Paul seemed the most natural thing in the world. They had done nothing about it, though, until her husband agreed to a divorce. Out of spite, he had refused for months. The day it became final, she and Paul were married, and, fifteen years later, they were still as happy, still as much in love.

Bonny and Tom were equally happy. She had fallen in love with Tom after their first date, while he'd considered her nothing more than a casual girlfriend, pleasant company for a few hours each weekend. When she got pregnant, even those weekend dates had stopped. It wasn't until she was three months pregnant that he finally proposed marriage, and it had taken her another two months to say yes. She had planned her strategy well: fearful that she was going to turn him down, Tom had finally realized how much he loved her. After almost five years of marriage, he still treated her as if she were a precious gift.

Despite the problems, everything had worked out well for Amelia and Bonny. Why shouldn't Caitlin have the same luck? she asked, and in her next thought, she answered the question.

Amelia and Bonny had one thing going for them that she didn't: Paul and Tom loved them. Jess didn't love her, didn't trust her, and wasn't the least bit interested in loving her. He liked her, and he wanted her, but he didn't love her. Last night she had told herself that was enough; she could settle for that. But when she saw the way Paul looked at Amelia, the way Tom looked at Bonny, she wanted desperately for Jess to look at her that way—with love.

"Cait?"

Slowly she turned to Jess. Her eyes were dazed, not quite focusing until they reached his face.

"The rodeo—it's over." He was standing up, but when he saw the sheen of wetness in her eyes, he sat down again beside her. "Cait, what's wrong?" he asked softly.

"Nothing."

"You guys go on," he told Tom. "We'll catch up with you later." He moved to sit on the bench in front of her, facing her. "Cait, don't lie to me."

She took a deep breath, forced a smile and did exactly what he'd just told her not to. "Nothing's wrong, Jess," she lied. "Are you ready to go back to the park?"

She stood up, and he took her left hand, forcing her down again. "No, I'm not." His eyes, sharp with suspicion, studied her face. But by then the urge to cry had passed, and her eyes were clear and calm. It bothered him. He knew she'd been upset about something. Why wouldn't she tell him? Why was she lying to him?

He let her stand up, and he got to his feet. "Are you sure you're all right?"

With a soft laugh, she put her arms around him and laid her head on his shoulder. "I'm sure. I'm a little bit hot and a little bit tired—someone was in my bed last night—but I'm fine."

He chuckled softly. "Would you prefer that I stay in my own bed?" he asked, sliding his hands behind her to play with her braid.

She stared at the center of his chest, where a button in his cream-colored western shirt had almost worked loose. It shifted with every breath he took; a deep one would free it. The small round button seemed to fascinate her, but she knew it was just an excuse to avoid his face. She didn't want him to see just how much she wanted him in her bed.

"Last night..." She stopped to clear her throat; she couldn't produce more than a hoarse whisper. "Last night was special for me."

He tilted her face up and smiled sweetly. "It was special for me, too, honey," he assured her. Then he kissed her: a brief taste of his mouth, a promise of what was to come later. "We can skip out on the others and go home, or we can see how much restraint we have and wait until tonight. What do you think?"

"Let's wait," she whispered. His lovemaking could easily become addictive, yet someday she might have to do without it again. His first leaving had devastated her. How could she bear it a second time?

The fireworks that night, paid for largely by Grant Pierce, were impressive. Caitlin caught Jess's grimace at the announcement of her father's name, but he said nothing. Restraint, she thought with a solemn smile.

On the way out of the park they got separated from the others when Jess chose an angling path that led to the parking lot. They reached his truck first and got inside. Never one to waste good time, he pulled Caitlin into his arms and kissed her hungrily. Driven by a need that made him shake, he pulled her shirt from her shorts and slid his hand underneath the soft pink cotton to cup her breast. "Oh, Cait," he whispered as her breast swelled to fit his hand. "I want—" He bit off the words and kissed her again.

He had almost blurted it out: I want to marry you. This wasn't the time or the place to propose marriage to a woman who had more reasons to say no than she did to say yes. He hadn't figured out yet where or how he would propose to her, but it wouldn't be in the heat of passion. He would be clearheaded and cool minded, so she would know that he meant what he said, that he hadn't been carried away by lust.

Tom's discreet cough warned Jess and Caitlin of the others' approach. Reluctantly, Jess released Caitlin and pulled her shirt down. A moment later Paul helped Lupe into the truck, and they were on their way home.

Lupe hadn't missed the changes in her son and Caitlin. She didn't altogether approve of their being lovers—she would much

rather see them married—but she was happy to see them together. Anyone could see that they were made for each other.
When they got home, she excused herself and went to bed. She
didn't want to interfere with any plans they might have.

Caitlin went into the kitchen to rinse the dishes they had used
for their picnic. Jess leaned against the counter and watched her.

"Bonny and Tom have invited us over for dinner Wednesday," he said.

"Okay."

He grinned at her vague answer. She didn't seem to realize
the significance of that day. A lot of people dreaded their thirtieth
birthdays, but she seemed to have forgotten hers was coming. He
couldn't remember his, either. He hadn't celebrated birthdays in
the years he was gone; he'd just gotten older.

"Jess?" She shut off the water and dried her left hand, then
turned, the towel dangling from her fingers. "How long are you
staying?"

He stared at her. Was she afraid he would leave again? Or
afraid he wouldn't? He remembered the day she had told him
that the sooner his house was finished, the sooner he'd be out of
hers. Later she had claimed she hadn't meant it, but what if she
had? He could have been reading too much into her recent behavior. Sleeping with him didn't necessarily mean she cared for
him. After all, Caitlin was a warm, wildly passionate woman who
hadn't been with a man in eight years.

He shook his head. He knew Caitlin: she hadn't been with a
man in eight years because she hadn't cared about any man in
eight years. She wouldn't have made love with him if she hadn't
cared. He had to believe that he meant something to her, that he
was something more than a warm body in her bed. "I don't
know," he finally replied. It wasn't a lie. He intended to stay
until he died, and he didn't know how long that would be.

His answer told her nothing, but it satisfied her. She offered
him her hand and a pair of scissors. When he had removed her
splint, she wrapped her arms around him and hugged him tight.
"How about a little help getting my clothes off?"

"I think your hand's getting better. You got along pretty well
today."

"It is," she agreed. "Do you want to take my clothes off or

not?"

He laughed softly. "Of course I do. Do I look like a fool?"

Dinner at Tom and Bonny's Wednesday night turned out to be a surprise birthday party, and Caitlin truly was surprised—not altogether pleasantly. She didn't mind birthdays, but she didn't usually celebrate them. There were always gifts from Lupe and her father, but without Jess, the day had had no special meaning.

Thirty years old, she thought, staring at the cake, with its burning yellow candles. The last birthday she'd had with Jess had been her twenty-first. She had had such plans for her life then. After she and Jess were married, she was going to get pregnant right away; he would support them while she continued with her art, looking for the break that would make her a success. They would have a baby every year—a big, happy, loving family.

But Grant had pushed too hard, and Jess had pushed back, and Caitlin had gotten caught in the middle. Now she was thirty, and she had no husband, no children, no big happy family.

She might still get the family—at least one child. Jess came to her every night, and they spent the dark hours making love. Each time her chances of getting that child increased. She didn't think Jess was being careless; he probably assumed that she would take the responsibility for birth control. But she'd had no need for contraceptives in the past, and she had no desire for them now. A child might be the only part of him she could have. It was definitely a part of him she wanted.

She'd given it a lot of thought. Being illegitimate wasn't easy; Jess's life had shown her that. Grant's fears about her own illegitimacy had been part of the wedge that drove her and Jess apart. But times were different. There would be gossip in a small town like Isabel, but in a city the size of Albuquerque, no one would care that her child had no father. Financially, she could provide everything a child needed; emotionally, she could give all the love a child could ever want. She could love him so much he wouldn't even miss his father.

"If you don't blow those candles out soon," Jess whispered in her ear, "the cake's going to be ruined. Make a wish—and I'll make it come true later."

"Arrogant," she whispered back, and he merely chuckled. She took a deep breath and blew. With help from the children around the table, she managed to extinguish all thirty candles. She cut the cake, ate a piece and opened her gifts. Jess's was last. She stared at the silver-and-mussel shell earrings with misty eyes, then leaned up to kiss his cheek. "Thank you," she whispered. "Thank you all."

When she went out to the patio for a moment's fresh air, Jess followed. "What were you thinking about in there while your candles burned down?"

"Babies. I was supposed to have about seven before I turned thirty."

"It's not too late to start."

Precisely what she had been thinking. With a little cooperation from Jess and nature, by her next birthday she would have her first baby. Jess she knew she could count on. Nature was something else.

What would he think if she told him that she was planning to get pregnant? To have *his* baby? She would assure him—in writing, if necessary—that she would make no claims on him. But was that the assurance he would want? Jess had grown up with the stigma of illegitimacy coloring every part of his life. He probably wouldn't be willing to let his own child share that experience. He would probably insist on marriage; regardless of his feelings for her, he would insist on being a part of his son's or daughter's life.

Caitlin paled. Was she trying to trap him? Deliberately planning to get pregnant because she knew he would demand that they be married right away?

"Cait, are you okay?" Jess pulled her into his arms. She felt so cold, and her face was colorless. "Caitlin?"

"I—I'm all right. Hold me, Jess. Please, just hold me." She hid her face against his shirt, her eyes squeezed shut. It was wrong. She wanted Jess to love her, wanted him to stay with her forever, but forcing him to marry her was wrong. He would hate her, and he would never forgive her. She would lose him forever.

The next day she went to see Dr. Ramirez. The following morning, while searching for new blades for his razor, Jess found the small packet of pills in her bathroom drawer. He opened the dispenser case and stared at its contents. There were none missing; she hadn't started taking them yet, he noted with relief.

Or she could have been taking them all along; it could be a new package, suspicion told him.

He stormed into the bedroom, where Caitlin was still lying in bed, a pale yellow robe wrapped around her, and threw the plastic case on her stomach. "What the hell are these?" he demanded.

Her throat was suddenly dry. "Birth control pills."

"I know that! Why do you have them?"

Her own temper flared. "Usually they're taken to prevent pregnancy," she retorted. "I hadn't noticed you taking any precautions, so I did, okay?"

He responded with an ugly curse. *"Precautions."* It sounded like a dirty word. "You don't have to take those. If you're so damned scared of having my baby, why the hell don't you just lock me out of your room?"

She knew it was a mistake, but the words came out anyway. "Because I happen to like sleeping with you."

"You like sleeping with me?" he repeated. The flippant reply infuriated him. "Let's see how well you like it this time!" His hands went to the belt he had fastened just minutes earlier. When he unzipped his jeans, Caitlin started edging across the bed, away from him. She had almost reached safety when he lunged for her, catching her arm in a bruising grip.

He held her down with his body, but even in anger he was careful not to hurt her. His smile was without pleasure, bitter and mocking, and it frightened her. "I like sleeping with you, too, Cait. I like it so much, I'm going to show you now. I like it so much, I'm going to keep doing it until you *do* get pregnant. Does that make you sick, the thought of my baby growing in your belly?" He pulled her robe open, his hands rough but not painful. He was so intent on what he was doing that he almost missed her answer.

"No," she said.

The soft word stopped him, slowly penetrating the rage that filled his mind. "No?" he echoed weakly.

"No," she repeated. "The thought of your baby growing inside me doesn't make me sick. I want...I want your baby, Jess, but I don't want you to feel...trapped or obligated. I was going to get pregnant anyway, without telling you, but...it wouldn't be fair. So I saw Dr. Ramirez yesterday.''

"Trapped?" He stared at her for a long moment, then dropped his head to her breast. "I wasn't taking any 'precautions' because I was hoping you would get pregnant. Then I could ask you to marry me, and you'd have to say yes. Then not even Grant could stop us. Please, Cait. Marry me.''

Caitlin's breathing was slow and even. She was quiet, calm, though she wanted nothing more than to hide her face and cry. He was willing to marry her because of a baby. He was willing to marry her because of Grant. Why couldn't he marry her just because he loved her?

Jess knew he had made a mistake. He could feel it in the stiffness of her body. He had known he shouldn't propose to her in the heat of passion because she wouldn't believe he really meant it. So instead, like a fool, he had done it in the heat of anger. Now she definitely wouldn't believe him.

He moved off her, closed her robe and tied the belt with clumsy hands. "That isn't the way it was supposed to come out," he explained quietly, avoiding her face. "I was going to point out all the reasons you and I should get married—all the reasons a marriage between us would be good. Then I was going to ask you if you would marry me. I didn't intend to ask it like this."

Caitlin still said nothing. She sat up and smoothed her robe, then got to her feet and went about the task of gathering clothes to wear. Jess sat in the middle of the rumpled bed and watched her. He couldn't gauge her reaction: if she was pleased or angry, if she was considering his proposal such as it had been, or if she had ruled it out immediately. All he knew was that she wasn't particularly thrilled with the idea.

Silently he cursed himself for being an idiot. What kind of woman *would* be thrilled by a marriage proposal that came after a rape attempt? The birth control pills were none of his business; he'd had no right to even ask her about them, much less blow up the way he had. He just hadn't been able to stop himself. He wanted so badly to see Caitlin carrying his child that the disappointment had cost him his self-control.

Caitlin felt fragile as she went into the bathroom to dress. If she moved too quickly, smiled or even tried to talk, she was afraid the mask she wore would shatter and Jess would see how deeply his proposal had hurt her. She had prayed that he wouldn't suggest marriage, because marriage to him was the one thing she wanted more than life itself—and the one thing that could destroy her. Now he had done it, and to make matters worse, he had mentioned her father in the same breath.

Then not even Grant could stop us. She had known he was using her as a tool against her father. She had known the only reason he could possibly want to marry her was to show Grant that he could. Mistakenly, she had told herself that she could handle it. She could handle being used, being wanted but never being loved, she had assured herself, and she had lied. Dear Lord, she couldn't stand it! She couldn't let him touch her again and know it meant nothing to him. She couldn't make love with him again, let him touch her very soul and know that for him, it was just part of a plan.

She brushed her teeth, washed her face, combed her hair. She dressed in the clothes she had chosen—a pale blue T-shirt and navy blue running shorts—clothes that had no buttons or zippers that required Jess's help. She even managed to put her splint on and tape it in place. She couldn't let him do it. If he touched her right now, she would scream.

Jess slowly left the bed and zipped his jeans, then refastened his belt. He went to the bathroom door and knocked. He didn't try the knob; he had heard the click of the lock when she closed it. "Cait? Are you okay?"

Okay? She almost laughed, but if she did, she would dissolve into hysterics. *Okay?* She had never been less okay in her life!

When she didn't answer, he tried the knob anyway. "Caitlin."

She opened her mouth several times before sound came out. "I'll be out in a minute." She sounded so normal. She looked so normal in the mirror above the sink. What she wouldn't give if she could *feel* normal!

She berated herself sternly. Jess had admitted from the beginning that he wanted vengeance on Grant. She had known all along that she was a part of that vengeance. Now that she had proof of it, why did she feel so shocked, so taken aback?

Because love played funny games with its victims. As long as he made no overtly vengeful steps, she could pretend that it wasn't true. She could pretend that he simply wanted her, that he liked her, as he claimed, and that someday he might even love her. Love had let her ignore the truth and focus on the fantasy. Now the fantasy had been ripped away, and she had to face the truth.

Jess knocked again. "Cait, please..."

She opened the door and stepped out. Her eyes didn't quite meet his when she raised her head, and her smile wasn't quite genuine.

What an arrogant bastard he had been when he'd decided so easily on Sunday that convincing Caitlin to marry him would present no problems at all. She looked as if her world had just tilted and wasn't ever going to be set right again. He couldn't imagine a woman less pleased with the prospect of marriage.

"Cait, I'm sorry. My timing was bad—"

His timing could never be good as far as she was concerned. She interrupted him. "If you don't eat breakfast soon, you're going to be late for work."

"Can we talk about this tonight?"

She looked away.

Jess laid his hands on her shoulders. When she tensed and would have pulled away, he held her tighter. "Please, Cait. We need to talk. Promise me."

She nodded. It was the best she could do.

She skipped breakfast, going straight to her studio. The reference books sat untouched, though; she couldn't make sense of the words in them. After several hours she got in her Jeep and drove out of town. She had bought the Jeep because it could be driven off-road; she was able to leave the rough dirt-and-gravel road and drive right out into the desert. She left it parked at the foot of a volcanic hill and climbed to the top, where she sat for hours, unaware of the sun beating down on her head. Unaware of everything.

As the sun began setting, she climbed back down the hill and returned home. Jess was already there, in the kitchen helping Lupe with dinner. He examined her with worried eyes, relaxing only slightly when she greeted Lupe with a hug. His tension eased more when she gave him a hug, too.

She hadn't found an answer to his proposal out there on the hilltop, but she had decided to hear him out. He felt there were reasons, other than Grant, for them to marry, and she wanted to hear what they were. She knew the main one, of course—children—and she agreed with it. Jess wanted children, and she wanted his children. That was one thing she was certain of. She wanted to hear his other reasons. Maybe she could agree with them, too.

After the dinner dishes were done, she suggested they go out on the deck. Jess suggested they take a ride out into the desert. He wanted her someplace where she couldn't run away from him if she decided she'd heard enough. He took her to the same spot they'd gone his second day back, after they'd had lunch with Lupe. When he shut off the engine, the silence seemed to echo and magnify, broken at last by his low voice.

"I really screwed things up, didn't I?" he asked, not expecting a reply. Caitlin gave him one anyway.

"It wasn't the most romantic proposal a woman could get," she agreed.

"Have you ever been with another man, Cait?"

She didn't answer.

Jess turned sideways in the seat, leaning back against the door. "Please, tell me. Have you ever made love with any man other than me?"

She remembered the first time they'd made love Saturday evening. He had even commented in husky tones about how tightly she fitted around him. She blushed deeply with the memory. "You know I haven't."

"You never found anyone else you wanted to make love with, did you? You waited all those years, never knowing if I would come back. You waited for me."

She couldn't think of any flippant remark, and she knew it wasn't the time for flippancy. They were here to talk, to work out their problems. Hiding behind sarcasm wouldn't do either of them any good. She simply kept quiet until he spoke again.

"I had waited a long time for you, too."

The significance of that took several minutes to sink in. "You told me there had been other women," she reminded him.

"There were, at first. But I hadn't been with another woman in almost two years, Cait. I couldn't find anyone to replace you. I couldn't find anyone I wanted the way I wanted you. I don't think I could have sex with another woman now if my life depended on it. You're the only one I want."

"And wanting is supposed to be enough?" She compressed

her lips together. She wasn't going to ask him to love her, because then she would have to admit her own love. She couldn't do that. He would use it against Grant, and he would ruin it.

Jess knew what she was asking. He could lie. He could tell her he loved her. Men did it all the time to get what they wanted from their women. But whatever honor he had left wouldn't let him. If he lied—and of course it would be a lie—and claimed to love her, it would taint everything they shared, and it would eventually destroy them.

"Yes," he said slowly. "Wanting can be enough. It's more than a lot of people ever have. We get along well, don't we?"

She didn't answer until he prodded her. "I suppose so."

"And you can't deny that we're perfect together in bed."

She agreed.

"And you and my mother get along very well."

"And you and my father hate each other." Which was precisely the reason they were having this conversation, she reminded herself. If Jess hadn't wanted revenge, he wouldn't have suggested marriage, and he wouldn't be thinking of reasons to convince her.

He waited a moment before using his strongest argument. "And we both want a family. Children. You said this morning that you wanted my baby. I can't think of anything I'd like more than to see you growing bigger every day with my child. I've been alone a long time, Cait. I don't want to be alone anymore. I want to spend the rest of my life with you, with our children."

She turned to face him and drew her knees to her chest. "The rest of your life?" she repeated. That was something that hadn't occurred to her before. She had always assumed that when his vengeance was complete, he would leave her. "You want to marry me and stay married to me until one of us dies?"

She sounded so skeptical. Jess was surprised. Of course he meant to stay married. He wasn't as devout in his faith as his mother was, but he had been raised a Catholic, and some of the beliefs had become part of him. He didn't believe in divorce—not for him. Once he married Caitlin, he would remain married to her for the rest of his life.

"Yes," he replied. "Forever."

"What if you're miserable? You're going to stay that way for the next forty or fifty years?"

"I won't be miserable."

"What if *I'm* miserable?" It was a very good possibility, she admitted silently. It hurt to love Jess now, knowing that he didn't love her. How much more would it hurt in two years, or five, or ten? How long could she bear to be the wife of a man who couldn't, or wouldn't, love her?

He said the words softly. "I don't believe in divorce, Cait, but I would never force you to stay with me if I made you unhappy."

Wonderful, she thought forlornly. He wanted to marry her to punish her father, to gain the children he'd always wanted, and to get a lover, and he would stay married to her because he was Catholic and the Church didn't approve of divorce. The Church probably wouldn't approve of a lot of the things Jess had done and was doing, but that didn't seem to matter to him. It must be nice to be able to choose what you wanted to believe and discard the rest.

"I'll be good to you, Cait."

How good? How good would he have to be to make up for not loving her? She felt tears stinging the insides of her eyelids, and she squeezed them shut.

Jess understood part of her sorrow. She had expected so much more when she got married. She had expected love—wonderful, bright, shining love—and he was asking her to settle for friendship and desire. They were a poor substitute. But he had no clue as to the worst hurt. He'd forgotten Grant, forgotten her ideas of revenge, forgotten that she expected him to use her against her own father. He had forgotten all of that, so he didn't understand her response when he asked, "Is it your father?"

Caitlin laughed, and then the laughter dissolved into tears. Helplessly, he reached out to stroke her hair. "Talk to me, Cait," he pleaded.

"Take me home." The words were muffled, because her head was lowered to her knees. "Please take me home."

There was nothing else he could say, not now. With one last pat, he turned in the seat and started the engine.

That night he stopped her at the door of her room. "Don't give me an answer yet," he softly requested. "Think about it. I know it's not everything you want, but it's the best I can offer, Cait. Think it over, and let me know later. Okay?" He kissed her forehead, then continued down the hall to his own room. It was the first time in a week that he hadn't spent the night with her, but he knew she wouldn't welcome him, not this time.

Caitlin couldn't sleep. She lay in bed and cried, muffling her tears with her pillow. She paced the length and breadth of her room; then she stepped through the French doors and continued her pacing outside. In his room—in Grant's room—Jess lay awake through the night, too, listening to the soft creak of her footsteps. At sunrise she left the deck for a long walk in the desert.

She had settled nothing when she returned. The idea of marriage to Jess thrilled her. The idea of marriage to him under the circumstances he dictated sickened her. If she told him no, he would leave her alone, and she would die without him. If she told him yes, she would probably die anyway, from loneliness and lack of love, but at least it would be a much slower death.

What would it do to Grant to come home and find her married to Jess? A little pocket of bitterness inside her thought it would serve him right. She had forgiven him for driving them apart the first time—at least, she thought she had—but there was a part that would like to win, even eight years later. To show him that he couldn't control her life any longer.

For the first time since Jess had returned, she understood his need for revenge. It wasn't pleasant or good or right, but she imagined there would be a certain satisfaction in bettering someone who had cost him so much in the past. If only he didn't have to use her to do it!

When she returned, Jess was waiting for her in the kitchen. Despite the early hour, he was drinking his second can of beer. His eyes were dark with concern, but he made no effort to touch her when she walked past.

She got a glass of juice from the refrigerator and sat down across from him.

"You didn't sleep." It was a statement, not a question. She still wore the same clothes she had worn the night before.

She shook her head. From the look of him, neither had he. Was it that important to him that she say yes? She sipped her juice, and Jess drank his beer. When her glass was empty, she laid her hand over his. "Come to bed with me."

He stared at her, not quite sure he understood.

"Please, Jess." She stood up and waited. "I need you."

His own need, unleashed by her words, exploded through him. He had feared for several long dark hours that he might never get to make love with her again. Now he followed her willingly to her room.

The bed had remained unmade from the last time they'd shared it. In the jumble of sheets, Jess found the plastic dispenser case he had thrown at her the morning before. He picked it up and wordlessly offered it to her.

Caitlin looked at it a moment. Those pills would practically guarantee that, if she wasn't already pregnant, she wouldn't get that way. She took it, opening the case and running her finger over the small round pills. After a moment she snapped it shut, tossed it into the wastebasket in the corner and turned back to face him, pulling her shirt over her head as she did so.

Their lovemaking was tinged with desperation. Caitlin wanted to be convinced that everything would be all right, that whatever decision she made would be the right one. Jess wanted to assure her that marriage wasn't just the right decision—it was the only one. She demanded, and he responded. She took, and he gave. Their mating was stormy and wild and violent, and when it was over, nothing was changed. Caitlin wasn't sure of anything except that she loved this man. Jess had convinced her of nothing, but he was more sure than ever that he couldn't live without her. He wouldn't.

Exhausted, he fell into a deep sleep. Caitlin lay beside him for several hours, then got up and gathered fresh clothes. Down the hall, in the master bath, she showered, washed her hair and dressed, then went looking for Lupe. Lupe could help her. Even if she told the older woman nothing, merely being with her would calm Caitlin and help her to think clearly.

She found Lupe sitting in the small circle of shade on the deck, a pitcher of iced tea on the table next to her. "Get a glass and join me," she invited.

After a long silence, Lupe asked, "Jess is sleeping?"

Caitlin nodded.

"What is it you want to talk to me about?"

"Tell me about Roberto."

Lupe was as surprised by the request as Caitlin, but she was also pleased. "What would you like to know?"

"Everything. Where did you meet? When did you fall in love? What was it like?"

Lupe's expression turned soft, as it always did when she thought of Roberto. "Jess looks like his father did then, though I've never told him so. I don't think he would be pleased," she said softly. "He never understood.... He always blamed Roberto for what happened. It wasn't his fault. It wasn't anyone's fault."

Lupe had been twenty-three when Roberto and his wife Ana moved to Isabel from Mexico City. She had been instantly attracted to the handsome young man, even though she knew that he was married. She had never expected the attraction to be mutual.

"I never met Ana. I don't think anyone in town did. They brought their own servants, their own nurses. They moved here because their families owned property in this area, and Roberto was going to manage it."

"Nurses?" Caitlin questioned softly. She had known Lupe all her life and about Roberto for at least twenty years, but she had never known the full story. She had always assumed it was a simple case of falling in love with the wrong man. Lupe had never volunteered the facts, and Caitlin had never asked until now.

"Ana was sick. According to Roberto, she was beautiful, but very frail, weak. It wasn't a physical illness—it was her mind."

Lupe fell silent for a moment, remembering; then she continued in her softly accented voice. "Ana's grip on reality was fragile at best. Roberto was her life, her reality, her reason for living. When she was distraught, only he could calm her. When she was despondent, only he could cheer her. His was the only voice that could penetrate the fantasy world in which she lived. No one else could reach her.

"He was a good man. He no longer loved his wife, but he felt a genuine fondness for her, and he couldn't abandon her, because of her precarious mental state. If Ana ever lost him, her psychiatrists in Albuquerque told him, she would be lost forever in her other world."

He hadn't wanted to love Lupe. He had fought the attraction desperately. If she had been stronger, if she had been able to say no, or if his marriage hadn't been a sham almost from its start, maybe the affair wouldn't have happened. But one night their passion broke free of its restraint, and they had been unable to end their relationship for many months after that.

They were discreet, but gossip always found its way. Ana had never known. Roberto doubted that she was even capable of understanding affairs, infidelity and divorce. But the townspeople and Lupe's family understood. They were disapproving at first, then scandalized, when she became pregnant.

When she told Roberto she was going to have a baby, he swore he would leave Ana. She would slip into her unreal world, but at least she was happy there. She felt no fear, no pain, no need. He would divorce the woman he'd married, who couldn't give him children or share his life or his bed, and he would marry the woman he loved, who carried his child.

But each time he tried to take action, Ana's condition would worsen. He couldn't help comparing the two of them: poor, gentle, sweet, sick Ana, and strong, capable, healthy Lupe. Without him, Lupe would survive. She would have their child, and she would survive. Ana wouldn't.

It broke his heart to tell Lupe he couldn't marry her. He offered her money and she took it, knowing she'd need it to raise their child alone. She saw him only once after that, when Jess was born. He came to see his son and to tell Lupe goodbye. Ana was at her worst ever; there was a clinic in Pennsylvania doing wonders with cases like hers. He had to try.

He made her a promise, and she had treasured it for thirty-one years. She repeated it softly, word for word, to Caitlin. "You are the wife of my heart," he had vowed. "If Ana ever gets better, I'll come back. I'll return for you and for my son."

She never saw him again.

Caitlin wiped a tear from the corner of her eye. "Oh, Lupe," she whispered. How Jess's bitterness toward his father must have hurt her over the years! "Does Jess know?"

She shook her head. "I've tried to tell him, but he never wanted to know. He preferred to blame Roberto." She smiled, teary eyed. "He's a lot like his father. He's a fine, handsome man. Roberto would have been proud of him."

"It cost you a lot to have him. Did you ever regret it?"

Lupe gave a definite no. Jess could have made her family proud, in addition to his father, if he'd been given a chance. But Ernesto Trujillo was a strict man—religiously, morally, ethically.

He could find no reason for pride in a young daughter who had gotten herself involved with a married man, or in the grandson who had resulted from that involvement. She had brought shame on herself, her son and her family, and the only way Ernesto could deal with it was to pretend that neither his daughter nor his grandson existed.

Lupe laid her hand over Caitlin's. "Be careful, child. Your mother loved your father dearly, but Grant kept them apart, and she lost him. I loved Roberto with all my heart, but I lost him to Ana. Before you give up anything, be sure you want to live without it." She smiled fondly at Caitlin, then closed her eyes and tilted her head back. "The sun feels good today, doesn't it?"

In a few minutes Lupe was asleep. Caitlin sat with her a few minutes longer, then went into the house. She met Jess, just up from his nap, right inside the door. She looked up at him, her gaze moving slowly over the face that she loved so well. "Yes, Jess," she said softly. "I'll marry you." With that, she continued through the room and down the hall.

Jess stared after her, then slowly turned his gaze outside. His mother was sitting in one of the lounge chairs, her head tilted back, her eyes closed, her mouth turned up in a satisfied smile. What the hell...?

A memory he wished would stay buried pushed its way into his thoughts, a memory of something Caitlin had told him one day at the building site. He had asked for her help with the house when it was finished, and she had agreed readily. "There's nothing I wouldn't do for Lupe," she had told him.

Was that true? Was there really nothing she wouldn't do for his mother? he wondered bitterly.

The question he had to ask next made him ache so deep inside that, for a moment, he couldn't feel anything but the pain. A few hours ago she had been so lost, so unhappy—hurt and distressed over his proposal of marriage. Now she had accepted him. He didn't want to face it, but the question forced its way out anyway.

If Caitlin would do anything for Lupe, would she marry Jess for her? If that was what it took to make his mother happy, would Caitlin agree?

Dear God, he prayed. *Please don't let it be true.*

Chapter 7

After church Sunday morning, Lupe informed Jess that she was going to spend the afternoon with Carmen. She wasn't sure what had happened between him and Caitlin, but she was sure that they needed some time alone to settle it. He kissed her forehead and climbed into his truck, heading home alone.

Caitlin was getting ready to leave the house. She'd left a note on the dining table saying where she would be; now she just hoped she could get away before church let out. Her timing was off.

"Where are you going?" Jess asked quietly.

"To the Coronado State Monument." She hesitated only a second, then asked, "Would you like to go?"

Jess didn't have the vaguest idea what the monument was, but he agreed. He would go anywhere to spend time with her. He changed into faded jeans and a cream-colored T-shirt. Just before leaving his room, he went to the closet, found what he was looking for and tucked it into his pocket.

Caitlin handed him the keys to her Jeep, then settled into her seat. "Where is your mom?"

"She's spending the day with Carmen. Where do I go?"

"Take the interstate into Albuquerque; then take I-25 north to Highway 44. Turn west on 44, and it's just a couple of miles."

She was giving him the directions all at once—to avoid having to talk to him during the drive? Jess cursed himself once more for his rash behavior Friday morning. Even though she had agreed to marry him, he was beginning to wonder if she would ever feel comfortable with him again. Already he missed the closeness they had shared.

"What are we going to see at this place?" he asked.

"The ruins of Kuaua Pueblo."

He repeated the unfamiliar name: Koo-ah-wah. "How old is this pueblo?" If he asked enough questions, she would start talking, and the sound of her voice would be enough to ease some of the hurt inside him.

"It was built at the end of the thirteenth century. Part of it was destroyed by fire around 1350, but the ruins of the rest are still there." She gave him a warning glance. "Not enough to be able to tell a lot about it. You can see the basic outline of the structures; the walls that have survived are no more than a few feet high."

"Is this part of your research for Morgan's paintings?" He couldn't avoid the resentment that tinged his voice at the mention of the other man.

"No. I just like to go there." She looked away from him, squeezing her eyes shut. She felt so strange with him. She had to get past that and get comfortable with the idea that she was going to marry him. After so many long years, she was going to be his wife. She had made her choice—no one had forced her to say yes—and now she had to accept it.

Before you give up anything, be sure you want to live without it. Lupe's words, more than anything else, had settled the matter for her. She didn't want Jess to look on her as a means to an end—as a weapon to gain revenge against her father, or as a way to get the children he wanted. She didn't want him to stay married to her because his religion forbade divorce. She didn't want to live with him, year after year, loving him and knowing that he didn't love her. But, more than any of that, she didn't want to live without him. That much she was sure of.

She looked back at him. "Kuaua was the northernmost village in Tiguex province. At its peak it had more than twelve hundred rooms. It's located on the west bank of the Río Grande, with a view of the Sandía Mountains. It's believed that Coronado spent the winter of 1540 and '41 at Kuaua while he was searching for the fabled Seven Cities of Gold. Probably the biggest attraction there now is a restored kiva, or ceremonial chamber; that's open to the public. When it was first excavated, they found that the walls had been decorated with fresco murals. They had been plastered over eighty times, and they found murals, or parts of them, on about seventeen layers. Some of them are on display in the gallery at the Visitor's Center.''

By the time she finished, he was smiling. It was such a warm, pleasant thing that she couldn't help but respond. ''Do I sound like a guidebook?''

''No. You sound like you're talking about something that interests you very much.''

''It does. Every time I go there I...'' She was embarrassed to continue. ''Maybe you'll feel it, too. If you don't, there's no sense discussing it.''

He was a bit puzzled by that, but before he could question her, the turnoff to the ruins came up. They paid the admission fee at the Visitor's Center, looked at the displays set up there, then went outside to the ruins.

The wind had picked up force. Caitlin's hair flew wildly around her face while she searched for a clasp in her purse. When she found it, Jess took it and pulled her hair back, catching it at her neck.

Paths led through the ruins, past walls of adobe bricks—some only inches high, others several feet—and past depressions that had once been kivas. ''When a kiva fell into disuse,'' Caitlin explained, ''they sometimes used it as a garbage dump. That's one reason why they were able to date the ruins fairly accurately.''

''How are you able to remember all these things?'' he asked with a hint of admiration in his voice. There were informative plaques set up around the ruins, but she hadn't even glanced at them.

''It's my history,'' she replied with a shrug. The answer seemed inadequate, but she couldn't explain it any better.

When they reached the restored subterranean kiva, Jess climbed down the peeled-log ladder first. When Caitlin was several feet above the floor, he lifted her down. He was reluctant to remove his hands from her waist, but she stepped away.

Most kivas were circular in shape, but this one was square. Peeled beams layered with twigs provided the ceiling, and flagstones covered the dirt floor. On the walls were reproductions of the original murals.

While Jess studied the paintings, Caitlin leaned against the ladder. "Religion was a part of their everyday lives—it still is. The goal is a balanced relationship with nature and the world. Harmony." She sighed wistfully. "I can't even achieve harmony with you and my father, much less with nature and the world." Her voice grew choked as he approached her. "When Dad comes back and finds you here, he's going to be furious. He won't want us to get married."

He put his arms around her, his hands stroking her hair and down her spine, comfortingly, soothingly. "When he comes back, Cait, we're already going to be married, and you're going to be carrying my baby. He won't be able to hurt us this time."

"I don't want to hurt him," she whispered.

"I know you don't."

"He'll be so angry."

"He'll get over it. You're his only child, Cait. As much as he hates me, he isn't going to give you up because you married me." He stroked her hair back from her forehead and placed a kiss there. "Caitlin, you can't live your life for your father or anyone else. You have to do what makes *you* happy." He hoped that was what she had been doing when she accepted his proposal—making herself happy—but he couldn't forget that she hadn't been able to say yes to him until she'd talked to Lupe. He couldn't forget how much Caitlin wanted her to be happy.

They left the kiva and continued along the path around the ruins. Caitlin stopped beside a series of rooms, staring over them. The wind rustled through the sage—an eerie sound, she'd always thought. Jess moved to stand behind her, his arms around her, his chin resting on top of her head.

"Can you imagine what life was like for these people?" he asked softly. "So long ago. They lived in these buildings, their children played here, and they probably raised their crops over there." He gestured toward the river on their right. "If you close your eyes, you can almost feel them, can't you? Their spirits, their souls, their force." He released her and grinned sheepishly. "I sound a little crazy, don't I?"

She turned to face him. For the first time in two days her eyes were calm, peaceful. "That's what I meant on the way here. I didn't know if it was my imagination, or if I really felt something. This place seems so *alive* to me, even though I know it's been abandoned for so many years." She was pleased that he'd shared the same sensations. It made her feel somehow closer to him.

It was as good a time as any, Jess thought. At last she wasn't looking at him as if he were some kind of monster, her brown eyes so sad they almost broke his heart. He reached into his jeans pocket and pulled out the slender gold band, keeping it hidden inside his hand. "Have you changed your mind, Cait?"

She knew he meant about the marriage. She couldn't explain to him why, but here in this place, where her people had lived hundreds of years ago, she had finally found peace with the idea. She could marry him and do it happily. "No, Jess, I haven't." The wind whipped her hair over her shoulder, and she impatiently brushed it back. "Have you?"

"Never." He cleared his throat. "If you're sure—if you're sure this is what you want, will you wear this?" He opened his hand to reveal the gold-and-diamond ring.

Caitlin recognized it immediately as the ring he'd given her eight years ago. The diamond wasn't large—less than a carat—but it was exquisitely perfect. It had meant more to her than any dozen diamonds ten times bigger.

She swallowed past the lump in her throat. "You kept it."

He nodded.

"Oh, Jess."

He held out his hand, and she placed hers in it. The solemnity of the moment was broken, though, when he tried to slip it onto her fourth finger. It wouldn't fit.

Caitlin laughed. It seemed as if weeks had passed since she'd laughed, and it felt so good. "I've gained some weight," she said unnecessarily when the ring got stuck above her knuckle.

Jess's eyes lifted to move caressingly over her breasts. "I know. It looks good." He removed the ring and slid it easily on her little finger. "I'll take tomorrow afternoon off, and we can go into Albuquerque to get it sized, okay? We can also pick out your wedding ring."

"And yours. I want you to wear one. Please." She suddenly hugged him tight, then cradled his face in her hands. "I'll be a good wife to you, Jess," she promised. Her lips sought his for a kiss that was given as fiercely as her words had been spoken.

Her vow and her kiss filled him with a sweet ache. He touched her mouth with a trembling finger and replied, "I know you will, honey. I know."

Dinner that night was a quiet family celebration. Jess noticed with some dread that Lupe didn't seem too surprised by the announcement of their engagement. Because Caitlin had already told her? Because she had encouraged Caitlin to marry him?

He didn't know that Lupe hadn't needed confidences to see what was happening between her son and Caitlin. Anyone with eyes could see that they were meant for each other, Lupe thought—anyone except Grant Pierce, and he was a cold, selfish old man who saw only what he wanted to see. She hoped fervently that they were safely married and out of Grant's house before he returned from the Middle East.

"Have you set a date yet?" she asked.

"Soon," Jess replied, at the same time that Caitlin answered, "Late January." Slowly they turned to stare at each other. "Late January?" he repeated incredulously. "Cait, that's six months away!"

"My father won't be home until the middle of January."

"Your father—"

"I won't get married without him, Jess."

"Don't be ridiculous. We can't wait that long."

She slowly stood up from the table. "Wanting my father present at my wedding isn't being ridiculous." Her tone was cold and icy, warning Jess to be careful.

He got to his feet and pulled her into his arms. "I don't want to fight with you, honey, honest, but...we can't wait six months. You know that."

He was referring to the baby they both wanted, the one that might already be growing inside her. Caitlin laid one hand on her flat stomach. If she was pregnant, by the time Grant returned home, she'd be in her sixth or seventh month. For herself, she didn't mind. But people would talk, would say that she had trapped Jess, that the marriage didn't stand a chance because of it. She didn't want him or their child to face that kind of gossip and speculation.

And she didn't want to get married without her father, the only family she had in the world. Besides, she probably wasn't even pregnant yet. "He's my father," she said stubbornly.

Sensing a fight brewing, Lupe spoke up. "Caitlin."

She turned in Jess's arms to look at the older woman.

"Jess understands that you love your father. Of course you want him at your wedding. But...he also understands what happened the last time you two tried to get married. I know that for many years you blamed both of them for what happened, but you can't deny that it never would have ended that way if Grant hadn't been so unreasonable."

"He was trying to protect me," she said in her father's defense.

"Trying to protect you from the man you loved? He was protecting his reputation. He didn't want you associated with the Trujillo bastard because he didn't want anyone to know that his precious daughter was illegitimate. He didn't want anyone to find out that the only heir to the exalted Pierce name wasn't his and wasn't a Pierce, but was instead a half-breed Indian bastard."

Caitlin drew back in shock, against the solid wall of Jess's chest. "Mom," he commanded sharply, unable to believe that his own mother would use those words to describe Caitlin.

Lupe raised her hand for silence. "He was protecting himself, Caitlin. He was controlling you."

Caitlin sat down in Jess's chair, and he laid his hands on her shoulders. Was that what it had been like for Jess all his life? she wondered. Hearing that word over and over? No one had ever called her a bastard before, because Grant and Lupe had kept Claire's secret well. She had never imagined how deeply it could hurt.

Lupe leaned forward and took her hands. "I'm sorry. It's an ugly word, with ugly meanings. But it's suitable for the way Grant feels about Jess. If you wait, Caitlin, until your father comes home, you'll never be married. He will not let you marry Jess. He'll keep you apart for the rest of your lives, the way he helped keep you apart the last eight years."

The way he kept her mother and her natural father apart, she thought. They had died apart. "Why can't you believe I'm strong enough to stand up to him?" she asked, looking from Jess to Lupe.

"Do you think you are?" Jess asked quietly.

She hesitated, then shook her head. Standing up to him would mean ending her relationship with him. If she knew Jess loved her, she could face anything, but she wasn't sure she could break off entirely with her father for a man who didn't love her. "Let me think," she said tiredly.

Jess kissed her lightly when she stood up. "Go on. I'll clean up in here." A few minutes after she left the room, he sent his mother to bed. He could handle the dishes alone.

Caitlin lay on the couch in the living room. There was some sense to what Jess and Lupe were saying, but she knew he had an even more important reason for wanting the marriage to take place before Grant returned: it would make his revenge so much sweeter if he and Caitlin were already married when Grant came back to Isabel, rather than just engaged. Engagements could be broken, as their first one had been. Marriages could be broken, too, but that was harder, took longer. Jess's victory would be greater if he could claim her as his wife.

She sighed tiredly. She wasn't going to make a decision now. She would think about it later.

Jess joined her on the sofa when the kitchen was spotless. "Roll over," he commanded. She turned onto her stomach, her head pillowed in his lap, and he rubbed her back, unkinking tight muscles. After several long minutes he turned her and continued the slow, easy massage across her stomach.

Caitlin was afraid to breathe. His fingers were cool, but her skin was hot. His hand was steady, but she quivered everywhere he touched her. Her heart was pounding so hard that she could feel it in her throat, and the blood was rushing through her body, spreading heat and hunger with every heartbeat.

His hands were like magic. No matter how she felt—happy, carefree, troubled, depressed, sad, or angry—the simple touch of his hands could make her forget everything except him and how much she wanted him. How much she loved him.

She whispered his name, and he smiled. His eyes were almost closed, and his breathing was as ragged as Caitlin's. He looked undeniably sexy.

She turned her head toward him, pressing a kiss to his denim-covered belly, then another and another until she reached the rigid flesh that pulsed beneath her slow, biting kisses. He groaned her name and lifted her away, then knelt on the floor in front of her. She reached for him, but he caught her hand and placed it on the couch. "This is for you, Cait. I want to please you. I want to make you feel good."

The low, husky flow of words stopped when he removed her clothes. She lay naked in front of him, taking pleasure in his obvious pleasure at the sight of her. His groan was deep, filled with pain and yearning, and his expression was reverent as he touched her with skilled, gentle, teasing, soothing fingers.

His mouth followed his hands with kisses: warm, wet, dark, painfully sweet kisses. His hands caressed her breasts, and her breathing quickened. His teeth tugged at her nipples, making her cry out. His fingers slid between her legs, parting her and stroked inside, and she moaned, capturing his hand between her thighs. "Jess?" she gasped.

With his other hand, he rubbed across her stomach. "It's all right, Cait," he assured her.

Her legs parted, and he continued his kisses, dipping lower, lower. She whimpered, raising her hips to meet him, wordlessly demanding more, pleading for more, and he gave it to her until she was on fire, gasping, crying, pleading, then shuddering with low groans and hoarse whispered sounds that meant nothing yet said everything.

"Oh, Jess!" she cried. She had to bite her tongue to stop the words that naturally wanted to follow. *I love you.*

He gathered her into his arms, pressing her to his chest, rubbing her with slow, easy strokes that relaxed her tightly coiled muscles, allowing her to sag bonelessly against him for support, and he soothed her with quiet words.

At last she found the strength to raise her head and open her eyes. He was grinning smugly. "You think you're something, don't you?" she softly taunted.

"I know I'm something." He moved her against his hips so she could feel exactly what he meant. "I know I'm aching to be inside you. I know I'm going to die without you. Come to bed with me, Cait. Give yourself to me."

"Yes, Jess." Her whisper made him shiver. She had already given herself to him. For now, tonight, and forever.

"Is it good news or bad?"

Caitlin stared at the diamond ring on her left hand for a long time before raising her face to Dr. Ramirez. She was smiling so happily that he didn't need to hear her answer; he could read it in her eyes. "Good. Very, very good."

"Then congratulations. Will you be seeing a doctor in Albuquerque?"

"Why would I do that? You've been my doctor since you took Dr. Cooper's place twenty years ago."

Ramirez smiled. "I'll want to see you once a month for the next five or six months. I don't need to tell you all the rules, do I? No alcohol, no smoking, no strenuous exercise?"

"I think you just did. That's all right. I don't drink, I don't smoke, and I don't care much for exercise."

"Except certain kinds," he added with a grin.

His joke surprised her. He had been her doctor for such a long time that she tended to forget that he was only about fifteen years older than she was. She laughed softly, then asked, "How's my finger?"

"The X rays say it's fine. You can throw that splint in the trash now. I'm sure that pleases you."

"More than you can imagine."

He stood up from behind his desk and walked to the door with her. "Tell me, Caitlin. You're just barely a month pregnant, and you have none of the usual symptoms yet. Why did you suspect it?"

She shrugged. "I just...felt it. There were...changes."

"You've stopped taking those pills I gave you?"

She laughed again. "Actually, Doctor, I never started. It seemed such a waste." Impulsively, she gave him a hug. "I'll see you next month."

She lingered on the sidewalk outside his office. She was only half a block from Carmen's store; she could go there and tell Lupe the good news, but somehow that didn't seem quite fair. She decided to go by Tom's office and find out if Jess was working at the house that day. As the father, he had the right to be the first one she told.

Tom sent her out to the site, where Jess was checking the work that had been completed so far. She stopped at the café, got sandwiches, chips and drinks to go, then drove to the house.

"I must be living right," Jess said when he came out of the house. "I was just thinking about you."

"You must be." She handed him the bags of food she'd brought, stood on tiptoe and kissed him. "Have you eaten lunch yet?"

"No. Are you offering yourself?"

"Not yet. Sit down, Jess. We need to talk."

They went into the back room that would soon have walls of glass—the room that Jess had promised to her for a studio. Sitting on the concrete slab, Caitlin divided the food, then opened her can of Coke. Jess gave her time to take a long drink before asking warily, "What is it you want to talk about?"

He sensed it was about their wedding. Though the waiting had driven him mad at times, he had given her almost a month to decide on a date. He had kept himself from asking, from pressuring, but she hadn't brought the subject up herself. Now she was going to.

"I've done a lot of thinking about the things we said the night we were discussing our wedding date. I asked for time to make a decision, and you've given it to me. I appreciate that." She leaned over and kissed his cheek. "Now I've made up my mind."

He had difficulty swallowing the food in his mouth. He washed it down with a gulp of Coke, then waited. The rest of his life might depend on her decision. If she had chosen to wait until Grant returned, Jess knew he would never have her. Please, he prayed, let it be soon.

"Is the eleventh of September a good date?"

With a whoop of elation, he lifted her into his lap and gave her a hard, fast kiss. "Are you really serious? That's just a little over a month away. Do you mean it, Cait?" he demanded.

She smiled. "Yes, I mean it. I take it you approve?"

"You're damned right I approve. God, honey, I was really starting to worry. I was afraid you would insist on waiting until Grant came home. I was afraid I would lose you." His expression saddened, then grew very serious. "What I said that night, Cait—I meant it. I don't believe in divorce. If you marry me, it will be for the rest of our lives. Forever. Are you sure that's what you want?"

She looked equally serious. "You said if we were unhappy, you wouldn't force me to stay with you."

Jess's heart squeezed tighter. What kind of response was that to his question? Was she already so sure that she wouldn't be happy as his wife? "I meant that. I would never force you to live with me, but I wouldn't allow you to divorce me. It would be a separation, Cait. You'd never be able to marry anyone else."

She reached up to trace her fingertips over his face. "I know that. And yes, Jess, I'm sure it's what I want." After a brief kiss, she continued. "There is one other thing I need to tell you. I hope you're as happy about it as I am."

His first thought was that Grant was returning early and that was why she had set an earlier date. But he forced himself to sit quietly and wait for her to tell him.

First she held up her right hand. "I saw Dr. Ramirez today. He said my finger is fine."

He pressed a kiss to the back of her hand. "That's great. Now you can get back to work."

"He also said I'm pregnant."

Jess sat motionless for a moment. For all his talk of wanting a baby, it was a hell of a surprise. He was filled with trepidation. What if something went wrong with her pregnancy, or her delivery? What if he was an awful father? After all, he'd never had a father of his own to teach him how to be a good parent. Maybe it was a mistake. He'd heard of false positives on pregnancy tests before.

Then common sense took hold. Nothing was going to go wrong. Caitlin was healthy, and smart enough to take care of herself; if she didn't, he would do it for her. And he didn't need anyone to teach him how to be a good father; his love would take care of that for him.

Slowly he smiled; then his mouth covered hers in a long, deep, loving kiss. When he raised his head again, he laid his hand over her stomach. "A baby," he whispered. "Oh, Cait."

The emotion that made his voice heavy and ragged was the twin of the one that filled her eyes with tears. For the first time in years her world was as right, as perfect, as it could possibly be. The injury that had kept her from her painting was healed without permanent damage. She was with Jess, his arms holding her close. In a month she would be his wife, and in eight months she would have his baby. She didn't have his love, but with everything else that she did have, there was no reason to be greedy. Besides, love could grow. In time it might be there. And until he learned to love her, or even if he never learned, her love would be enough. Her love was strong enough for them both.

The church was quiet. There was little to show that the people in the pews were gathered for a wedding rather than the weekly Sunday service. Caitlin hadn't wanted a lot of flowers; she had chosen only a bouquet for herself and a single rose for the lapel of Jess's jacket.

He hated wearing a suit—it had been Caitlin's idea. So was the church. He would have preferred driving in to the courthouse in Albuquerque and having a very simple, very brief ceremony in front of a judge, but she had insisted on the church—not for herself, he knew. It was for Lupe. It was important to Lupe, Caitlin had insisted, that they get married in the small church she attended. All their friends had been invited too; that was also important to Lupe.

And that was why he hated it. The only things Caitlin had been adamant about were things that mattered to his mother. At times he had gotten so frustrated that he'd wanted to demand to know if the marriage was Lupe's idea, too. But he never had. If Caitlin was marrying him to please his mother, he didn't want to know.

The sound of the organ was his and Tom's cue to leave the small room and join Father Sandoval at the front of the church. As soon as they were in place, Bonny and Caitlin would walk down the long aisle to meet them.

Tom gave him a smile, but Jess didn't even try to return it. Did he look as sickly as he felt? He half expected something to go wrong—for Grant to appear and stop the wedding, or for Caitlin to decide she was making a horrible mistake and change her mind. Until the ring was on her finger—and the matching band on his—he wouldn't feel good about this.

"Wow."

Jess looked at Tom, then turned toward the back. There was Caitlin. His mouth went dry, and his hands, he was sure, would have trembled if they weren't clasped together.

She was beautiful. He knew he had thought that so many times before, but today she was truly breathtakingly beautiful. Her dress fell to mid-calf. It was made of a soft, gauzy ivory-colored fabric that made her look ethereal, like some dark angel. She had chosen not to wear white—"I'm hardly a virgin," she had scoffed, though Jess couldn't think of anyone more innocent or pure than she. And she had voted against a formal-length gown— "Keep in mind that I'm two months pregnant," she had laughed. Still, she looked more beautiful in her simple dress than any bride he had ever seen.

This was it, Caitlin thought. If nothing went wrong within the next ten minutes, she was going to be Mrs. Jess Trujillo. She had waited such a long time to call herself that. *Please, God, let it happen.*

Her throat was dry, and her bouquet of delicate pink roses was shaking slightly, but she was smiling when she stepped into place next to Jess. He looked down at her and finally managed to smile a bit himself. He was incredibly handsome in his dark suit, she noted. He hated suits, hated ties, but he had gracefully agreed to wear it. This would be his one and only wedding, he had said. He could make the sacrifice.

His one and only wedding. He was taking a big risk—marrying a woman he didn't love, a woman who, as far as he knew, didn't love him. Of all the women he could have, he had chosen her for his wife, the only wife he would ever have.

Her cynical side pointed out that Jess's marriage proposal hadn't exactly been a great honor. After all, she was Grant Pierce's only daughter. His only means of punishing Grant. But that was something she preferred not to think about, especially today.

She hoped that she wouldn't disappoint him. She wished that everything in their lives would be good—not perfect, but happy. And she prayed that he would forget his need for vengeance against her father and would simply let her love him.

The service was brief. They repeated their vows, made their

promises to love and honor for the rest of their lives, and sealed them with a gentle kiss.

Caitlin gave a sigh of relief. It was over. They were married, and nothing had happened. Jess was now her husband, and no one, not even Grant, could change that.

The celebration following the ceremony was held at the Mendez house. There was cake and wine, feasting and toasting, dancing and laughter—and not a single chance for the newlyweds to be alone for even a minute. After several hours, though the party showed no signs of ending soon, Jess claimed Caitlin in the middle of a conversation with Melly Wilkins and took her outside.

"That was rude," she said when he lifted her into the Jeep.

"There's nothing rude about a man wanting to be alone with his wife," he disagreed. "We've been married three hours and twenty-four minutes, and we've been surrounded by people the entire time. Now it's our time."

"Where are we going?"

He glanced at her. Her head was back against the seat, and she was smiling dreamily. For what seemed like the hundredth time that day, he was struck again by her beauty. Did other men find her so gorgeous? he wondered. Or was it just because he knew her and cared for her?

She repeated her question, bringing Jess out of his thoughts. "Matt has a cabin up north," he said. "We're going to spend a few days there."

It was late in the evening when they reached the cabin. It was small and not overly clean, but it offered the only two features that mattered to Jess: privacy and a bed. He didn't need anything else when he was with Caitlin.

He carried their suitcases inside, set them down and faced Caitlin. His wife. He gently smiled. She looked as scared as he felt. They had been lovers for so long, but somehow this, their first night as husband and wife, was different.

She had changed into a white cotton skirt, a bright-blue tank top and huaraches before they left Isabel. She looked as lovely as she had in her wedding dress.

"Would you like to take a walk?"

She nodded.

Jess got their jackets, and they left the cabin, walking through the bright moonlight in silence. When they came to the edge of a stream, without speaking, they sat down on a flat boulder that overhung the water. He spread his jacket out to protect her white skirt.

"This place is beautiful."

Jess answered with a nod.

After another few minutes Caitlin turned to face him. She was twisting the new gold band on her finger. "Are you nervous?"

"Yes," he said with a smile.

"So am I. I wonder why."

"As the old saying goes, Today is the beginning of the rest of our lives." He laughed softly. "I don't think I ever really believed it would happen—that we would get married. While I was waiting at the church, I could think of a hundred different reasons why you might back out."

She shook her head. "I didn't want to back out."

Jess reached for her hand, clasping it between his. "I know you wanted your father to be there, Cait. I'm sorry it couldn't work out that way." He was hesitant about discussing Grant with her. He still couldn't keep the resentment out of his voice, and he knew that bothered her.

"Do you think he'll ever accept our marriage?"

She sounded so wistful; he longed to tell her yes. But that would be a lie. As long as there was breath in his body, Grant would hate Jess, and now that they were married, he would never give them a moment's peace.

He knew what would happen eventually: just like in the past, one day Caitlin would have to choose. She couldn't have both Jess and Grant in her life, and she would have to take one or the other. He only hoped that, when that day came, she would care enough about her husband to choose him. He couldn't bear to lose her a second time.

Jess never answered her question. He wasn't ignoring her; he had decided it was kinder not to answer than to point out what she already knew. But that wouldn't satisfy her, and after a little while she said, "Surely after the baby's born..."

He hugged her close. "Honey, do you think he's going to accept that baby?"

"This is his grandchild."

"No, it's not. It's the Trujillo bastard's kid."

"And mine. He won't overlook that it's mine, too." She

stroked his face gently. "You'd be surprised what a baby can do to a mature adult. Maybe the baby is what we need to make Dad forget the past."

"He'll never forget that he hates me," Jess warned her. "And he's not going to acknowledge my baby as his grandchild." His next words were as hard as the tone in which they were spoken. "The only thing your dad's going to do when he finds out we're married, Cait, is look for ways to break us up. He will lie to you, and he'll treat me worse than he ever has before. That's why I want you to understand one thing: you're mine now. I am not giving you up—not for your father, or my mother, or anyone else in the damn world. You belong with me, and that's where you're staying."

She shivered and pulled away from him. After staring at the water for a minute, she looked back at him and said accusingly, "You talk like I'm your property."

Jess smiled a bitter smile. "No, Cait. You're my life." He moved to stand beside her at the rock's edge. "All that talk about not believing in divorce—I'm not stupid, Caitlin. I know that if you want to divorce me, there's nothing I can do to stop you. That will be the first thing Grant suggests when he comes back, and someday you'll probably do it. But it won't mean anything. In my mind, and in my heart, you'll always be my wife."

"I told you I wouldn't ask for a divorce," she whispered.

But she had never said she wouldn't leave him. She had never said she would stay with him for the rest of her life. "I'm sure you meant it, too," he said quietly. "But things change. Hell, Cait, you've already had doubts about marrying me. What makes you think you can say no to Grant when he demands that you leave me?"

She stared up at him. "Why did you marry me if you believe I'm going to divorce you?"

He touched her face, with just the tips of his fingers. "I need you," he said simply.

She laid her hand over his, trapping his palm against her cheek. "I need you, too, Jess." She rose on her toes to kiss him, then picked up his jacket, shook it out and handed it to him. "Let's go back to the cabin now."

* * *

"Take your clothes off."

Jess turned his head slowly to look at his wife of two days. "What?"

She repeated her request without looking at him. She was rummaging in the heavy canvas bag that held some of her supplies. A sketch pad rested in her lap, and an assortment of pencils had been dumped on the quilt in front of her.

They had taken a picnic lunch out to the stream, along with the fishing gear Matt kept at the cabin, but neither of them was interested in fishing. Caitlin had decided to do some sketches, and Jess had chosen to watch her. Now she wanted another subject.

"You want me to take my clothes off out here?"

She looked around with exaggerated patience. "Why not? There's no one else around for miles. Nobody will see you."

"Why should I?"

"Remember the day I broke my finger?"

He smiled slowly. He remembered it, more for what had happened later than for the accident. The building site hadn't been the most romantic place for a seduction, but it had been perfect.

"I decided that day that I would paint you. Naked. In the desert."

He stood up from the rock where he'd been sitting and placed his hand on his hips. The stance made him look aggressive. "This isn't the desert."

She waved her hand as if it didn't matter. "That part will be filled in later. Come on, Jess. Please?"

He laughed softly and began unbuttoning his shirt. He had adored her since they were children. He had still been very young when he had learned that he could deny her nothing—not the six-year-old child, not the sixteen-year-old girl, and not the thirty-year-old woman. Certainly not his wife.

The shirt was tossed onto the rock behind him. He sat down on it to remove his shoes and socks; then his jeans and briefs joined the shirt. He stood there, tall and strong and naked, his body lean and softly bronzed under the warm September sun. Yes, Caitlin thought, she had to paint him without clothes. He was too magnificent, too perfect, to allow clothes to cover him.

"What do I do?" he asked, a little self-conscious with his

nudity. He wasn't embarrassed about being naked, but being naked outdoors while she was fully clothed—that wasn't quite fair.

"Sit down, if you want. Or you can stand up, or you can come over here and lie down, and I'll work from the rock. It's up to you."

He settled in a reclining position on the boulder. "I ought to make you take your clothes off, too," he muttered.

Caitlin looked up at him and smiled slyly. "I will. Soon enough."

He had never really watched her work before. He was impressed with how absorbed she became in her sketches, rarely noticing the slight breeze, the warm sun, the singing birds or the rushing water. She studied him for long moments, her manner almost clinical, until he was positive she could draw an exact image of his body without another look.

She made several sketches, occasionally asking him to change positions. She did more than she needed, because her subject was so handsome, so pleasing.

The longer she worked, the less detached she became. Jess watched her, saw her eyes turn that liquid color that made him think of heat, made him feel the heat that was flowing through her. He saw her breasts swell, her nipples grow hard. He noticed that her breathing had quickened, and he responded, a pure, sweetly painful swelling.

Caitlin somberly closed her sketch pad and put away her supplies. With hands as steady and sure as her love, she reached up to remove the cotton knit shirt she wore. She rose fluidly to her feet and undid the buttons down the front of her skirt, until enough were loose to allow the skirt to slide off her hips to the ground. Her panties, a tiny scrap of white silk with tinier scraps of lace, followed.

She moved unhurriedly, as graceful as any dancer, her long legs slowly closing the distance between them. With a groan, Jess opened his arms to her, opened himself to her, and she took him, completely, utterly.

He looked up at her as she blocked the sun, her shadow covering him, her body blanketing his. This, he thought with a deep satisfaction, was what it was like to love.

* * *

Caitlin's eyes finally focused on Jess's hand as it soothingly stroked her stomach. His fingers were long and slender. They were calloused, but they were still gentle, even more skilled at arousal and at comforting than ever before. How many times in the past had his touch taken her to the brink of tears because it was so good, so right? Blinking back the moist haze, she knew he still held that power—the power to arouse, to soothe, to hurt and to destroy. She wouldn't take it from him for anything, because it was that power that gave her life and happiness, and that was worth any amount of pain.

"Caitlin?"

"Hmm?"

"A long time ago I told you...there's a big difference between having sex and making love. Do you remember?"

She nodded. A high school boyfriend had been pressuring her to have sex with him. Jess had told her that if the boy cared enough to make love to her, then he would care enough to wait until she was ready. The boyfriend had failed the test. But Jess hadn't. She had gone to him a virgin, and he had been the sweetest, gentlest, most tender lover a woman could ever have.

His hand drifted up to her hair, untangling the long, heavy strands, and he continued in that low, husky voice that she loved. "You're the only woman I've ever made love to, Cait," he said softly. "I just wanted you to know that."

His admission touched her deeply. She had to bite her tongue to keep from blurting out her love for him. Fear and pride kept her from it. She didn't want to hear him say he didn't love her— and saying nothing would mean the same thing—and she didn't want to give him another weapon in his fight against Grant. If Jess ever learned of her love, he would have to be the one to bring it up. He would have to be the first to admit it.

"I missed this," he said. "Holding you...being with you... making love with you."

"Then why didn't you come back?"

She sounded so wistful, so full of longing, that for a moment Jess believed that if he had come back, she would have welcomed him. But that was only wishful thinking. "I was angry," he answered. "I thought you had betrayed me by choosing to stay with Grant. I thought you wanted to be his daughter more than

you wanted to be my wife. I thought you meant what you said—
that you never wanted to see me again.''

"How could you believe any of that?" she asked in a dis-
mayed whisper. "Jess, I *loved* you."

He chilled at her use of the past tense. He wanted to hear her
say it in the present: I love you. He had no right—he was certainly never going to love her again—but he wanted her love,
wanted it as much as he wanted her. "You were pretty damned
convincing, sweetheart." He lifted her away and stood up, reaching for his clothes. "We'd better head back to the cabin."

Caitlin wanted to continue the conversation, but clearly he
didn't. Reluctantly, she got to her feet and quickly dressed.

Jess picked up the picnic basket and the canvas bag. Inside
the open bag was the sketch book. "Can I see your drawings?"

She hesitated. She had no problems with people seeing her
work in progress, but none of that work had ever included Jess.
What if he could see her feelings for her subject? Critics had
often said that her emotions shone through her paintings. If that
was true, and she believed it was, what would Jess see in the
sketches of him?

He bent his head to kiss her forehead. "That's all right. Just
promise I can see the finished painting, okay?"

She gave him a relieved smile. "Okay."

The remaining four days of their honeymoon were unreal. Everything seemed so perfect; they never argued—they didn't even
need words to communicate. Whatever one wanted, so did the
other. Whatever one needed, the other gave. It was hard to believe, there in the private little cabin, that anything bad had ever
happened between them in the real world.

It was hard to believe, Caitlin thought, that Jess was using her.
He seemed as happy, as pleased, as much in love, as she was. It
was a dangerous illusion. If she began believing that Jess cared
for her even half as much as she loved him, she was dooming
herself to a lifetime of heartache when he proved it wasn't so.

It was with mixed feelings that she climbed into the Jeep Saturday morning for the long drive back to Isabel. The past week
with Jess had been the best seven days of her life, and she didn't
want them to end. But they hadn't been real days, and she wanted

too much to believe the illusion. She needed to get back to every-day life, where she knew that Jess didn't love her. Where she could protect herself at least a little against the inevitable pain.

She chose not to tell Grant about their wedding. He had friends in town, none of whom had been invited to the ceremony, but they would have heard about it anyway. They might tell him, but Caitlin wouldn't. Not yet. Not until it couldn't be avoided any longer.

She didn't want to talk it over with Jess. He always tensed at the mention of her father's name, and she hated to see that. Besides, she knew he would agree with her decision. He probably wanted to deliver the news in person so he could see Grant's face. His satisfaction would be so much greater that way.

Work on the house continued at a steady rate. Tom rarely sent Jess out on other jobs; he knew how important it was to get this house completed—both for Jess and Caitlin's sake, and for Lupe, as well. Sometimes Jess felt guilty about it—he knew he wasn't fully earning the salary Tom paid him—but he would make up for it when the house was completed. He would work harder than ever then, in gratitude for his friend's help and understanding.

It was still hard for him to accept that he was a married man, and soon to be a father. He was uncomfortable with Caitlin sometimes, until she touched him or kissed him or made him laugh. The adjustments weren't as easy as he'd expected. After so many years of being on his own, he now had responsibilities.

Then he scolded himself. He had always had a certain responsibility to Caitlin: years ago, before the wedding, and now. Nothing had changed. He had been living in her house since June, had shared her room as her lover since July; now he was sharing it as her husband. Nothing else had changed.

Some days she surprised him at the site with lunch. At first the men on the subcontractors' crews often teased him about his pretty wife, but after a few months the jokes stopped. They liked Caitlin and they respected her husband, but those weren't the reasons for the new respect they extended her. It was the simple matter of her pregnancy. As each week passed, it became more visible. She was so slender that every pound she gained seemed to show up immediately. By the fifth month it was something that no loose-fitting blouse and baggy trousers could hide. Everyone could see she was pregnant, and the men on the crews, mostly family men themselves, didn't make even good-natured jokes about expectant mothers.

Jess loved looking at her. He loved seeing the rounded curve of her belly get bigger every week, knowing that it was his baby that caused it. He was already certain that he was going to love this child in a way he had never loved before. If only he could love the mother, too, his life would be perfect.

He knew he could love her, if he only let himself. Sometimes, when they made love, she seemed to become part of his soul, and he knew then that the love was there, deep inside him. It was fear that kept it inside. Self-preservation. If he loved Caitlin, he had to trust her; if he trusted her, she could destroy him. He wasn't ready to take that chance. Not yet. Maybe not ever.

Chapter 8

The week before Christmas they moved into the new house. It had meant rushing to get the interior work finished, buy the furniture and get it delivered, and get Caitlin's and Lupe's personal things packed and transferred from the Pierce house, but Jess had wanted to spend Christmas there. It seemed fitting to him to start their life in their new home with the holiday celebrations.

The day before Christmas Eve, Caitlin announced to Jess, "I need some sand."

He had awakened in bed alone and gone searching for her. He found her sitting on the dining room floor, surrounded by lunch-sized paper bags and dozens of candles. "Sand?"

"For the *farolitos*."

He sat down in front of her, picking up one of the bags. He hadn't seen *farolitos*, or *luminarias*, in years, although they had always been a tradition at his house. Brown paper bags were filled with a few inches of sand to anchor the short votive candles. They were placed along sidewalks, driveways, porches—even on the roofs of the flat-topped adobe houses—and the candles were lit at dusk. "All right," he agreed. "I'll get some today. How many are you going to have?"

"A hundred or so."

He rolled his eyes, then pulled her to her feet. "And who is going to have the honor of going out in the cold and lighting these 'hundred or so' candles?"

"Why, Jess, I'm six months pregnant. Surely you don't expect me to do it," she said with wide-eyed innocence.

He laughed even as he kissed her. "No, surely not you. Tom's giving me the afternoon off, so I can help you get ready for tonight. You get all the bags and candles ready, and I'll bring the sand back with me around noon, okay?"

"Okay." She kissed the tip of his chin. "You're a pretty good guy, you know that?"

The casually given compliment touched him. Before he could think of a suitable response, the baby kicked, the sensation passing through Caitlin and into Jess through the contact of their bodies. "He's pretty active for this early in the morning," he said.

"She takes after her father," Caitlin teased, putting a slight emphasis on the "she." "I've seen many early mornings when you were far more active than this."

She was referring to the many times he had awakened her with kisses and caresses, followed by sweetly drowsy lovemaking. He couldn't help it, he thought in self-defense. Was it his fault that waking to find her curled up next to him was the most erotic experience he'd ever had? Was he guilty because simply looking at her made him want her? Because touching her made him need her? Was he to blame because the more he had, the more he craved?

"Sorry, lady," he said, not meaning it one bit. "You knew what you were getting when you married me. What makes you so sure that this one's a girl?"

"Ever hear of woman's intuition?" she asked dryly. "I *feel* it, Jess. I really do."

"Are you going to be disappointed if it's a boy?"

She knew all mothers were supposed to say they didn't care about the sex, as long as the child was healthy, but she really wanted a girl—a pretty, delicate little girl, dressed all in ruffles and lace. But a boy—a rough, tough, sturdy little boy like Jess had been—that would be wonderful, too, she conceded. "Of course I won't be disappointed. We'll just have to try again."

He liked the idea that she would be around long enough for

them to try again and again, but he wasn't going to pin his hopes on it. His mother was getting weaker; she'd had to cut her hours at the store, and she spent more and more time in bed, too weak to do much of anything. Soon she would be gone, and when she was gone, Caitlin would have no reason for staying. At the thought, the laughter and joy disappeared from his eyes, replaced by bleakness.

Sometimes, Caitlin thought, he looked so sad that her heart ached for him. She wished he would tell her what was wrong, what brought that sorrow to his dark eyes. But when she asked, he always said "Nothing" and turned away. This time she didn't ask; she simply held him close and offered him wordless comfort. At last she gave him one more pat and straightened. "It'll be all right, Jess," she whispered.

He smiled bittersweetly. Did she have any idea what was bothering him at times like these? He thought not, or she wouldn't be giving him reassurances she had no intention of keeping. Things would never be all right, not if he lost her again. He lifted his hand to brush lightly over her hair. "Cait—" What could he say? Don't leave me. Spend your life with me. Need me. *Love me.* He settled on something much safer. "I'd better get ready for work."

"Do you want breakfast? I can fix it while you get dressed."

"No thanks, hon. I'm going to be late if I don't hurry. But you be sure and eat, okay?" He kissed her forehead and left for their bedroom.

Caitlin settled down on the floor again and reached for the stack of paper bags. She worked slowly, folding the top two inches of the bags to the outside to help strengthen them.

After a few minutes Jess returned, carrying her robe and a pair of slippers. "If you're going to sit on the floor, you need these," he said, pulling her up and sliding the robe around her shoulders.

She laughed softly. "This is the desert, Jess."

"This is winter in the desert, Cait. It gets cold here, too—too cold for my pregnant wife to be sitting on the floor in a flimsy little nightgown."

"You used to like this nightgown."

"I still like the nightgown. I like you in it. But I also like for you to be warm." He tied the belt of the robe, bent and slipped the house shoes onto her feet, then stood up again and looked at her. Suddenly he pressed his mouth to hers in a fierce kiss. "I'll be home soon," he promised before turning away.

Caitlin finished with the bags for the *farolitos* before Lupe got up; then she fixed breakfast for herself and her mother-in-law. As soon as Lupe left for work, there was unpacking to occupy Caitlin's time until Jess returned from work shortly before twelve.

"You look tired," he commented when he saw her.

She patted her stomach. "I don't have as much energy as I used to. This extra weight slows me down a bit. I hate to think what it's going to be like in another two months. I'll probably stay in bed all the time."

"We'll get a housekeeper," he suggested. "You're doing too much, Cait: painting, getting settled in here, taking care of the housework and the cooking and watching over Mom. You need to take it easy."

"There's not much housework, we'll be settled in soon, and I can handle the rest. I don't want a housekeeper. Did you get the sand?"

"Yes, I did. You sit down, and I'll take care of it." He steered her toward a wooden bench against the dining room wall. When she was settled on its thick cushions, he brought in a bag of sand, setting it on the sheet she had spread on the floor.

She watched him work for about five minutes before she joined him. When he started to protest, she cut him off with a kiss. "I can help. I'm sitting down, so how can I get tired? Besides, it's Christmas. You do the sand, and I'll do the candles."

How could he tell her no? But he knew when to bargain. "You can help with this—but you lie down before the party tonight."

She readily agreed. Maybe, if she was lucky, she could get him to lie down with her. That would make an unscheduled rest worthwhile.

Jess didn't join her in bed. He arranged the *farolitos* outside, spacing them about twelve inches apart, on the porch, down the steps, along the sidewalk and the driveway. He cleaned the mess in the dining room and fixed a late lunch for himself and Lupe when she arrived home from work. He set out the boxes of ornaments in the living room, next to the live fir he had put up the night before; then he helped Lupe in the kitchen with the food for the evening's tree-trimming party.

Though their guests were all good friends, Caitlin dressed carefully for the party. She had visited practically every maternity shop and department in Albuquerque before she found her outfit for the evening, but when she saw herself in it, she knew it had been well worth the effort. It was exquisitely simple—black satin pants worn with a dazzling white satin blouse. The blouse was loose and flowed over the bulge of her stomach into a gathered hem that fell at her hips. It didn't hide her pregnancy—not even a tent could do that, she admitted—but it made her look wonderful. More importantly, the rich, lustrous fabric made her *feel* wonderful—even sexy and sensuous.

The tree was trimmed, the food was eaten, the carols were sung, small gifts were exchanged. Through it all, Jess's eyes rarely left his wife. When he looked at her like that, she could almost believe he loved her. She tried not to ever think such thoughts—her disappointment would be even greater if she let herself believe—but tonight she couldn't stop. There was such gentleness in his eyes—tenderness that, despite her awkward heaviness, was tinged with hunger. If he could want her, looking the way she did, he *must* feel something more than fondness.

Finally the guests were gone, Lupe was in bed, and Jess and Caitlin were alone. Only candles lit the living room, and one by one she was blowing them out. She stopped at the last one, next to Jess, and he put his arms around her.

"You are beautiful."

She smiled mistily. Did he know how much she needed to hear that? Not "You look beautiful," as if it were something that could easily change, but "You *are* beautiful." How easy it would be to tell him then, to say the three simple and most important words she knew. "I love you." But she didn't say them; she just continued to smile.

"Are you tired?"

"Not a bit."

"The party's over."

Turning her head to the side, she blew out the last candle, then wrapped her arms around him. "No," she corrected in a husky voice. "It's just become a private party."

The weeks following Christmas were busy ones for Caitlin. She had finished, behind schedule, the four paintings Christopher

Morgan had commissioned, and she'd made a start on the oil painting of Jess. The fatigue that had plagued her through the middle part of her pregnancy was gone; she had more energy and felt better than she had in months. Dr. Ramirez had proclaimed her disgustingly healthy at her last exam. Sometimes even Jess had trouble keeping up with her, and this, he knew, was going to be one of those days.

"Get out of bed," she commanded, her voice floating out of the closet. "We've got things to do today."

He rolled over lazily onto his back. "I can think of plenty of things to do," he said with a grin. "And not one of them requires getting out of bed."

She ducked out in time to see his leer and gave him a sly smile in return. "For heaven's sake, Jess, I'm a very pregnant lady. I waddle instead of walk, and I can't sit on low couches because I need help getting up again. How can you possibly think seductive thoughts about my body?"

That brought him out of bed to draw her into his arms. "I happen to like your body," he said in an erotically low voice. "And you have a cute waddle."

She feigned a jab at his jaw. "Thanks a lot. I really needed that."

"You're beautiful. You're wonderful. You're lovely." He got a handful of clothes from the closet and began dressing. "So what do we have to do today?"

"I have to deliver Christopher's paintings to Melly's."

He scowled, which she had expected, and she laughed, which he had expected. "I suppose he'll be there to pick them up?"

"Yes. And to hand over a check."

"Okay. Then what?"

"Then..." She knew that, in her condition, there was a very good chance he would turn down her "Then...." With her sweetest and most innocent smile, she tried it anyway. "There's snow in the Sandías."

He shook his head. "No."

"Please, Jess."

"No."

"The roads are clear—I called to check. Please."

"You're seven months pregnant. What if you fell?"

"You'll be right beside me. You wouldn't let me fall, would you? Please, Jess—*snow*. I haven't seen snow since last January. Please."

He tried to look stern and forbidding, but he knew he was going to give in. When was the last time he'd told her no and stuck to it? he wondered in disgust. "You'll stay right beside me," he said crossly.

"You won't be able to get rid of me."

"No sledding, no hiking through the woods. We'll just go up, see the snow and come home."

"That'll be fine." She was too smart to gloat over her victory. They weren't at the mountaintop yet, and Jess could change his mind any time before they got there. She gave him a light kiss and began putting on her clothes.

In the early months of her pregnancy she had been amused by the expandable waists of the jeans and trousers she found in maternity shops. Now she was grateful; she had outgrown her regular jeans three or four months ago. She pulled on an outsized sweater in vibrant red, a pair of jeans, heavy socks, and a pair of sturdy hiking boots. Sitting on the bed, she stuck her feet out so Jess could lace the boots for her. Another few pounds, she thought ruefully, and she wouldn't even be able to see her feet, much less put shoes on them.

Jess delivered Caitlin and the paintings to Melly's gallery, then went to find a parking space. He returned to the store just as Christopher Morgan was arriving. He warily answered Morgan's greeting, then held the door for the other man.

Caitlin was sitting behind the counter, talking to Melly and Tanya. Christopher greeted her with a smile that practically beamed. "Caitlin. You look wonderful. Melly told me about your accident. I hope everything's all right now."

She slowly got to her feet and came around the counter to take the hand extended. "I'm fine. Sorry about the delay on the paintings, but...things happened."

He looked directly at her stomach, then at Jess. "Yes. I can see that. Congratulations."

He sounded as sincere as Grant Pierce would, Jess thought viciously. He had to fight the desire to remove Caitlin's hand from the other man's grip; he hated seeing him touch her while he mouthed sentiments he didn't mean.

"Thank you. You've met my husband Jess, haven't you? Caitlin gently tugged on her hand, and Christopher released it.

"Yes, we met the last time. I guess it's you I should be congratulating. I hope you're very happy together."

Jess slipped his arm around Caitlin's shoulders. "We are," he agreed coolly.

Caitlin was amazed by Jess's jealousy. Here she looked like something that had been beached on the sand, and he was worried that Christopher Morgan might actually be interested in her. She gave him a reassuring smile before turning the conversation back to the paintings.

A half hour later they left both the gallery and a very satisfied customer behind. "Now the mountains," Caitlin said.

Jess still didn't think it was wise, but she looked so excited that he couldn't bear to let her down. "All right," he said, tucking her hand inside his. "Now the mountains. Do you want to take the tram or drive?"

The drive was scenic, but the tram to Sandía Peak was quicker. It took her only a moment to choose it.

The snow was about two feet deep, packed and cold and wonderful, she declared. She was all in favor of hiking the mile and a half to the crest, with its spectacular view, but Jess refused. It answered his question of that morning. He was finally able to tell her no and mean it.

After half an hour of tramping around in the snow, Caitlin turned to him. "Do you remember the last time we came here?"

He nodded. It had been a hot summer day, and they had decided to escape the heat with a picnic on the mountain. They'd made the winding drive to the top and hiked into the forest, far off the trails, far away from the other hikers. He had very quietly asked her to marry him, and he'd given her the ring, sliding it onto her finger. Then they had made love, swearing to love each other for eternity.

How short eternity had been. A few months later he'd been gone.

"We'd better head back," he said abruptly. He didn't want to remember anything else.

Before she agreed to go, Caitlin put her arms around his waist and hugged him tight. "I'm very glad you came back," she whispered. "I'm very glad you wanted me." Even if he could never love her again, she would be grateful that he wanted her.

When they arrived home a few hours later, Lupe was anxiously waiting, pacing the length of the living room. Her face was lined with stress, and she was mumbling a soft prayer when they walked in. Jess and Caitlin exchanged glances, then hurried to her.

"Mom, what's wrong?" Jess demanded, wrapping his arms around her. "Are you all right?"

"Yes, yes, I'm fine." She looked up at Jess, then swung her gaze around to Caitlin. "Your father's back. He got in today. He's looking for you."

Jess found Caitlin in her studio, staring out the window. The Sandía Mountains were out there, so far away that they were barely visible.

She looked up when he approached, but her face remained expressionless.

"We have to tell him."

She nodded once.

He took her hands in his. They were cold. "He'll wonder where you are. He'll worry about you."

She nodded again. He was right. She had to face her father today. Soon.

How many times in the months since they were married had she picked up the phone and dialed the number, only to hang up before the sequence was complete? How many times had she sat down at her desk with pen and paper to write to him? But she never had. Fear had kept her from it. "He'll be so angry."

"I'll go with you, Cait. I won't cause trouble. I promise." He managed a crooked grin. "Look, we'll handle it, all right? We'll deal with it."

"That's easy for you to say, Jess. He's always been angry with you. I don't know if I *can* deal with it."

"Oh, Cait." He wrapped his arms around her and held her as close as he could. "Do you want me to tell him?"

She had expected and dreaded his offer. If he wanted vengeance, saying yes would mean playing right into his hands. Having her permission to confront Grant with the news of their marriage would be the ultimate victory in his game. "No," she said with a soft sigh. "Maybe I should go alone."

"No." Twice in one day, he'd stood up to her. "I'm the one he hates, Cait. I'm the one he'll blame." He leaned forward to kiss her forehead and found her skin cool and sticky. "Let me change clothes, okay? It'll just take a minute."

His hands fumbled with buttons and zippers. It seemed to take him forever to get changed, and the more he tried to hurry, the longer it took him.

God, how he had dreaded this! His eyes fell to his wedding band for assurance. Caitlin was his wife. They were married, legally bound, and they were going to have a baby. Grant couldn't change that. By God, he wouldn't let him!

But it would take a fight, and a fight was what had driven him from Caitlin years ago. Jess was going to have to fight for Caitlin, their marriage, their baby, and his life, and he honestly didn't know whose side she would take.

The drive to the Pierce house was silent. Jess gripped the steering wheel until his knuckles turned white, and Caitlin sat huddled against the door. With her head bowed and her eyes open, she recited a silent prayer: *Prove me wrong, Jess. Show me it's not a game.*

He parked behind Grant's brand-new Cadillac and shut off the engine. A glance at Cait showed that she was pale and nervous and frightened. He wanted to pull her into his arms and hold her, assure her it would be all right. But he didn't. He wasn't certain that she wanted his assurances. At that moment he wasn't sure what "all right" would mean to her.

She wasn't ready. God help her, she wasn't ready. She had known for months that Grant was coming back in January, but she had preferred to ignore it. If she didn't think about it, maybe it would all just magically work out. But nothing had worked out; Grant was home, and in a minute she was going to tell him that she and Jess were married. She didn't have the vaguest idea how to go about it.

Grant answered her knock, opening only one of the double doors. Jess was out of sight behind the other. "Caitlin!" he exclaimed. "Oh, honey, it's good to see you!" He swept her into his arms for a hug, then felt the difference in her body. He set her down and stepped back, his eyes dropping to her rounded stomach.

His blond hair was almost completely gray, she noticed, but his eyes were as blue as ever. As sharp and as critical as ever. "Caitlin...you're pregnant." He sounded surprised and hurt that she had kept the news of her pregnancy from him.

She clasped her hands together as if she could hide her belly behind them. "Yes, Dad, I am," she replied softly. "About seven months."

"My God, honey—" Then he saw her rings. All the joy and happiness were gone, replaced by confusion. "Are you married, too?" he asked harshly. "Or is that just for show?"

"I'm married."

"For how long?"

"About five months."

He swore softly. "And where is this husband of yours? Is he afraid to come around?"

"No, sir." Jess stepped into view, laying his hands on Caitlin's shoulders. "I've never been afraid of you."

Grant stiffened. He straightened to his full height, putting him on eye level with Jess. He cursed again, then took a step toward them before stopping. "You bastard," he said in a low, deadly voice.

Caitlin felt every muscle in Jess's body go taut. He was hard as rock against her back. Please, she prayed. Please don't do it, Jess.

The mere sight of Grant filled Jess with hatred. He was amazed that he had the capacity to feel any emotion besides his desire for Caitlin so intensely. He clenched his fists and gritted his teeth while he fought for control. He had promised her that he wouldn't hurt her. He had promised that he wouldn't cause trouble.

But Grant had started this trouble, his anger reminded him, over fifteen years ago. Jess only wanted to end it.

"How could you do it, Caitlin?" Grant asked. "Was it the baby? Did you marry him because you're carrying his brat? There are better ways to take care of problems like that, Caitlin. You could have had an abortion. You *should* have had an abortion."

Jess's control had reached its limit. "Let's go, Cait," he commanded.

"She's not going anywhere with you." Grant reached out to grasp her arm, his voice softening when he spoke to her. "Come inside, honey. We need to talk."

Jess tightened his hold on her. "She's not going anywhere *without* me," he warned.

"It'll be a cold day in hell before I'll invite trash like you into my house!" Grant roared. His face was mottled red, and his eyes were wild. He seemed almost insane, out of control. Jess was deeply grateful he hadn't allowed Caitlin to come alone.

"That's what you told me about marrying your daughter, too," Jess said with an easy, dangerous smile. "Let go of her now, before I break every bone in your hand."

Caitlin was numb. If Jess hadn't been holding her so tightly, she probably would have collapsed. Her father's hatred of Jess was far more vicious than she had expected. She was stunned by its power.

"We came over here to tell you that we're married and that Cait's all right. Now we're going home." Jess's voice was cool and commanding. "When you've calmed down, when you can speak and think and act in a rational manner, you can see her again. Until then, stay away from my wife."

When he turned to leave, he had to guide Caitlin's footsteps. She looked back at her father just before they reached the corner. The hatred in his face made her wince. Sadly she turned back to Jess, leaning against him for support.

He'll be so angry. That had been a masterpiece of understatement. She wanted to laugh, but if she did, she would cry, too. She had expected anger; she hadn't expected outrage and fury, hadn't expected such consuming, violent hatred—or such pain.

Jess lifted her into the truck from the driver's side. He wanted her close. He wanted to feel her next to him on the way home. She was grateful for that. She was grateful for him.

Her prayer had been answered. He hadn't taunted Grant, hadn't gloated over their marriage. Maybe a few of his remarks had been a little smug, but she could accept smugness. Still, that didn't mean that her theory of revenge was wrong. It didn't mean that he might possibly want Caitlin for herself. He could still be planning to use her somehow, some way.

When they got home Jess switched off the engine, then put his arm around Caitlin. "It's all right. Give him a little time."

"A little time?" she echoed. "It'll take the rest of our lives! Jess, he hates us!"

"Not you, Cait. He'll never hate you. Honey, he's angry. He never expected to come home and find you married and pregnant, and he sure as hell didn't expect me to be the one responsible. Let him get used to the idea that I'm back, that we're together again. He'll come around."

She shook her head, her hair rubbing against his chin. "He'll never get used to it. He'll never accept it. For God's sake, Jess, he thinks I should have had an abortion!"

He didn't argue, didn't try to convince her of anything. He just held her and stroked her. "Don't worry, honey," he whispered. "Don't worry."

She wearily shut her eyes. In one short day her life had changed from almost perfect into a nightmare. How could she *not* worry?

The next few days were tense in the Trujillo household. Lupe tried to talk to Caitlin, but nothing she said could make a difference. Jess tried to comfort her, but she was too worried, too hurt by her father, too unsure of her husband, to be comforted.

Tuesday, when she went to the office to meet Jess for lunch, she saw her father again. Unable to find a parking space near the building that housed Tom's company, she had to walk a block. A few yards from the entrance, she met Grant coming out of the newspaper offices.

For a moment she thought he was going to walk on past without acknowledging her, and her heart sank to her toes. Was this what it had been like for Lupe when she was pregnant with Jess? Had her family pretended not to know her?

Then he lifted his eyes to her face and said in a low, cool voice, "Hello, Caitlin."

"Hi, Dad." She shivered, more from the chill in his eyes and his voice than from the weather, and pulled her coat tighter. "You—you look good."

"You don't."

Her first instinct was to pull the coat even tighter, to try to hide inside it. Her second, the one she followed, was to stand straighter. "Yes, Dad, I do. I look better and feel better than I have in years."

"You're a fool, Caitlin. You don't even have the sense to know that he's using you," Grant said with a sneer. "He's not interested in you, not after all these years. Not after what you did. You should have gone with him that night. If you had really loved him, you would have. He wants to hurt you, Caitlin. He wants to hurt both of us."

She felt as if he had struck her, but she managed to hide it. Was he right? Was it obvious to everyone but her that Jess didn't love her, didn't even want her? Could everyone else see that he wanted only to avenge himself on the Pierces?

"You're wrong, Dad," she said, her voice soft and shaky.

"You could have done so much better than him."

"I don't believe that. I don't believe there is anyone better."

Grant stared at her, his eyes hard. Then he sighed. "You're in love with him again, aren't you? Or did you ever stop loving him?" His warning was delivered in a soft, concerned voice, but it hurt just the same. "You're a fool, Caitlin. He's going to break your heart—just like the last time."

Inside the office, Jess paced restlessly. Tom watched for a minute, then reached for a trade magazine. "She's only a couple of minutes late," he pointed out.

"Caitlin is rarely late, and never without a reason."

Tom didn't try to pacify him. He knew that his friend had been under a lot of stress since his father-in-law's return. If he wanted to get a little paranoid, that was his right.

Jess went to the door and looked out at the street. Then he saw her, standing with her father, in front of the store next door. He cursed softly and reached for his coat.

Tom came to stand beside him. "Let them talk."

"Are you mad? He's trying to convince her to get rid of me and the baby and come back home to him. I don't need that, Tom."

When Jess reached for the doorknob, Tom grabbed his arm. He was smaller, but he was strong.

"He loves her, Jess, in a weird kind of way. Maybe she can

work things out with him if you're not around. You know you make the old man crazy. Let her talk to him alone."

Jess could have freed his arm if he'd really wanted to. But what Tom said made sense. The sight of Jess was liable to send Grant into a rage—the same way the sight of Grant set him off. Maybe Caitlin could talk to him. Maybe she could make him understand.

"You don't need to worry, Jess," Tom said, talking in a low, calming voice. "Caitlin's not going to leave you because that's what Pierce wants."

"She did before."

"That was years ago. She was hardly more than a kid. Things are different now."

Different how? Jess wondered bitterly. For better or worse? Eight years ago she had been in love with him, but she had still chosen her father. This time they didn't even have the bond of love, just that of marriage. Would it be enough? Would it keep her with him?

He stood at the door and watched them talk, and wondered where he could go if he left New Mexico again. He had promised himself that he wouldn't leave Isabel, and he knew he couldn't go while his mother still lived. But once she was dead, if he lost Caitlin, too, he knew he couldn't stay.

She loved her father so much. If she loved *him* even half that much, maybe he'd stand a chance against Grant. Maybe the baby would be enough to keep her with him. Maybe, maybe, maybe. The most useless word in the English language.

"What happened the last time wasn't all Jess's fault," Caitlin said softly. "It was your fault, too, and mine. You had no right interfering in my life. You have no right to do it now."

"I was trying to make you see the truth! He's a bastard, Caitlin—"

"And so am I!" she interrupted. "Why does that make him such an awful person? Is it his fault Lupe and Roberto didn't marry? Is it my fault that Mom and my father didn't marry?"

Grant looked stricken. Not once, in the almost nine years that she'd known the truth, had she ever brought up the circumstances of her birth. Not once had she ever referred to Claire's lover as her father.

"You hate Jess because he's Roberto's son, because Lupe chose Roberto over you," she went on gently. "You hate him because he's illegitimate, and it would damage your Pierce pride if anyone ever found out that I'm illegitimate. By attacking him, you draw suspicion away from me. Those are ridiculous reasons for hating someone, Dad. You've never been able to see all the good things about him. He *is* a good man. He's kind and gentle and loving and proud and honest and hardworking. I *do* love him, Dad."

"It'll never last. He'll never stay with you."

She smiled sadly. "Then I'll have him for as long as he does stay. I'll have his child, and I'll have my love for him. I will always love him, Dad."

"We'll see how long your 'love' lasts when he walks out on you," Grant said confidently. "You'll come back home then—back where you belong. No matter how many pretty words he tells you, he'll never be able to love you the way I do." He smiled, but it was a cold, emotionless thing. "You'll come back to me, Caitlin."

He stepped around her and walked toward his car. Caitlin turned and watched him, her forehead wrinkled in a frown. He was wrong, she insisted. Jess wouldn't leave her. He might never love her, but he wouldn't leave her. He had promised. Then the absurdity of that statement struck her, and she laughed. She was putting a lot of faith in the promises of a man who didn't love her, who might very well have married her only as part of a game.

Grant was right about one thing, at least: she *was* a fool. A fool in love.

As soon as she stepped inside the door, she knew Jess had seen her with Grant. It had taken every bit of his willpower not to join them on the sidewalk; she could see it in his eyes. He hugged her, warming her with his body, but he made no reference to her father.

After a long time he stepped back, but he didn't release her. He studied her face while his hands moved caressingly over her arms; then he smiled faintly. "Let's have some lunch," he suggested softly.

* * *

Isabel was a small town—Jess realized that—but it seemed that every time he and Caitlin left the house together over the next week, they ran into Grant. Each time it was harder for him to be civil to the man. On Saturday he gave up trying.

They had gone to the grocery store and met Grant there. Ignoring Jess, he had invited—no, commanded—Caitlin to come to dinner that evening. Alone. Maybe if she hadn't seemed to be considering the invitation, Jess wouldn't have gotten angry. But she was considering it.

He put his arm around her shoulders and pulled her to his side. "I told you last week: my wife isn't going anywhere without me," he warned in a soft, almost friendly voice.

Finally Grant looked at him. "You don't own her."

"Oh, yes, I do. She's mine now, Grant. My wife. My property. You thought you would never have to give her up, but I took her from you. Now she's mine." He smiled smugly. "I can call you 'Grant.' There's no reason for me to call my *father-in-law* 'Mr. Pierce,' is there? I'm part of the family now."

"You'll never be part of my family!" Grant snarled. "Caitlin may have been stupid enough to marry you, but she's not stupid enough to stay with you. It won't be long before she realizes what you're doing. Then she'll leave you."

Jess felt a twinge of pain deep in his stomach. Of course Grant would know that was his biggest fear—losing her. He would torment him with it if Jess showed how much it hurt. So he smiled broadly, as if he couldn't care less whether Caitlin left him, and said, "She may leave me, but you'll never have her back—not the way you used to have her. You'll never be able to forget that she married me, that she slept with me, or that she's carrying my baby inside her. You can never make her clean again, Grant."

It was true, Grant realized. He could never forget. He seemed to age ten years with that realization. He looked defeated. "Why did you do it?" he asked softly. "Caitlin, why did you give yourself to that bastard to be used against me?"

The sorrow in his voice could have broken her heart, if Jess's words hadn't already completed the job. He *had* used her. He didn't care if she left him, if she went back to her father, because knew Grant would never forget that Jess had had her. He 'd live with the shame forever. So would she.

She was going to be ill. "I want to go home," she said. But she couldn't find her voice, so the words had no sound and went unheard. She tried again. Clutching at Jess's arm, she forced his attention to her. "I want to go home. *Now*. Take me home, Jess. I want to go home!" Tears were streaming down her face, but she didn't notice them, didn't feel them. She didn't feel anything but the overwhelming urge to be sick.

He grinned sarcastically. "Excuse us, Grant. I'm going to take *my wife* to our house. We'll see you soon."

They were walking down the aisle when Grant called out one last question. "Trujillo, they say revenge is sweet. Is that true?"

He looked over his shoulder and smiled. "Very true," he replied, and Caitlin's world shattered. She had lost everything: her dreams, her trust, her faith and her future. It was all gone, with nothing left except a love that was full of pain and empty of hope.

Jess glanced at Caitlin frequently on the drive home. Her tears hurt, but he knew instinctively that if he touched her, she would pull away. She had to be angry with him. He had promised—he had promised so much. To be good to her, not to start trouble, not to hurt her. The scene in the store must have disgusted her; it had sure as hell left him disgusted with himself.

This time he couldn't blame Grant, or Caitlin. He was the one responsible. He shouldn't have resented being ignored; he shouldn't have minded if Caitlin wanted to have dinner alone with her father. He shouldn't have called her his property. And he certainly shouldn't have displayed her like a prize he had won in battle.

He had done it all because he was afraid. Sure, there had been some satisfaction in having the upper hand with Grant for once, but the deeper reason was fear. If he lost Caitlin... He needed her. Didn't she understand how much he needed her to live? How much he loved her?

He smiled bitterly. This was a hell of a time to get the courage to put that name to his feelings. He'd known it for a long time, but he had chosen to hide behind words like want and need and like. Now it was probably too late. If he told her now that he loved her, she wouldn't believe him—or, worse, she wouldn't care.

As soon as the truck stopped in the driveway Caitlin slid to the ground and rushed inside the house. Jess was right behind her. "Cait!" he called.

She made it to the bathroom just in time, where she was miserably, violently ill.

Jess knelt beside her with a cool damp washcloth. She pushed his hand away, but he was insistent. He bathed her face, then lifted her into his arms. As he settled her into the bed, his words whispered over her. "I'm sorry, Cait. Honey, I'm sorry."

She cried, and she let him hold her, although she found no comfort in his arms, or in his soft words of apology. She was too cold inside. He couldn't touch her—not with his words, not with his gestures. But he wanted to hold her, so she let him.

At last, when she was calmer, he released her and sat up. "I'll apologize to him, Cait. I'll go over there now."

She blew her nose on a tissue. "What good is an apology, Jess?" she asked with a weary sigh. "The damage is already done." Feeling light-headed, she raised herself awkwardly from the bed and went to the window to stare out.

Jess watched her for a long time, dread growing in his stomach. He needed to talk to her, to apologize, to make her understand, but he didn't have an idea in hell of how to go about it. How could he make her understand the way Grant made him feel? How could he make her understand his fear? How could he make her accept his love?

"You couldn't resist it, could you? You were just waiting for the right time—the time when you could hurt him the most."

"No, Cait, that's not—" He ran his fingers through his hair. "Yes, I did want to hurt him. But not you, Cait. I never wanted to hurt you. Honey, please... I was mad, okay? I shouldn't have said any of those things, and I'm sorry I did, but I was mad! For God's sake, Cait, haven't you ever lost your temper and said something you didn't mean?"

They both thought about the night he'd left her when she had told him that she didn't want to see him anymore. On their honeymoon she had claimed that she hadn't meant it. She knew he was waiting for her to agree, to say, yes, she sometimes said things in anger that were the opposite of the truth. Instead she smiled coldly. "No, Jess, I haven't."

She had lied to him on their honeymoon, he realized in a sickening rush. Everything she had told him, everything she had done—even her lovemaking—had been a lie. That deepened his pain, and his eyes became empty black pools of nothingness. "How do you keep all your lies straight, Caitlin?"

She heard the pain in his voice, and it pleased some perverse, mean spirited part of her. Now Jess could pay. Now he could be the one who was hurt. He had hurt her so deeply that she wasn't sure she could survive, but now it was her turn to inflict a little pain on him. Let him see how it felt. "It comes naturally," she replied.

He walked to the door, then came back. There was a question he should have asked months ago, but he hadn't had the courage. He wasn't any braver now, but he had to have an answer. He had to know the truth. "Why did you marry me, Cait?"

The answer came straight from her heart. *I love you, Jess. God help me, I never stopped loving you. I wanted you, wanted anything you could give me, any part of you I could have.*

She clenched her jaw so the words couldn't get out. He didn't want her love. He didn't want her. But he was waiting for an answer, and she knew he wouldn't leave her alone until she gave it. "I wanted a baby."

"You didn't need marriage for that."

"I wanted her to have a father. I didn't want her to be branded a bastard, like you." As an afterthought, she added, "Or like me." The fact that her illegitimacy had been kept a secret didn't matter; she knew, and so did others.

He could accept that. It didn't make him feel any better, but children were one of the reasons he'd given for marrying her. He could live with that.

But he couldn't leave it alone. He had to push. He had to be sure. "Is that all?"

She couldn't meet his eyes. If she looked too long into their soft, dark sadness, she would break down and tell him the real reason. Then he would know that he had achieved everything he'd set out to do. She turned to look out the window.

"Are there any other reasons?"

If she continued with the lies, she would drive him away as surely as Grant had done before. But Jess was driving her away— he had admitted to using her; he'd even seemed amused by it. There was nothing left between them but her love, and she would not, *could not,* let him know about it. Then his victory would be complete. So would her loss.

She turned slowly and looked at him. "Your mother is dying," she said quietly. "I would do anything in the world to make her happy."

She had no way of knowing that her reply was the one thing he had feared from the day she'd agreed to marry him. She had never known of his suspicions, as he had long ago forgotten hers. She didn't know that, with those soft-spoken words, she had destroyed his world, as his angry words had destroyed hers.

He walked to her, brought his hands up to her face, lowered his head and gently, slowly, hungrily kissed her. The way he held her kept their bodies apart, blocked by his arms, so the only contact they made was through their mouths and his hands. That was enough for Caitlin. She kissed him back, unwillingly at first, then with the full passion of her anger, her pain and her love.

Jess raised his head. Still holding her face, he looked down into her eyes. "Tell me now, Cait. Tell me you married me only to make my mother happy."

Heated longing had rushed through her, shutting down her mind, swelling her breasts, making her need. It took a long moment for her to comprehend his soft demand. When she did, she felt cold again, as if all the warmth was gone forever from her life. She shivered, and he saw it as distaste for his touch. Still, he didn't let her go.

"Tell me."

Unwilling to lie anymore, she avoided answering. "Leave me alone, Jess."

His hands tightened. "Tell me, dammit."

"Let go of me!" He was inflicting real pain on her, his palms squeezing her head, his fingertips tangled in her hair. Tears returned to her eyes. "Leave me alone!"

"I want to know the truth. Just once you can tell me the truth, can't you?" he demanded nastily. "Have you told so many lies, lived so many lies, that you don't recognize the truth anymore? Did you marry me because of my mother?"

She shrank back from the anger in his voice—the same way she shrank from her father. Furious with her cowardice, she drew herself tall. "Yes!" she shouted. "Yes, I did! Now are you satisfied?"

He turned and walked away from her, closing the door behind him without a click. He walked through the house, out to his truck and drove away.

Satisfied? He could never be satisfied with less than her love, and that was one thing he could never have. Why had he asked? Why had he forced an answer from her? For months he had suspected the truth, but he had been happy not knowing. Now he wished to God that he still didn't know. Not knowing was better than losing everything.

Caitlin listened to the truck leave, then sank to the floor, not caring that she would find it almost impossible to get up again without help. She was an awful, horrible person. So he had used her. What did it matter? He had been good to her. He had been kind and gentle, and he had treated her better than most men treated wives they claimed to love.

She couldn't blame him for not loving her. He had apologized—God, he had apologized over and over and over—but that hadn't been enough for her. No, she'd had to punish him, had to hurt him. She'd had to drive him away.

She wanted to run after him, to tell him the truth, to beg him to forgive her. She wanted to beg him not to leave her.

But it was too late for that. He was already gone.

Chapter 9

Jess didn't return home that evening. Caitlin didn't even try to explain his absence to Lupe. How could she repeat the lies she'd told her husband? But explanations weren't necessary. Her puffy eyes and red nose were enough to tell Lupe that something was seriously wrong between Caitlin and Jess.

"Did you see Grant today?" Lupe asked while Caitlin set the table for dinner.

"Yes, we did."

"Was it bad?"

Caitlin closed her eyes for an instant and saw Grant's anger and Jess's triumph. "Yes, it was."

"There are always problems, Caitlin, but they can be worked out. It takes effort and patience and compromise, but it can be done."

She sadly shook her head. "Not when there are three people involved who want different things, and two of them have never heard the word compromise." Suddenly tired, she sank into the chair across from Lupe and rested one hand on her stomach.

"Being pregnant takes a lot out of you, doesn't it?" Lupe asked with a sympathetic smile.

"It's just the stress. I really felt great before..." Before Grant returned. Before she'd ruined any chance of success for her marriage.

Lupe patted her hand. "They'll settle their differences, Caitlin. They'll probably never like each other, but they'll learn to get along."

"How can you be so sure of that?"

"Because they'll both learn that the only way they can be part of your life is to accept each other. Neither of them wants to give you up, so they'll learn to tolerate each other."

"I wish that were true. Right now I don't think Jess can tolerate *me*, much less my father." She rose from her chair when the timer went off and took a casserole from the oven. It was one of Jess's favorites; she hadn't realized it when she put it together. Now it served as just yet another reminder that he wasn't home.

Neither of them ate much. Lupe's appetite had become nonexistent with the progress of the disease; she forced herself to eat each day for the sake of living. Caitlin was too upset to be hungry; after a few bites she pushed her plate away. "I hurt him, Lupe."

She had found no pleasure in his pain; it served only to increase hers. She had accused him of seeking revenge, but wasn't that what she had done by lying to deliberately hurt him? She had refused to accept his explanation—that anger was responsible for the things he'd said to her father—while at the same time her own anger had been prompting her to lie.

"Hurting is part of loving. If you give yourself to another, you also give that person the power to hurt you. In return, you get the power to forgive."

Caitlin opened her mouth to point out that Jess didn't love her, but the words wouldn't come out. If Lupe wanted to believe he'd married her for love, let her. It was easier for both of them: it made Lupe happy, and it prevented Caitlin from admitting the truth. As long as she didn't say it or hear it, it was easier to ignore, easier to pretend.

"What if he doesn't come back?" she whispered.

Lupe smiled soothingly. "Of course he'll come back. He isn't going to abandon you or the baby—or me, for that matter. He'll be back when he's calmer. You're tired, Caitlin. Go lie down. I'll clean up in here."

Caitlin changed into a nightgown and got into bed, but she couldn't sleep. The bed seemed so big, and the sheets smelled faintly of Jess. Where was he? What was he doing? Would he come back to her?

She knew he would come home—but not to her. Lupe had been right about one thing. He wouldn't abandon his baby or his mother. He was angry with Caitlin—he probably hated her—but he wouldn't leave as long as his mother lived.

Once Lupe went to bed, the house grew silent. Caitlin lay on her back, staring at the ceiling. The moon rose, casting its shadows through the window, and continued its journey through the sky. The hours passed slowly.

The bedside clock showed five-thirty-five when the sound of Jess's truck broke the early morning silence. Caitlin sat up in bed. Her hands were shaking; her throat was dry. What was she going to say to him? How could she make him understand that she had lied? The truth seemed the logical choice. She could tell him that she loved him, that she'd been so hurt to find out for sure that he'd married her to repay her father that she'd wanted to make him suffer, too. And he wouldn't believe a word of it. Not now. If she had loved him, he'd reason, she would have said so sooner. She wouldn't have waited until their marriage was falling apart.

No, she couldn't admit her love, not yet. All she could do was apologize and hope—no, pray—that it would be enough.

Jess didn't turn on any lights; he knew his way well enough. He walked slowly to his bedroom and opened the door. Damn, she was awake. He had stayed out so late hoping that sheer exhaustion would make her fall asleep, so he wouldn't have to talk to her.

He said nothing. He sat down on the bed and removed his boots, setting them neatly on the floor. Next he pulled his shirt free from his jeans and unsnapped it. It landed in a heap on the floor, followed by his socks. He didn't take his jeans off before he lay down.

That hurt Caitlin more than anything. She could understand him not wanting to talk to her, or even look at her, but she couldn't stand it that he wouldn't even undress to go to bed. If either of the extra bedrooms had a bed in it, she had no doubt that he'd be sleeping in it instead of with her.

"Jess?"

He turned his back to her.

"Jess, please."

He closed his eyes and deliberately slowed his breathing. Maybe she'd give up and leave him alone, so he could get some sleep. God knew he needed it.

"Jess, let me talk to you. Please."

Finally he rolled onto his back, but he didn't look at her. "I'm tired," he said, pronouncing the words distinctly. "It's almost six o'clock in the morning, and I am drunk, and I am tired, and I really don't want to hear anything you have to say."

Tears filled her eyes. "That's not fair, Jess," she softly accused. "I've been waiting all night..."

Then he looked at her. The room was dark, but he could make out her features. "There are a lot of places I could have spent the night," he said coldly, "and I'd prefer any one of them over this house and this bed with you. But my mother is here, and she would worry if I didn't come home. That's the only reason I'm here. Not for you, not for your baby, but for my mother."

Your baby. The words and the meaning behind them chilled Caitlin so thoroughly that she could do nothing. She wanted to cry, but the tears wouldn't come. She wanted to run from the room and the house, but her legs wouldn't move. He hated her so much that he also hated their baby. Her baby. Had all his claims of wanting children been lies, or had his love for this baby been destroyed simply because it was also a part of her?

She mumbled something and forced herself out of bed. The wood floor was cold beneath her feet, but she didn't notice. She found her robe on the back of a chair in the corner, slipped it on and left the room.

Jess rubbed his eyes, feeling the moisture there. He was just tired. It had been a long night, and he was tired. He wasn't crying. He had nothing left to cry over.

Since business was never booming in Isabel, Tom Mendez often made bids on construction projects in Albuquerque; over three-quarters of their work was in the city. Jess had rarely been sent on any of those jobs; because of Lupe's illness and Caitlin's pregnancy, Tom had always kept him in Isabel, close to home.

Now, though, Jess began requesting work out of town. When Tom questioned him about his reasons, he said he didn't want any special treatment from the boss. Besides, now that Lupe had quit her job at Carmen's store, she was home with Caitlin. If anything happened to either of them, the other would be there to help, and Jess was just a phone call or two away.

Tom knew those were lies. He could see the truth in his friend's eyes; he could hear it in his voice. He was hurting— hurting badly. There was no more casual conversation between Jess and the rest of the crew, most of them old friends. Dinner invitations for him and his wife were turned down without exception. There was never any mention of Caitlin, no more lunch dates, no interest in getting home each day. No more laughter, and no more joy.

Tom couldn't question him. His moods were changeable: one day surly and argumentative, the next distant and withdrawn. Whatever his problems, Tom couldn't help him unless he asked for help. All he could do was grant his friend's requests for the out of town jobs.

Caitlin hated the new jobs. They meant Jess left the house earlier and got home later, if he got home at all. More often than not he didn't come home, and he didn't call. She assumed he was all right; apparently he always made it to work the next morning, or Tom would have called.

If she could talk to him, she would offer to move out of the house. It wasn't fair that he felt it necessary to avoid his own home because of her. She didn't know where she'd go, but she had plenty of money to find a place for herself in the city.

But she couldn't talk to him. The few evenings he did come home, he showered, ate dinner and stayed in whatever room she wasn't in until bedtime. He still slept in their room, but he never seemed to notice that she was beside him. He never looked at her, never talked to her, never touched her. He was punishing her, she thought unhappily, and he was doing a damned fine job of it. She had thought nothing could be worse than living without him, but this was.

This was the most horrible existence she could imagine.

It was morning, and Jess was home. Mornings when he woke up in his own bed were rare, but last night he had forced himself to return to the house after an evening at Rusty's Bar in town. He'd been too tired to make the drive to the nearest motel on the outskirts of Albuquerque, so he had come home and pretended that Caitlin wasn't there. He was getting pretty good at that.

His alarm on the nightstand was set to go off in ten minutes. He reached over to shut it off, then turned onto his back. He rolled his head slowly to the left, knowing what he would see, needing to see it.

She was still so damned beautiful. In sleep her expression was gentle and relaxed, open and unguarded. For once the sadness was gone from her face. In sleep she could forget the bad—and everything in her life right now was bad, he bitterly acknowledged. Soon she would be free. Soon everything would be right again, because she would be free of Jess.

Dear God, how could he stand it? How could he lose her a second time—not just her, but also their child—and survive? He told himself that he would learn. Every hour he spent away from her, every day he made it through, every night he spent without her—each was a victory, however small. He was learning to live without her, but he was dying inside.

It was time to get up, but he didn't move. Just a few more minutes. He needed a few more minutes.

He wanted to make love to her. Despite her pregnancy, he wanted her so badly. If he could make love to her one more time, maybe she would see or feel how much he loved her. Maybe she would want him, the way he wanted her.

He turned to face her, supporting his weight on one bent arm. With a hand that trembled, he lifted the sheet and the blanket from her, moving them to her waist. She slept on her back, unable to lie on her stomach and uncomfortable on her side. His hand moved slowly inside the V-neck of her nightgown to gently cup one swollen breast, and his thumb stroked lightly over the tip.

Caitlin awoke almost instantly to find Jess staring down at her. The emotions in his eyes were fierce. Hunger. Desperation. The same feelings surged inside her. "Jess?" Her voice was a mere whisper. She couldn't find the strength to raise it.

He continued to stroke her breast for a moment, feeling it respond, feeling himself respond. Then, when his need was hard and demanding, he removed his hand, smoothed the silk with his palm and left the bed. It took him less than a minute to grab a set of clothes. Only a minute or two later, he left the house.

He had wanted her. The knowledge filled her eyes with tears. He had wanted her, but he hadn't taken her. She wished she could believe it was because he knew her pregnancy was too far advanced to allow any lovemaking, but she knew that wasn't it at all. There were other ways she could have satisfied him, if he'd been interested. But he hadn't been.

She met her father for lunch that day at the Goldmans' restaurant. He greeted her with a kiss and asked her to sit down. While they waited for their food, he kept the conversation flowing with talk of his year in the Middle East. Then he stopped suddenly and said bluntly, "I hear you and Trujillo are about to split up."

Caitlin stared at him. In the past few weeks she'd had lunch with him several times. Without Jess, she was desperately lonely, and she couldn't face her friends—their friends—so she had turned to her father. This was the first time he'd mentioned Jess at all. "Where did you hear that?" she asked softly.

"Around town. Everyone's talking about you and him."

She clenched her hands in her lap, out of sight, forcing all the tension into her fists so her face could remain emotionless. "And what are they saying?"

"That he doesn't go home much at night. When he does go home, it's only after he's gotten half-drunk at Rusty's. Some say you used the baby to force him to marry you; others think he used you to get back at me. Whatever the reason, he's tired of you now, isn't he? He doesn't want anything to do with you anymore."

She kept the tears from her eyes only by biting the inside of her lip until it bled. She shouldn't have been surprised that her problems were known to most of the people in town. It was a small place; gossip was their favorite pastime. Still, it hurt to know that she and Jess were the prime topic of conversation these days.

Grant's sharp blue eyes were boring into her. "How much of it is true?"

She loosened her hands long enough to take a sip of water. "That's none of your business."

"He doesn't come home at night, does he?"

She didn't answer.

"And when he does, he doesn't want anything to do with you. You know why, don't you?"

Caitlin tilted her head back. There was a throbbing behind her eyes that threatened to turn into a world-class headache. She wanted nothing more than two aspirin and a warm bed, in a dark room. If she went home now, she could have them. But that would be running away. Grant would see it as an admission that the rumors were true.

"He's seeing another woman, isn't he?"

She lowered her head again, looking into her father's eyes. God, he was taking such joy in this! He was happy that her marriage was over! Quietly she asked, "You don't give a damn about me at all, do you, Dad?"

Grant stared at her. "Wh—what?"

"If you loved me, you wouldn't be repeating these things to me. If you loved me, you would at least try to hide the fact that you're thrilled that my marriage is in trouble." She leaned forward, dropping her voice. It was husky with tears. "I love him, Dad. I *love* him, and I hate what's happening between us. And *you're* happy." She gave a sigh of disgust. "I'm going home now. I've lost my appetite."

Grant understood that she loved Jess, or that at least she thought she did. But he couldn't deny that he *was* happy that their marriage was falling apart. He had known all along that Trujillo wasn't the man for her; he had tried to warn her.

He caught her hand as she stood up. "You'll find someone else," he assured her. "As soon as you get rid of that bastard, we'll find a man who can make you happy. We'll make Trujillo pay."

She jerked her hand free. "Haven't we all paid enough?" she demanded angrily. "Haven't we lost enough?"

The other diners turned to stare openly, but she didn't notice. Fumbling in her purse for her keys, she hurried to the door and outside.

Home. She just wanted to get home, where she could hide from the gossip and the curious eyes. Where she could shut herself in her room, knowing that no one would bother her there— not even her husband.

She cursed him silently. He was responsible for the gossip. He had to know that the men he worked with would talk about the fact that he rarely returned to Isabel when the day's job was done. He had to know that every time he parked his truck in front of Rusty's Bar for hours at a time, half the people in town saw it, and they told the other half. Apparently he simply didn't care about the gossip. Why should he? He didn't care about her, either.

Caitlin watched the TV channel sign off, her eyes blurring from fatigue. With a sigh, she pointed the remote control unit and punched a button, and the screen went dark.

It was one o'clock in the morning, and Jess wasn't home. Just like so many nights before. She could hardly remember the last night he'd spent at home. No, that wasn't true. She remembered it vividly. It had been two weeks ago, and she had awakened the next morning to find him watching her, touching her for the first time in weeks. He'd been home since then—to pick up clothes, to see his mother—but he hadn't spent the night, and he hadn't seemed to notice Caitlin at all.

She didn't know where he was staying. The one time she had gotten the courage to ask, he had simply said that if Lupe needed him, they could tell Tom, and he'd get the message to him. If Lupe needed him. He'd said nothing about Caitlin. If she needed him, would he come? When their baby was born, would he be there, or would she have to go through that alone? She hadn't asked him that, afraid of the answer he would give.

Where was he? What was he doing? Who was he with? They were questions she had asked herself nightly for weeks, questions that nagged at her until her head ached and her eyes watered. She was hurt that he so obviously preferred someone else's company to hers. She was angry that he didn't care who knew he rarely went home anymore. And she was jealous.

Lord, how she envied the people he spent time with. To be able to look at him, talk to him, maybe even touch him! Did they appreciate him? Did they enjoy their time with him? Did they know that she would give anything in the world to trade places with them, whoever they were?

Slowly, with a weariness that was more mental than physical, she got to her feet. She had to slide to the edge of the sofa, then push, to lift herself. She might as well go to bed. Jess wasn't coming home tonight.

A few weeks ago she had denied Grant's suggestion that Jess was seeing another woman. No matter how much he hated her, she was certain he wouldn't do that. But tonight, as she undressed for bed, she looked at herself in the mirror, and what she saw wasn't pleasing. There was no sign of the slender figure she'd had six months ago. Her belly was distended, with faint lines spreading across it. Stretch marks that Dr. Ramirez had said would never go away. Her breasts were large, swollen and tender. She was heavier all over—her face and arms and legs and hips. If Jess had turned to another woman when he'd turned away from her, could she blame him?

She pulled her nightgown over her head. Hell, yes, she could blame him. She was his *wife*. Tears of self-pity slid down her cheeks as she switched off the light. At least in the dark she couldn't see herself. And in the dark she couldn't see that she was alone. But, Lord, how deeply she felt it

"You need to go home."

Jess didn't raise his eyes from the dark-amber liquid in his glass.

"Come on. You got a home?" The bartender looked pointedly at the gold band on Jess's left hand. "You've got a wife, you've got a home. You've got to go home."

He scowled at the man. "Why?"

"Because *I've* got to go home. Your wife's probably worried about you. Why don't you give her a call and tell her you're on your way?"

His scowl deepened. "Why?"

The bartender looked sympathetic. "Having problems at home?"

Grumbling to himself, Jess pulled some money from his pocket, tossed it on the bar and started toward the door.

"Hey, are you okay to drive?" the man called. He had served him only a couple of drinks in the three hours he'd been there, but he didn't want a lawsuit on his hands if the guy had a wreck.

Jess didn't turn. "I'm fine," he said, raising one hand in a farewell wave. He stepped out into the night. After the warmth and smell of cigarette smoke and booze, the cold air felt good. It smelled clean, refreshing.

I'm fine, he'd answered the bartender. That was one of the biggest lies he'd ever told, and lately he'd told a lot. He was far from being fine. He was losing everything he'd ever wanted— his mother, his wife and his baby—and when they were gone, he would lose his soul.

He ached. All the time. Nothing he did made any difference. Working fourteen-hour days made him tired, but the pain was still there. Drinking all night only gave him hangovers. It didn't lessen the hurt.

He had stopped at this bar—his third of the evening—intending to get stinking drunk. It had been hard finding a bar where a man could do some serious drinking without everyone in the place wanting something—the men to talk, to commiserate, and the women...

His lip curled in disgust as he remembered the suggestions of the women who had approached him. How could they really believe that he'd go to bed with any of them, when his wife was sitting at home?

His wife. Caitlin. He savored the sound of her name. It had been so long since he'd been with her, so long since he had really talked to her, since she had smiled at him. He wondered what she would think if she knew how badly he wanted to be with her. Did she know he drank to forget her? He tried so damned hard to forget her, but he only wanted her more with each passing day.

If he weren't such a coward, he would tell her how he wanted her, how awed he felt each time he looked at her, her rounded belly filled with their child. He would tell her that he didn't care why she'd married him, that her reasons didn't matter as long as she would stay with him.

He would tell her that he loved her.

The refreshing night air had seeped into his bones, chilling him through and through. He started across the parking lot to his truck.

He *was* a coward. Their marriage would end soon, without Caitlin ever knowing that he loved her. He would move on, returning to the travel that had filled the worst eight years of his life, and he would never see her again, would never see their child.

"Dammit, no!" He hit the steering wheel, starting a dull ache in his hand. He might lose Caitlin, but he wasn't giving up his child. He would stay around Albuquerque, even if it meant the pain of seeing Caitlin and knowing he couldn't have her. By God, he was going to be a part of his kid's life.

At last he started the engine. The Central Avenue motel where he stayed was cheap and shabby, worse even than the boarding-house rooms he had lived in before. He didn't care. It was better than going home. Better than seeing Caitlin and not being able to touch her.

Underneath the bed was the small wooden box that he'd carried with him all those years while he was gone. Each night he opened it and went through its contents. The letters were old, written by a much younger, much happier Caitlin. The only thing new was a photograph, a wedding picture. It was starting to show the effects of too much handling. He looked at it for a long moment, then carefully replaced it and closed the box. He didn't need to look at the picture to see her—she was in his mind all the time.

Now he was ready to sleep. Now he would see her in his dreams.

He dreamed that night of going back to Isabel, back to Caitlin, and the joy he felt stayed with him all through the day. She had welcomed him in the dream. She had even said she loved him. He knew none of what he'd dreamed was real—just an indication of how strong his yearnings were, even in sleep—but the dream left him with a desire to see her that he couldn't overcome. He had to go home.

The day dragged. A delivery came late; that meant the entire crew had to work several hours overtime. By the time Jess got back to his room, cleaned up and changed, it was almost eight o'clock. He didn't let the late hour deter him. He was going to see Caitlin tonight.

He considered stopping for a drink or two, but quickly vetoed the idea. He could use a little bottled courage, but he didn't want to go to Caitlin with his mind befuddled by booze. He drove past the countless bars to the interstate and turned toward Isabel.

Toward Caitlin. Toward home.

Grant walked slowly around the living room. He hated to say anything nice about Jess, but the man had done a good job on the house. It was nicer, even, than his own. Too bad Caitlin wouldn't be living in it much longer.

"Here." She entered the room and held out a glass. She didn't bother being too friendly. She still hadn't forgiven him for that day at the restaurant.

When he pulled into the driveway next to Grant's Cadillac, Jess gave a vicious curse. It was just his luck that the one time he got the courage to see his wife, Grant would be there. He was tempted to reverse the truck and head back to Albuquerque, but sheer obstinacy refused to let him. He got out and used his key to let himself into the house. Purposely, he made as little noise as possible. He wanted to know what Grant was telling Caitlin. He stopped in the darkened hallway outside the living room to listen.

Grant accepted the drink. "Where's Trujillo?"

"Is that why you came here? For more gossip?" She sighed deeply. "Stop it, Dad."

"It's true then, isn't it? He's moved out."

"No." She didn't elaborate. For all practical purposes, Jess *had* moved out. They rarely saw him, and only a few of his clothes remained in the closet. But she wasn't going to tell Grant that. It was none of his business.

"Where's his mother?"

"She's visiting Carmen Mendez." The hostility in his voice when he mentioned Lupe made her wince. According to the story Jess had told her—a story Grant hadn't denied—her father had been in love with Lupe when they were young. How could love turn to such unrelenting hatred? Because she had rejected him? Caitlin couldn't accept that. Jess had rejected her, too—twice— but she would love him until the day she died.

Grant sipped his drink, while his gaze traveled once more around the living room. Jess stepped farther into the shadows to avoid detection.

Maybe Caitlin could take the house in the divorce settlement, Grant mused. He'd have to mention it to his attorney the next time they talked. It would be a shame to give it up to Trujillo. He owed it to her.

She didn't sit down while she waited for him to get to the point of his visit. She didn't kid herself that he'd just wanted to see her. She was beginning to learn, as Jess had long ago, that Grant never did anything without a reason.

She was uncomfortable with him. It hurt her to admit that about the man who had raised her from infancy, but it was true. She had always been able to accept Grant's possessiveness toward her, and even his hatred for Jess, because she loved him. But she didn't want to accept it any longer; her love wasn't enough anymore. When she had desperately needed his love and sympathy, he had been mocking and smug, reveling in her unhappiness. He had disappointed her at a time when she couldn't bear any more disappointment.

Grant set the empty glass on a table, then swung around to face his daughter. "Come home with me."

Caitlin simply stared at him.

"There's nothing keeping you here. Your husband sure as hell isn't. When was the last time you saw him, Caitlin? When was the last time he slept here?"

She still said nothing. Her silence damned her in Jess's eyes. She offered no defense for him, as a wife should for her husband—but could he blame her?

"People in town are still talking about you. They laugh behind your back. Everyone knows that he's left you. Don't you have any pride, Caitlin? You offered yourself to a bastard like him, and he's made damned sure everyone knows he doesn't want you. How can you sit here, waiting for him to remember you exist?"

"This is my home."

"No, it's not. Your home is with me. I tried to warn you. told you he was using you. I told you he'd walk out on you when he was through. He'll never love you, Caitlin, not the way I do. We're family—families stick together. You don't need him. Come home with me, where you belong."

Caitlin ran her hand through her hair, mussing it. "And what about the baby, Dad? Does she belong in your house, too? Are you going to love Jess's daughter the way you love me?'' She wasn't considering his offer; she just wanted to hear his answer. She wanted to know if he would accept her baby.

Grant obviously found the idea of having Jess's child in his house distasteful, but he knew that saying so would destroy his chances of getting Caitlin back. Like Claire, like Lupe, she would never give up her child. ''The baby is as much a part of you as of him.''

She knew what his answer meant: he didn't want the baby, but he would tolerate her if he had to. That wasn't the kind of life she wanted for her child. Grant would eventually come around, but he would make it impossible for Caitlin to teach the child anything about her father; it would be impossible for her daughter to have a relationship with Jess. Grant would try to teach her to hate Jess the way he did, and as she grew older, he would try to control her life, as he'd done with Caitlin. As he was still doing with Caitlin.

Jess had heard enough. Angry with Caitlin for listening to Grant, angry with himself for believing they might still make their marriage a success, he stepped into the room. He didn't look at Caitlin—his dark eyes went straight to Grant—but his words were directed at her. ''Surprised to see me?'' he asked harshly.

Grant's smile was triumphant, and it made Jess sick way down deep inside. From the day she had admitted her reasons for marrying him, he'd known he couldn't make a go of it with Caitlin, but he had continued to hope, to want, to need, to love. All these weeks he had been mourning her, missing her, dreaming of coming home to her, and she had apparently been keeping company with her father—the man who had been the source of every problem they had ever had. That she could even consider Grant's suggestion was proof of how little she wanted Jess. She had to look ahead, he supposed. Lupe had only a few months left; soon Caitlin's reason for the marriage would be buried along with his mother. Once her duty was done, she had to make sure her precious daddy would take her back, would forgive her and welcome her into his home.

Caitlin realized that he'd heard too much. She should have refused her father's offer outright, in no uncertain terms. She knew she had no intention of ever returning to Grant's house, but Jess didn't know that, and he wasn't likely to believe it now. Why did she keep making these terrible mistakes in dealing with him? Just once, why couldn't luck be on her side? she lamented.

He still refused to look at her, but that didn't stop her from drinking him in. He was so incredibly handsome. He hadn't changed at all. Being away from her for so long hadn't had any effect on him that she could see. He hadn't lost any weight; he wasn't wasting away; he didn't look sad or heartbroken or even mildly put out. He just looked angry.

Grant's smile was wide. In his triumph, he could afford to be friendly—sort of—to Jess. "It's been a long time since we've seen you. You look good."

Jess's smile was ugly. Grant was too insensitive to see anything, but he knew that if Caitlin looked into his eyes, she would see how much he'd missed her, how miserable he'd been the last few weeks. That was why he continued to look at Grant. "What are you doing in my house, Pierce?" he asked softly.

"I came to get my daughter."

Caitlin took a step forward. "Jess..."

From the corner of his eye, he glanced at her. "Aren't you packed yet?"

She caught her breath. Surely he wasn't going to throw her out without talking to her, without listening to her! "Jess...!" The sound of his name was a trembling entreaty.

"Go on, Cait. God forbid you should disappoint your daddy." Jess's voice was heavy with sarcasm and hatred. "It's not so hard to do—you've done it before. Take your things and your father and get out of my house."

She looked at her father, standing near the patio doors, then at Jess, who remained just inside the hall door. Maybe Grant was right. Maybe Jess had no further use for her. After all, he'd accomplished his goal; he'd gotten his revenge, and he'd said it had been sweet. He had used her, and when he was finished, he had left her.

"Let's go, Caitlin. You can pick up your things later." Grant took a step toward her, but she turned away, facing Jess.

"Can we talk?" she whispered, her brown eyes searching his face.

At last he looked at her. He had thought she could see the pain and sadness in his eyes, but all she saw was indifference and anger. It almost took away her courage. "I came here tonight to talk you," he said in a harsh tone. "But I wasn't expecting to find Daddy here."

"Please, Jess."

He hardened himself against the plea in her voice. "No. There's nothing to say."

Caitlin felt her heart sink. She wanted to cry out that he was wrong—there was so much she needed to say! But he wasn't interested in hearing it.

His next words returned a measure of hope to her. "You have to decide, Cait. Now."

She looked up at him quickly. She'd heard those words before—almost nine years ago. *You have to decide, Cait. Tonight. Now. I can't put up with this any longer.* That night she had pleaded with him, had pleaded with her father, but it had gotten her nowhere. Jess had refused to listen to her, and Grant had seen no reason to listen; he'd known what her choice would be before she made it.

Grant remembered the words, too, and they also gave him hope. Caitlin was his daughter; she loved him. She might think she loved Trujillo, too, but Grant was sure he'd taught her well. Trujillo couldn't be allowed to interfere with family. A lover, even a husband, could be replaced. A father couldn't. She would choose him. Just as she'd done all those years ago, she would choose to stay with her father.

Jess had known that night would be repeated; he'd known Caitlin would be forced to choose between them once more. He just hadn't known that he would be the one to force it this time, too. He had thought the ultimatum would come from Grant.

The circumstances were different this time, he told himself. Caitlin was a grown woman. She could make choices for herself. They weren't talking now about a boyfriend, but about her husband, the father of her baby. And there was more at stake here than their relationship; her decision this time would affect the life of their child. Just because the ultimatum was the same, that didn't mean the result would be, too.

Jess and Grant were both watching her. Jess's face was expressionless; Grant was smiling, certain of his victory. Caitlin looked from one to the other, then stared down. Her belly blocked the view.

You have to decide, Cait. Decide what? What was Jess asking her to do? The last time the issue had been clear: go away with Jess to be his wife, or stay home and be Grant's daughter. This time she wasn't sure what he wanted. Did he want *her*? Or did he just want to see her separated from her father?

She could choose Grant, and the rest of her life wouldn't be worth living. That much she was sure of. Jess would never forgive her for betraying him a second time. He would never have anything to do with her again. She would have her father, but the price would be more than she could bear.

She could simply go—live on her own with the baby in the city—but that would have the same result. Jess would still be out of her life.

There was only one thing left. She could stay. She could stay in Jess's house as long as he would let her, stay his wife until he forgot his views on divorce and asked for one. It would mean cutting her father out of her life completely, refusing to ever see him or talk to him or acknowledge his existence. It would mean giving up the only family she had for a man who couldn't love her, a man who right now couldn't stand to live in the same house with her.

With all his faults, at least Grant loved her. It wasn't necessarily a good love, not even a healthy one, but it was love. Could she give that up for Jess? For more lonely nights? More tears? More heartache?

She raised her eyes to her father. He didn't even notice her gaze, because he was too caught up in his smug satisfaction. He thought he had won, once and for all, over Jess. She made her decision, and calmness settled over her.

She walked to her father, smiling, and spoke softly when she reached him. "There's an old saying, Dad: *Contra amor y fortuna no hay defensa alguna.*"

Jess translated it silently. *Against love and fate, there is no defense.* Was it her fate to be with him? he wondered fearfully. Or with her father? He didn't even consider the first part of the saying. Thinking about love in connection with Caitlin was too painful.

Grant sputtered. "Wh—what do you mean by that?"

She cupped his face in her hands, lifted herself on tiptoe and kissed both his cheeks. "Goodbye, Dad."

Jess was positive he couldn't have heard her correctly. If he had, that meant she was choosing *him*, and she couldn't be choosing him over her father!

But that was exactly what she was doing. Slowly, but with grace in spite of the cumbersome weight she carried, she moved to stand by Jess's side. Not in front of him, to act as a shield, not behind him, to use him as a shield, but at his side.

She had chosen him. Jess couldn't believe it, but he could see her, could feel her only inches away. *Contra amor y fortuna...* Was he her love, or only her fate? At that moment he was so grateful, he didn't care. All that mattered was that she had chosen *him*.

"You're crazy, Caitlin!" Grant exclaimed. "You can't mean this—you can't possibly want him! He's just a bastard—"

Her slender hand reached out, tucking itself neatly into Jess's big palm. The simple gesture stopped Grant mid tirade. It was no mistake. He and Trujillo had once again forced her to choose, and she had done so. The first time Trujillo had lost. This time Grant had lost—lost everything. His daughter. His grandchild. His family. His power. He had been pushed aside for Lupe's bastard son.

Jess could have gloated. He could have rubbed it in the way Grant had done before. And it wasn't the knowledge that doing so would hurt Caitlin that stopped him. He didn't do it because he understood how the old man felt. He could read it in the slumped shoulders, in the tired lines of a face that had aged twenty years. He knew what it was like to lose Caitlin, to face life without her. He knew how it hurt. He didn't say a word.

Caitlin felt peaceful, serene. She had made the right choice. Her father was walking out of her life, and she would miss him terribly, but she had made the right choice. The only choice.

They stood silent for long minutes after Grant left. Neither knew what to say to the other. Jess was confused, bewildered, by what had happened. He needed a few minutes to get his thoughts straight.

When she at last tried to pull her hand free, he tightened his hold. He turned to look at her, his eyes searching her face. He couldn't quite accept that she had chosen him. He didn't understand. If she loved him, that would have made a difference, but she didn't love him; she had married him only for his mother's sake.

So why had she rejected her father? If she was going to leave *him* when his mother died, why had she sent Grant away? She had to know that Lupe had only a few months left, at most, and then she would be free to leave Jess. Knowing that, why had she chosen him over the father she loved?

The answer was there, but Jess refused to see it. He had hoped for so long, had been disappointed so much, that he couldn't even consider the possibility that she cared. He would have to hear it from her, would have to see the words come from her mouth, before he could believe them. Before he could say them himself.

Maybe he shouldn't ask. Maybe he shouldn't search for reasons, just accept that Caitlin had chosen to stay with him. Maybe he should be happy with what he had.

But he had to know.

Uncomfortable under his steady, searching gaze, Caitlin tried once more to pull away. This time he kept her right hand and claimed her left, too. "Tell me something, Cait," he said hoarsely.

She nodded.

"Am I your fate...or your love?"

Her smile was tremulous, her eyes damp. She had kept her secret for so long, wanting him to admit to love first. Now the time for secrets had ended. Jess was with her, waiting to hear her answer, and that gave her the courage to give it. She freed one hand and lifted it gently to his face. "Both," she whispered. "Loving you is my fate. I can't fight it or hide it anymore. I love you, Jess."

The fear and the pain he had lived with day after day dissolved, and peace and joy took their place. She loved him! God, he had waited so long to hear those words again—all of his life, it seemed. The simple little words made everything worthwhile.

"Are you sure?" he asked in an emotion-heavy whisper.

"Very sure." She moved closer to embrace him. She didn't wait for his response. She didn't expect a declaration of love from him, nor did she need one. She loved him, and that was enough.

He slipped his arms around her. She was so soft and warm against his body. It had been so long since he'd held her, and for a moment he just closed his eyes and savored her. "I thought I had lost you."

Caitlin made a soft sound that was almost a laugh. "I'm not easy to get rid of." She rested her head against his chest. He was so strong and solid. "God, I missed you," she whispered. "I love you."

He needed to see her face when she said that, so he tilted her head back and laid his hands against her cheeks. "Say it again," he commanded.

She repeated the words. Her eyes—eyes that haunted him, that were soft and gentle and trusting, that let him see into her soul— were glazed with emotion so intense he had to believe her. The raw edges of his pain began fading.

He smiled down at her, and it was the sweetest thing she'd ever seen, because there was life again in the dark brown depths of his eyes. "I love you, Cait."

Her smile was shaky. "You don't have to say that. It's all right."

"I do have to say it. I've been dying to say it for so long, but...I thought you wouldn't believe me. I thought I had waited too long." He pressed his cheek against the sweet fragrance of her hair. "I love you."

After another brief silence they spoke, both at the same time. "Jess, I lied about marrying you for Lupe—" Caitlin began as he said, "I never intended to use you against—" He placed his fingers over her lips. "I didn't want revenge, Cait, but I needed an excuse so I could touch you, so I could be with you. When you suggested that..." He shrugged, then touched his fingers to her cheek. "Caitlin, how could you love me when you believed I was using you against your father?"

She turned her head and pressed her mouth to his hand. "There's another old saying: *Amor viejo, ni te olvido ni te dejo.* Old love, I can neither forget you nor give you up. I had no choice, Jess."

"I didn't want to hurt you. God, I never meant to hurt you."

"I know," she whispered. "And I didn't marry you because of Lupe. I married you because I was already in love with you. I don't think I ever stopped loving you." Holding his hands tightly in hers, she started pulling him toward the door. "Come with me. There's something I want to show you."

She took him to her studio, flipping on the lights as she walked in. She went to an easel facing the wall and turned it to show him the painting it held.

It was the nude portrait of him that she had started after Christmas. She had never let him see it while she was working, and he'd left before it was finished. Now she presented it to him, nervously awaiting his judgment.

Jess was impressed. He didn't feel at all conceited in thinking that the man in the painting was breathtakingly handsome and incredibly sensual. The image she had created was one highly influenced by emotion and passion. One day at the gallery Tanya had told him that one reason Caitlin's work was so popular was because her feelings for her subjects were right there on the canvas for everyone to see. Now he saw exactly what she'd meant. Even if Caitlin hadn't said she loved him, he would have known it after seeing the painting.

He reached out to hold her, breathing her name on a sigh.

"Do you like it?"

"It's beautiful, Cait." He lifted his hand to touch her, and it trembled. He was trembling all over, inside and out. "Come to bed with me, Caitlin," he murmured thickly.

He held her so close that she could feel the swelling change in his body. It touched her and aroused her. It also amazed her that any man—even the one who loved her—could want her in her condition. "Jess!" She sounded scandalized. "I'm over eight months pregnant! We can't make love!"

He knew that, but it did nothing to ease the ache in him. "Then just let me hold you. Let me touch you and look at you. Let me love you."

He led her down the hall to the bedroom where she had spent so many nights alone. Now they would share it again.

The light from the studio spilled into the hallway and through the open door, allowing him to see her as he removed her clothes, then his own. With painfully gentle kisses, he lowered her onto the bed, where he did just what he'd said: he held her and touched her and looked at her. And with every touch, every look and every breath, he loved her.

Epilogue

It was quiet in the church. The worshipers made little noise; even the children were silent for the few minutes before the service ended. It was dark, too. There was no sun outside to shine through the stained glass windows, and the light inside, both electric and candle, seemed inadequate to brighten the gloom.

In Jess's lap seven-month-old Lucia lay quietly, her head pillowed against his bent knee. She held her favorite toy, a ragged stuffed rabbit that fit neatly into her small hands. It had been made by her grandmother and given to her when she was four weeks old. She played with it, slept with it, clutched it in her hand while she was fed and bathed, and had drooled on it when her first two teeth appeared a month ago.

She was a beautiful child, he thought, frankly prejudiced. Their friends took sides, some saying she looked like her mother, others declaring she took after her father. He didn't know how they could tell, since he and Caitlin shared the same coloring. Lucia was also dark; her eyes were a medium brown, the same as her mother's, but her hair was black, like her father's. Jess preferred to think that she took after her mother, because they were both so beautiful, and he loved them both.

Caitlin reached across, holding out a hand-knitted sweater in pale lavender. The service had ended while he was engrossed with his daughter. He held her in a sitting position while Caitlin put the sweater on over a lavender dress that was trimmed with delicate ruffles and lace. Even her socks, with tiny lace edging, and her shoes matched the outfit, a six-month birthday gift from Carmen Mendez. Carmen had appointed herself adoptive grandmother; she showered Lucia with gifts, spoiled her rotten, and babysat on a regular basis so Jess and Caitlin could have some time alone. They appreciated her thoughtfulness. She couldn't replace Lupe, of course, but a baby needed a grandmother, a family. The Mendezes provided that family.

By the time Caitlin got Lucia bundled up for the trip to the truck outside, they were surrounded by friends wanting to say hello and to see the baby. Lucia loved the attention; she smiled and showed off her two new teeth, and she greeted Carmen with the flow of gurgling sounds that were reserved for the special people in her life.

"Come to lunch today?" Carmen invited when she handed Lucia back to Caitlin.

Jess shook his head regretfully. "I've already made some plans. Next time, okay?"

"What plans?" Caitlin said as she wrapped a bright yellow quilt around Lucia. She covered the baby's head just before she stepped outside, and Lucia let out a wail of disapproval. Before they reached the truck a few yards away, she had freed herself and was grinning happily at her mother.

"It's a surprise." He held the baby while Caitlin got into the truck. While she strapped Lucia into the infant seat that sat between them, Jess went around to the driver's side.

The pickup was new. The old green truck had served him faithfully from the time he got his driver's license at sixteen, but it had lacked the necessary seat belt for Lucia's seat, so it had been replaced with the new model.

Jess drove west, a quarter mile out of town, and parked the truck next to a rusting iron fence. The cemetery looked bleak under the dark October sky. Plastic flowers that decorated some graves had faded in the hot New Mexico summer; live flowers planted around others had withered in the unexpected cold spell. Their drooping stems and wilted blossoms looked sad.

"Go ahead," Caitlin said softly. "We'll be with you in a minute."

He nodded with a faint smile and left the truck. The entrance to the *camposanto* was through an iron gate set in stone. Overhead, carved in the stone, was, *Dios da y Dios quita. The Lord giveth, and the Lord taketh away.* No English translation was provided; none was necessary. In the old New Mexico tradition, there were separate cemeteries for the residents of Isabel. The Anglo cemetery was in town. This *camposanto* was for the Hispanics.

The gate creaked when he pushed it open. Once it had swung freely, but now it hung crooked, and the iron was badly rusted. He left it open for Caitlin. The weeds crunched under his feet as he weaved his way around the graves to his mother's. There were no neat rows of uniform tombstones, no close-clipped grass, no concrete paths leading the way to the graves. There was no need for constancy here; if life itself isn't orderly and constant, the reasoning went, why should death be?

The graves were placed haphazardly, weeds grew free, rocks were left in place, and the markers were anything but uniform. Many carried no inscription; some were homemade, using every material from wood to concrete, sandstone to pipe. The only thing they had in common were the crosses. Each grave was marked with a cross.

Cerquitas, small fences of wood or iron that outlined the graves, were popular in this cemetery. Lupe had chosen one for her own grave. It was of iron posts a few feet high that curved gently at the top. She had chosen her marker, too—a simple white marble cross. The inscription had been left for Jess and Caitlin to choose. It gave her name, the dates of her birth and her death, then said simply, Beloved Mother and Grandmother.

The wind rustled through the weeds, making Jess shiver in his corduroy sports jacket. He pushed his hands into his jeans pockets, then immediately pulled one out again and bent to pull a weed from the base of the cross. The weeds and overgrowth weren't a sign of disrespect or lack of caring, Lupe had told him when they visited the cemetery shortly before Lucia's birth. They were a part of nature, a fact of life as natural as death.

It had taken Jess awhile to see death as a natural event. There had been nothing natural about a healthy, happy woman like his mother slowly wasting away. But she had peacefully accepted death, and that had helped him to accept it. Caitlin and Lucia had also helped.

They joined him then, Lucia again wrapped in a quilt. This time Caitlin had covered her black curls with a knit cap, tied securely under her fat chin. Jess smiled, brushing a curl that had escaped back in place. "I knew you'd give up trying to keep her head covered with the blanket," he said. "I bet it only takes her a few weeks to learn how to untie this thing and take it off."

"Then I'll tie it in knots." Caitlin sounded cross, but she wasn't. She was learning, much to her surprise, that even babies had very distinct personalties. Lucia was going to be headstrong and stubborn. It was cute now, but she could see some battles in the future. And Jess would be no help. All Lucia had to do was flash that snaggle-toothed grin at him, and he melted. He had already admitted that he would have no more success in telling her no than he did with his mother. It would be interesting, she decided with a smile, to see who he sided with when mother and daughter each wanted something different, and it was left to him to say no to one of them.

Jess took his daughter and hugged her, eliciting a high-pitched giggle. She looked so small and fragile against his broad chest, Caitlin thought, though she knew she'd never seen a sturdier child. While he held her, she knelt to place the small bouquet of flowers she'd brought at the foot of the stone. They wouldn't last long in this cold, but that didn't matter. Bringing flowers to the grave was a ritual that neither she nor Jess wanted to give up, not even for winter.

A short distance away were the graves of several of Lupe's relatives: an uncle, a cousin, a grandmother, a great-grandfather. Caitlin wandered over to look at them. Jess and Lucia followed, and he slipped his free arm around her. "Family is important," he said softly.

She nodded.

"She never heard from her parents or her brothers and sisters again."

"I know."

"It's been a long time since you've seen your father."

She stared off into the distance, absently agreeing. She hadn't seen Grant in almost eight months, not since the night she had chosen to remain with Jess. She missed him, for herself and for Lucia. Grant hadn't been an ideal father, and he wouldn't be an ideal grandfather, but he was the only family, besides Jess, that she and Lucia had.

But his hatred of Jess wouldn't allow her to see him. She had tried before to maintain a loving relationship with both of them, and she had failed. Jess had been willing to share, but Grant hadn't; he wanted all of her. He'd ended up with nothing.

Jess felt Caitlin shiver inside her coat, and he turned her toward the truck. "Let's go. We're going to be late for dinner."

That reminded her of his reply to Carmen's invitation, that he'd already made plans. Curiously she looked up at him as they made their way to the truck. "Where are we having dinner?"

"You'll see."

Jess knew that Caitlin missed her father, even though she never said anything. When Lucia was born, he had made sure that Grant was notified. He hadn't dared to see the older man himself; it had been only a few weeks since the confrontation over Caitlin, and he'd assumed that Grant was still angry and upset. He had asked Carmen Mendez to tell him, hoping that he might care enough to call or visit Caitlin and Lucia. He hadn't.

Caitlin's birthday had also passed with no word from her father. She had tried to hide her hurt, but Jess had seen it, had felt it. He was partially responsible, and he felt guilty. That wasn't a feeling he liked, so he'd decided to do something about it. After weeks of emotional and often hostile meetings, he and Grant had finally worked out a compromise. Grant still disapproved strongly of Jess and wished Caitlin had never laid eyes on him, and Jess could think of a few thousand men he would prefer for a father-in-law, but they could tolerate each other, because they had one thing in common: their love for Caitlin. Even though he was domineering and selfish and possessive, Grant loved Cait; she was the only person in the world he did love. And Jess loved her more than he loved life itself. Surely, with that going for them, they could learn to put up with each other.

"Do I look all right for wherever we're going?" Caitlin asked as they drove into town again.

Jess looked across at her. She had loosened her coat; underneath it she had on a full black skirt with a soft-pink sweater. She also wore the silver-and-pink mussel shell earrings he'd given her for her thirtieth birthday, along with a matching necklace that had been his gift for her thirty-first. "You're beautiful," he said simply. "I love you, Cait."

She could say the same about him, but she didn't need to; it was in her eyes for him to see. How she had ever thought she could hide her love for him, she didn't know. It was so obvious. But Jess hadn't been looking for love then; he had needed to recognize his own love before he could see hers. Thank God he had. She couldn't imagine life without him. Not even Lucia could have filled the emptiness created by his leaving.

The road began to climb, and Caitlin turned her gaze from Jess to look around. The road was so familiar, she could recognize it without looking, but it had been a long time since she had traveled it. She had never expected to travel it again, because there was only one destination, only one house, at its end. She looked back at her husband. "Jess?"

He only smiled.

Caitlin swallowed nervously. Normally, she trusted Jess implicitly, but this time she was afraid. What was he doing? He knew as well as she did that he wasn't welcome at her father's house; for that matter, neither was she, as long as she and Jess remained married.

He stopped the truck in the driveway, turned off the key and reached across for her hand. It was like ice. "Tell me you love me," he commanded with a lazy smile.

"I do love you, Jess."

He leaned across Lucia to kiss her cheek, kissed Lucia, too, then got out and went around to the other side. Caitlin protested, but he forcibly helped her down, then placed the baby in her arms. Then he dragged her to the door, where he knocked loudly.

In only a moment Grant opened the door. He looked from Caitlin to Jess, then back at Caitlin. Nervously he smiled. "Hello. Come on in."

Jess ushered Caitlin inside, holding the baby while she removed her coat and handed it to Grant, who hung it in the closet, then led the way into the living room. "Dinner will be ready in a few minutes," he said. "Would you like a drink, Jess?"

Caitlin was astounded. That was the first time she could remember her father ever calling Jess by his first name in conversation. In fact, it was the first time she'd ever heard Grant and Jess have a conversation; before, they'd always had fights.

Jess declined the drink, and Grant fell uncomfortably silent for a moment. His eyes kept going to Lucia, hidden inside the quilt on her mother's lap. At last, hesitantly, as if he feared a refusal, he asked, "Can I see my granddaughter?"

Caitlin stared at Jess, who was seated on the sofa next to her. He leaned over, removed the quilt, then pulled the cap from the baby's head. She grinned at him with an unmistakable look of relief. "This is Lucia," he said softly.

Grant's touch was uncharacteristically gentle. After a moment Caitlin offered the baby to him, and he carried her to the recliner.

Jess was grinning when Caitlin turned to him. "You did this, didn't you?" she asked.

He nodded, proud of himself.

Her eyes were moist with tears. "Why?"

Sobering, he put his arms around her and hugged her close. "Because family is important. Because, by making you choose, we were punishing you when you were the innocent one. Because you need your father, and Lucia needs her grandfather, and Grant needs both of you."

She touched his cheek gently. "And what about you, Jess? What do you need?"

Solemnly he considered the question. He didn't need much—just Caitlin and Lucia. He needed them to be happy. He needed them to love him.

He gave her a kiss, then a slow smile. "I have everything I need, Cait," he replied softly. "I have you."

* * * * *

SILHOUETTE®
Desire®

Do you want...

Dangerously handsome heroes

Evocative, everlasting love stories

Sizzling and tantalizing sensuality

Incredibly sexy miniseries like **MAN OF THE MONTH**

Red-hot romance

Enticing entertainment that can't be beat!

You'll find all of this, and much *more* each and every month in **SILHOUETTE DESIRE**. Don't miss these unforgettable love stories by some of romance's hottest authors. Silhouette Desire—where your fantasies will always come true....

DES-GEN

INTIMATE MOMENTS®
Silhouette®

If you've got the time...
We've got the
INTIMATE MOMENTS

Passion. Suspense. Desire. Drama. Enter a world that's larger than life, where men and women overcome life's greatest odds for the ultimate prize: love. Nonstop excitement is closer than you think...in Silhouette Intimate Moments!

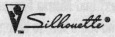

Silhouette®

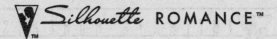
Silhouette ROMANCE™

What's a single dad to do when he needs a wife by next Thursday?

Who's a confirmed bachelor to call when he finds a baby on his doorstep?

How does a plain Jane in love with her gorgeous boss get him to notice her?

From classic love stories to romantic comedies to emotional heart tuggers, **Silhouette Romance** offers six irresistible novels every month by some of your favorite authors! Such as...beloved bestsellers **Diana Palmer, Annette Broadrick, Suzanne Carey, Elizabeth August** and **Marie Ferrarella,** to name just a few—and some sure to become favorites!

Fabulous Fathers...Bundles of Joy...Miniseries... Months of blushing brides and convenient weddings... Holiday celebrations... You'll find all this and much more in **Silhouette Romance**—always emotional, always enjoyable, always about love!

SR-GEN